Paula Roberts
Private Investigator
Johns Island (Sequel to The Paralegal)

Daniel Easterling

Paula Roberts
Private Investigator
Johns Island
(Sequel to The Paralegal)

©Daniel Easterling
December 1, 2012

FIRST EDITION

ISBN-10: 1481240498
ISBN-13: 978-1481240499

ALL RIGHTS RESERVED

No part of this book may be used or reproduced in any form, or means, without the written permission of the author, except in cases of brief quotations.

This is a work of fiction. Names, characters, places, and incidents are, either the product of the author's imagination, or are used fictitiously, and any resemblance to actual persons, living or dead, business establishments, events, or locales is entirely coincidental.

ACKNOWLEDGMENTS

Thanks to friends who encouraged me to keep at my craft. Developing, writing, and editing a good read is arduous, to say the least. The writer finds himself in a lonely place quite often. Special thanks to readers of The Paralegal who wanted to read more about the protagonist. This impetus pushed me forward.

Thanks for those of you who bought The Paralegal, whether hard copy, or by e-book, for your loyal support and for input you have given me. As always, please email comments to *dsetoday@aol.com*, or post them online at Amazon, or Barnes and Nobles where you will find the e-books.

Special thanks to Joe Perrone, Jr. for cover design and final formatting. Joe is an accomplished author, who also assists authors with a complete range of publishing services. The help he provided was invaluable in getting my work in print. It is great to have him as a friend and fellow writer, who provides encouragement and inspiration. Thanks to Peggy O'Neale for editorial assistance.

Finally, I thank God for His grace who gives me the inspiration to create and write stories. It is my sincere hope to entertain the reader, and to spark faith by certain events that occur in my stories.

Feel free to "friend me" on Facebook at Dan Easterling, Irmo, SC, to keep in the loop on the status of future novels and book signings. One additional sequel is in the offing for release in late 2014.

Paula Roberts Private Investigator Johns Island
(Sequel to The Paralegal)

By

Daniel Easterling

Paula Roberts P.I. - Johns Island

One

Russell Baxter waited up the street from where his client's husband, Mark Jennings, parked. Just thirty minutes earlier he had tailed Jennings and watched him parallel park along the secluded street lined with giant live oaks, branches draped with Spanish moss, then walk up to his girlfriend's driveway. Anna Leigh Jennings had hired Baxter two months prior, a local private investigator of some renown, hoping to obtain enough evidence for a divorce without the usual one-year waiting period in South Carolina. The smell of perfume on his clothes and the smear of lip-gloss and makeup on his collar, along with the late hours her husband kept, were all the signs she needed. She fully believed that her husband was guilty of adultery, but could not prove it in a court of law without concrete evidence.

Baxter glanced down at his watch, figuring that Jennings had enough time to get inside the house and into the bedroom with his mistress. He quietly opened the door to his forest-green Jeep Cherokee and slipped out onto the curb without disturbing the serenity that hung in the air like an early morning fog. Closing the door gently, he cupped the bill of his navy blue baseball cap, pulling it down over his forehead. He wrapped his London Fog of the same color around himself, cinching the belt to his waist. A small dog barked from a courtyard behind an adjacent brick wall. Baxter's black leather tennis shoes barely made a sound as he moved in a fast walk stealthily down the uneven seventy-five year old sidewalk. Sprigs of grass, with a little life left, grew up from the cracks in the sidewalk made from years of growth by the huge trees and their root systems.

    Baxter looked up for a moment at a street light where a mist was falling through the trees. The wet shroud resembled the glorious Milky Way. Ghosts seemed to whisper gossip at the sight of his presence. They reminisced about other affairs they had witnessed in times past, and spouses discovering the broken, sacred matrimonial trust. A crescent Carolina moon sporadically peeked through the darkened clouds as they floated by ignoring what transpired below. Keeping his body close to the outer walls that surrounded the exclusive older homes in downtown Charleston, Baxter stopped at the end of an outer wall next to Carol Allen's driveway.

    Carol did not intend to become anyone's mistress, but she was vulnerable shortly after her divorce when she encountered Jennings for the first time at the bank where he worked. She dressed provocatively that day when she went to change the name on her accounts and access her safety deposit box. After completing those two tasks, she was shown to Mark Jennings' office to apply for a loan. Finding her appealing, Jennings allowed himself to be charmed as she completed the application for a second mortgage. Hiding his wedding ring in his drawer, Jennings spoke of a happy hour where he met her for drinks. Shortly after this rendezvous, the extramarital affair began.

    Baxter peaked around the corner of the wall in the direction of the house and saw a light on in the back. Partially drawn curtains prevented him from seeing anyone inside. He needed to get closer for a better view. Crouching, Baxter ran swiftly through the cover of darkness to the side of the home by the lovers' bedroom. For a few seconds, he envisioned naval operations in Desert Storm when he led a strike-team to assault an Iraqi patrol bedded down in a building they had seized in Kuwait. Risking his life while in combat gave him a confidence to do this part of his investigative work without hesitation or fear. He positioned himself against the house in a flowerbed where he could see the couple, then pulled his video camera out of a small shoulder bag. Turning it on, he selected night mode, pointed, and began recording the lovebirds from his well-chosen spot shielded behind a tall, leafy Japanese camellia covered with blossoms glistening from the mist.

    Inside her bedroom, Jennings and his lover pulled apart from their steamy embrace to unbutton each other. Simultaneously, their fingers danced with sinful delight as each pair of hands glided from buttonhole to buttonhole. Continuing to kiss each other, Carol yanked Mark's shirttail from his pants, as he slipped her blouse from her skirt. Shirts hanging loosely from their shoulders, kissing and embracing from various angles, they allowed their garments to fall to the floor. Mark's bare hairy chest against Carol's breasts, wearing only a bra, now heated their passions to new heights.

Baxter had seen a bit of everything in his fifteen years of detective work. Consequently, he did not get much of a thrill seeing a woman half-naked in his camera. His mind remained purely on the business of gaining enough evidence to satisfy his client's needs. His wife and family were paramount in his life, and all that he did revolved around supplying a comfortable life for them. Focusing on his target, Baxter adjusted his stance slightly for a better angle and stumbled on a broken limb, which had fallen on the pine straw surrounding the shrubbery. He caught himself with his one hand against the windowsill to keep from falling headlong into the bushes.

"Shh, I hear something outside," Jennings said.

"It's just the wind, darling, Carol replied.

She paused for a moment and then continued kissing him. With Mark's help, her skirt fell to the floor on top of her blouse. Carol helped him unzip his pants, and he stepped out of them. They wrapped their arms around each other tightly, kissing passionately. Both of them now excited to yet another level. When it seemed like they would not be stopped, he pried himself away from their kisses long enough to peer around her and listen for any sound that he might capture from outside the home.

"I know I heard something just outside the window," he said, breathing deeply.

Her breathing had become heavy like his. "Forget about it Mark, it's just the wind blowing the trees. It does that all the time when the sea breeze kicks up at night. There's a camellia outside the window that's gotten tall; I need to cut it back."

"I guess you're right, sweetie, but you should have closed the blinds," he said.

"How could I, Mark, when you were draped all over me the moment you walked in? You didn't give me a chance."

Their lips found each other once again. Standing with her back against the bed, Carol stepped back a couple of steps to the edge of the bed. She reached with one arm and pulled the bedcovers back, her other arm around Mark. She put one hand on his shoulder, and the other on his lower back then pulled him down to her nest. Their bodies slid onto the cool, golden silk sheets. He reached behind and pulled up the sheet to cover the lower half of his body, their bodies now as one, as they delighted in forbidden pleasure. The lovebirds whispered sweet nothings in each other's ears until their ecstasy consummated.

Baxter collected himself after nearly blowing it, and managed to record most of the action on his camcorder, accomplishing the task that he set out to do. Carefully, he eased away from the window, squatting down and listening for his chance to run.

"I'm glad you came tonight, sweetie," she said, kissing him on his neck and ear.

"I am too, Carol," he said, kissing her neck and face.

Hearing nothing at the window, Baxter decided he would make a break for it. The detective sprang from his crouched position and ran full bore down the driveway toward the sidewalk.

"Wait, said Jennings, "I hear footsteps; it sounds like someone running." He jumped up and peeked out the window, but Baxter had turned the corner by the outer wall of the residence, and was already out of sight. Satisfied that Carol must be right about the shrubs, he closed the blinds and returned to bed. His mistress waiting anxiously for his return was alarmed by her lover's disquietude.

"Sorry, sweetie, I guess I'm freaking out for no reason."

"It's okay, dear. I'm glad you're back. It's scary sometimes with the noise the wind makes blowing the shrubs against the house, as I told you," said Carol.

Jennings settled in with his mistress for a brief nap until he awakened and left her sleeping an hour later.

Baxter entered his Jeep and started the engine. Efficiently, he made a three point turn on the narrow brick street and traced his way back out of the neighborhood. Glancing up, he checked his rear view mirror to make sure no one was following him, and then flipped open his cell phone. Dialing from a saved contact, he reached his client on the second ring.

"Mrs. Jennings, this is Russell Baxter. Did I wake you?"

"No, you didn't Mr. Baxter. I was reading a little before going to sleep. What's going on?"

"I'm glad I didn't disturb you. Listen, I just left the residence of the woman that your husband has been seeing. I was able to get substantial evidence recorded tonight."

"What type of evidence, Mr. Baxter?"

"I tailed your husband from downtown to near Poinsettia Park by the Battery. He parked and entered the home of a woman that I have seen him with on a couple of other occasions at a bar near the Market District. They drove different cars on those nights and left without meeting at her home," he said, pausing, not sure how much to share with her on the phone.

"Is that all?"

Realizing she wanted details, Baxter continued. "Tonight was different. I followed him to her residence and recorded them in her home kissing and then going to bed together. I'm quite sure this is all the court will need for you to get a ninety-day divorce on grounds of adultery. I'll review it when I get back to the office for clarity, and give you a call tomorrow, Mrs. Jennings.

"Well, I can't say I'm glad to hear it, but I'd rather find out sooner than later. So, this is the same woman you told me about earlier?"

"Yes, it is," he said. An awkward pause followed. Baxter resumed. "As far as I know, this is the only woman he's been seeing. I'm sorry, Mrs. Jennings."

"Thanks for your call. You did your job well. Good night, Mr. Baxter."

"Good night ma'am."

Anna Leigh placed a tasseled bookmark to save her place in the novel she was reading, slapped it shut, and turned off the bedside lamp. Flopping onto the bed, she nestled in her pillow, exhaling a sigh of exasperation and bewilderment at her husband's actions. She thought about what life would be like for their children without their father at home. Realizing that there was nothing else she could do to fix the problem, she drifted off to sleep to face her battle another new day.

Although Baxter knew he did his job, he felt empty inside and bad for Mrs. Jennings. He hated to see a couple torn apart by the foolishness of a fleeting affair when it put an otherwise solid family into shambles. The divorce would likely be a slam-dunk for Mrs. Jennings, who had done her best to be what her husband wanted. She bore him two children, and was a good mother. She stayed in shape, kept house, and cooked better and more often than most married women that she knew. Still, she inexplicably suffered the fate of dealing with an unfaithful husband, and she did not intend to live with it any longer than was necessary. She wondered why this had happened to her, but there did not seem to be a reason.

Baxter headed back to Crescent Moon Investigations in downtown Charleston to put the evidence in a secure location. He pulled into a parking spot behind his office and let himself in the back door. After rewinding and viewing enough of the recording to be satisfied with its clarity, he locked the camera in a file cabinet. Switching off the light, he exited out the back door and looked at his watch.

"Geez, it's almost two in the morning. I need to get home and rest," he muttered.

He wanted to get someone else to help him do detective work. Since he had hired Carla, a College of Charleston student, for clerical duties, business was picking up better than expected. Now, he found himself overworked because she, unlike the previous temporary workers he hired, took the calls on a timely basis, and handled them much better. She was a rising senior and had the intelligence and maturity to view her job as a stepping stone, not just a paycheck.

Baxter hoped that a referral for a potential detective that Luke Bradley, a local attorney, had given him would work out. On his drive home, he mulled it over. From a phone conversation on the previous day, she sounded okay, but he was not sure if she would follow up with faxing the resume he requested. He also had reservations about having a female detective working with him, but from their conversation, he felt that she could be an asset. He figured if Paula Roberts would go to work for him, he could use her for some of the routine cases, and that he would take the tougher ones. Having someone more mature with experience to listen to clients might help him pick up even more cases and grow his business the way he envisioned could happen one day when the right pieces fell together.

Two

Shortly after moving to Charleston, Paula Roberts began to look for employment as a paralegal. After four separate interviews, she still had not received a call for a second interview. Given her experience, she had no idea that it would be this tough to secure employment. Second interviews, background checks, and long waits were not the norm for her. In the small town of Georgetown, where she had most recently worked, after one interview she was hired. *Had I not worked for J. Thomas Denby, with his sometimes twisted methods to win cases, none of this would be happening to me,* she thought.

She remembered how easy it was going to work for the Denby Law Firm in her early thirties. Now though, her past employment there put a dark cloud on her chances. Word of mouth had spread quickly in the Charleston legal circles about how she was involved in a blackmail plot that nearly had her serving time in federal prison. The law firms simply could not afford to risk their reputations when a good name means acquiring new clients, and retaining old ones. The death of Judge Parks had rocked the legal community and anyone who tarnished his legendary memory was looked down upon. Paula had witnessed at least two attorneys take one look at her resume and glare at her as if she had personally killed Judge Parks.

Jim Roberts, her husband of one year, kept his furniture business going in Georgetown for the past two months since closing on their house in Charleston, but planned to move the business as soon as he found a suitable building with a good location. The drive from Georgetown was a little long, which took him through several small towns, but he enjoyed the scenic trip down the winding Highway 17 adjacent to the South Carolina coast.

Gargantuan live oaks with huge branches, as large as a normal tree's trunk spread in all directions and draped with Spanish moss, hanging serenely, seemed to whisper that giants once occupied the land. The fresh salt air drifting in from the Atlantic cleared his head as Jim drove with his front windows down, his hair lifting from the breeze. The marshlands, which surrounded the road in many places, were dotted with white egrets high stepping as they inspected the shallow waters for shad. Seagulls graced the Carolina blue skies as they swooped down, poking the water for fish. A formation of Brown pelicans glided from above to dive bomb the inlet for fish beneath the surface. Jim took it all in glancing to one side of the road then the other. No matter the tasks that faced him at work, the drive to the city was therapeutic and charged his batteries to take on each new day with gusto. *Being married to Paula is inspiration enough*, he thought, *but this low-country scenery is spectacular.*

After putting in a long day organizing, selling, and looking at the paper for possible locations to relocate his business, the return trip from work was nearly as nice, allowing Jim to collect his thoughts and unwind. Arriving at home, he entered the front door of the hundred-year-old stucco home they had purchased near the Charleston harbor. He dropped his worn tan windbreaker on the metal hook of an antique oak coat rack tucked inside the front door. Turning left and walking out of the foyer, Jim found his wife sitting at the oval-shaped mahogany kitchen table thumbing through a magazine.

"Hi, honey, how's the job hunting going?" said Jim.

He leaned to kiss her on the cheek. She turned and pecked him on the lips, a delight for him after a long day at work, and an hour's drive home. He dropped his large ring of keys in a catchall ceramic bowl, hand-painted with colorful fruit, and then joined her at the table.

"Slow Jim, very slow. I'm getting rejections, or no responses, from all the firms thus far. When I call to follow up, I get the run-around with something like," "Sorry, Mrs. Roberts, but we are fully staffed right now, blah, blah, blah"... "I'm so frustrated."

"Things will work out, Paula. Hang in there. With your experience, not to mention great looks, you'll find something soon."

"I appreciate the encouragement, Jim. I really do, but I am entertaining another possible vocation. I'm thinking of applying for work as a private investigator with a small agency that Luke recommended." She looked over to catch his reaction.

Jim squared his shoulders, crossed his arms, and raised an eyebrow. "What's my nephew doing referring you to that type of work?"

"Now, now Jim, I phoned him and inquired. It wasn't as if he called me. He was just trying to be helpful. Besides, I was already doing a good deal of those duties for the Denby Law Firm. I'm fascinated with investigative work and if the truth be known, and I can handle it," she said, with a sense of finality.

"Honey, that's not what I'm concerned about. I know you can handle anything you put your mind to. It's just that when you worked for Denby, you worked on cases that weren't so dangerous, except for the last one. If you go to work for a detective agency, there's no telling what you'll be doing."

"Aw, Jim, that's sweet. I appreciate that you are trying to protect me, but you know I cannot sit at home. I have tried that now for six months, and have been patiently waiting for a positive response on the job front, and nothing has happened. It's driving me stir-crazy."

Jim rolled his eyes and changed the subject. His business was doing well enough to support them, but he had to admit that it would help to have a secondary income. His two sons lived in New York with his ex-wife, and it took a lot of money to keep everything going, especially to set aside for a college fund for his kids and her two daughters.

"What are the girls doing, honey?" Jim inquired.

"They're upstairs doing homework, or better be. I can hear their music playing, so I cannot tell for sure if they are studying, or just playing around. Maybe I'd better run up and check on them."

"They're alright until dinner time, aren't they, honey?"

"I suppose you are right, Jim. Do you want a glass of wine, or something else to drink?"

"No thanks, I'll wait for dinner. Speaking of that, what's cooking? It smells great," Jim sniffed the aroma in the air as a hound would when tracking its target.

"Can't you tell? It's one of your favorites. I picked up a pot roast from the grocery store, and put it in the oven on a medium temperature when I ran by the house earlier this afternoon.

"Hmm, it smells delicious," said Jim, smiling. "What are you cooking with it?"

"The usual, you know… potatoes, carrots, onion, and celery."

Paula hopped up, and opened the oven to check the contents of the blue metal cooker. She slid the metal rack out and pulled off the top of the cooker by its handle. With a mitt on one hand and with a fork in the other hand, she poked the roast, potatoes, and carrots for tenderness. She shook the mitt off her hand, grabbed a sharp knife, and then cut a small piece of the succulent meat, blowing on it before putting it in her mouth.

"Hmm, tastes good. It's ready. Jim, would you call the girls please?"

"Sure Paula. Wow that smells delicious!" Jim walked to the bottom of the stairs, and then looked up to the top of the landing. He cupped his hands around his mouth to amplify his voice above the music. "Girls, time to eat."

"Yes, sir," said Rachel, responding for both of them. With a couple of quick clicks, Rachel saved her work on her laptop. Christine dropped her pencil on the page she was writing. Hopping up, they scampered down the stairs on each other's heels finding their places at the table. The family began to enjoy dinner with the usual banter.

"Mom, I want to be a cheerleader next year," said Christine. She forked a piece of roast mixed with rice and gravy into her mouth quickly followed by lima beans.

"Chrissie, slow down with your eating, hon. You're eating like there's no tomorrow," said Paula.

Rachel laughed at her little sister. "There might not be, Mom," Rachel interjected.

Paula glared at Rachel enough to ward off any more cute remarks. Christine put her fork down beside her plate and chewed her food more slowly like her mother had reminded her to do many times. Embarrassed, she looked up at her mom and smiled, lips closed and her mouth bouncing up and down. Paula grinned lovingly at her daughters.

"Now about cheerleading, just keep your grades up, and we'll need to enroll you in gymnastics soon so you can catch up with the other girls."

Recovering from her mouthful of food, she responded, "Why can't I just try out now, Mom?"

"Chrissie, you know, it's not like it was when I was in school. You have to be able to tumble pretty well to be a cheerleader these days."

"Okay, Mom. Well, can you give me a couple of weeks before I start gymnastics? We have finals next week, and I'm studying a lot right now."

"That's what I like to hear. You're thinking for yourself, and about what's most important, your education."

Pleased within at her mother's approval, Christine changed subjects suddenly, taking her mom off-guard. "Mom, who were you talking to on the phone when I got home from school today? You were telling them that you have experience as a private investigator."

"I was talking to a man about a job, dear. He was interested in interviewing me, if he liked my resume."

"What's a resume, Mom?"

Jim flinched then looked at Paula. "Did you arrange an appointment with him?" he asked, interrupting their conversation.

"Not yet Jim, I need to revise my resume first. He wanted me to fax it to him, and then call later to set a time to get together and go over it. That's why I brought it up to you when you got home, so we could talk."

"Oh, I see," he said, with a look of consternation.

Paula cut her eyes away from her husband and toward her older daughter. She felt Jim's uneasiness and wanted to buy time by changing the subject.

"How's school for you Rachel? Do you have finals to study for, also?"

"Yes, Mom, but I exempted two, so I only have two to study for this semester."

"That's great, honey. If either of you girls needs help, y'all let me know, okay?"

Rachel and Christine both responded in unison with their usual, "yes ma'am".

Jim finished his meal thinking about what had transpired at the table. He enjoyed his stepdaughters, and was glad to be a stepfather to them, but he often yearned to be with his boys. He felt that he had let them down, although the divorce was not his fault. He thought about the times past when he was an assistant coach for their little league baseball team. He found a little solace remembering that they would be visiting Charleston soon, the first time since he and Paula had married. He thought of them together. Images of them playing ball, and throwing a Frisbee at the beach ran through his imagination.

After completing the meal, and a family effort at cleaning the kitchen, Paula and Jim watched TV in the den while the girls sprawled out on the den floor and studied. An hour passed as Paula finished watching her shows, switched off the TV, then nudged Jim as his eyes were closing. Rachel and Christine closed their books and gathered up their things, prancing upstairs to prepare for bed. They did most things on their own, without prompting, a source of pride for Paula.

"Come on, Jim, let's go to bed. You must be beat."

"Uh, yeah, I am. I lifted too much today. My back is feeling it now."

Jim yawned as he sat up from his slumped position on his comfortable burgundy leather chair and matching ottoman. Following his wife of one-year up the stairs, she held his hand loosely while leading the way upstairs to the bedroom. They disrobed and eased into their king size bed, turning off the lights. Jim made himself comfortable facing the side of the bed away from his wife.

"Not going to read tonight, honey?" Paula asked. "You usually turn on your lamp."

"No, I'm too tired. What's the name of that private investigator who wants to interview you?"

"Russell Baxter. Luke uses his agency to help him with divorce cases and several other things. He owns a business called Crescent Moon Investigations. Luke said his business is growing rapidly from the quality work he does. He said he needed someone for the routine assignments."

"Routine assignments?"

"You know... looking up records, interviewing potential clients, delivering divorce papers, that type thing. He uses a college girl to handle most of the clerical duties."

"I see," he said.

"Is that all you have to say, Jim, "I see"?"

Jim pulled the covers over his shoulder without talking more or the desire to be amorous, settling down for sleep. He closed his eyes determined to shut Paula out. She knew her husband was brooding so she reached over the top of his broad shoulders, and kissed him on the cheek.

"Good night, honey," said Paula.

"Good night," said Jim. He adjusted his covers a little, burying his head in the pillow, not turning to face her for their usual kiss on the lips good night when they were not in the mood for anything else.

Jim knew her well enough to understand that she wanted to pull her weight of the proverbial wagon in the family's financial matters. He just could not fathom why she had to involve herself with a dangerous occupation again, especially after her plight with her last job.

Three

After seeing Jim off to work, and getting Rachel and Christine off to school, Paula sat down with her laptop to flesh out a revised resume that she hoped would impress her prospective employer. Her fingers raced across the keyboard as she slanted her past job descriptions and duties, transforming some of the redundant tasks of a paralegal to include more duties like that of a private investigator. She inserted her experience as a college student while working with her uncle, a highly respected private investigator from Savannah, Georgia. Completing the final touches, she printed two copies and closed her laptop, inserting it into its case. Excited at the possibility of a new job, she drove down to a local office store and faxed the resume to Crescent Moon Investigations by 11 AM.

Baxter was out of his office most of the morning, but dropped by before going to lunch to check his phone messages. He flipped through the stack of facsimile pages on the center of his desk that Carla neatly stacked and flagged with yellow sticky pad notations.

"Good, she did fax the resume after all. Maybe she's serious about a job here," said Baxter, louder than he intended. He lifted the two-paged resume vertically for reading ease and studied it with interest. Scanning over her past experience and job duties, Baxter saw a good fit for his business.

"What's that, Mr. Baxter?" Carla asked, overhearing him speak aloud to no one in particular.

"Oh, sorry, Carla, just thinking out loud. A prospect for private investigator I spoke with faxed me her resume."

"Yeah, I noticed that. Very impressive, I thought," she said.

"Me too, so far," he said, as he picked up the phone to dial Paula's number.

"Hello?"

"May I speak to Paula Roberts?"

"This is she."

"Yes, this is Russell Baxter with the Crescent Moon Investigations. I received your resume today and wondered if we could get together to talk it over?"

"Well, hello Mr. Baxter. I'm glad you received it so quickly. Sure, when would you like to meet?"

"How about today, say around one o'clock at the Hamburger Shack? We can do a working lunch, if that's good with you."

Baxter wanting to meet so soon took Paula a little by surprise. She looked down at her jeans, old college sweatshirt, and worn tennis shoes that she slipped on that morning, and thought about what she might quickly change into for a decent appearance. Not wanting to appear desperate, she hesitated a moment before responding.

"That's about two hours from now. Hmm, I think I can make it," she said, knowing that she could. "I have one other detail to finish up and will be glad to meet you there."

"Do you know where it is?"

"Yes, I do. Isn't it that place at the end of Market Street near the harbor?"

"That's the one."

"That'll work for me Mr. Baxter," replied Paula.

"Call me Russ, if you will. I'm not much on formality."

"Sure, I can do that, Russ. Call me Paula. What's the attire, if I may ask? It's rather short notice, not that I mind."

"Just come as you are. It's not a problem. I usually dress casual myself."

"Great, I love casual. See you there, Russ. By the way, what do you look like so I'll recognize you?"

"I'm six feet tall, and have sandy brown hair. I'll have on a pair of Khakis, and a pale blue polo shirt."

"Got it, I'll be in slacks, and a green pullover sweater, since you did say casual. I'm five feet seven, brunette with green eyes and shoulder length hair."

"I'm sure you'll be easy to recognize. I'll see you there, Paula."

Daniel Easterling

"I'll see you there. Good-bye now and thanks."

The Hamburger Shack, located downtown near the Market, had been voted Charleston's best place for hamburgers numerous times. The outside of the building was nothing much to look at. The exterior was made of heavy-gauge corrugated aluminum panels, the kind normally used for roofing, or an outbuilding of some kind. As a result, the restaurant stood out from the rest of the buildings on the block that were made of brick, or stucco. This unattached building at the end of the block was about forty feet in width and eighty feet in length, very functional for an in and out lunch atmosphere.

Two women with their hair in buns, wearing short-sleeved cotton dresses, mid-length to their shins, hovered over the long flat grill with their spatulas, as they pressed then turned the monstrous mounds of hamburger meat. They stood stoically, in their white socks and black leather walking shoes, shuffling on the thick black rubber mat, dutifully cooking the meat on medium heat to prevent carbonizing the outsides. It took considerably longer than your common fast food joints to get the centers of these huge patties done. The best thing about the burgers, besides their size, was that you could get them practically any way you wanted. Some people ordered the burgers with cheese, or pimento cheese, sautéed mushrooms, jalapenos, homemade chili, and numerous other options. Lettuce, tomato, and onion were placed on one side of the bun, and the burger on the other.

They were served with a dill pickle spear and a generous portion of fresh-cut French fries, unless potato chips were requested.

Market Street was busy with lunch and tourist traffic; drivers, hawk-eyed, looking for a coveted place to park. Baxter stood waiting on the sidewalk near the front door under the green canvas awning. As he looked at his watch, then side to side, an above-average looking woman with a fair complexion and shoulder-length hair curled under and bouncing, approached him. Before she could speak, he stepped forward with his hand extended.

"You must be Paula Roberts?"

He immediately noticed her engaging, intelligent eyes taking him in then glancing around at her surroundings. She stopped in her tracks catching herself on the balls of her feet—her hair on one side swathing across her face then springing back to its position, then extended her hand to his.

"That would be me," said Paula, smiling. She shook his hand vigorously with direct eye contact and a confidence that portrayed her sense of self-worth. "And you are Russ Baxter, no doubt."

"I am. It's a pleasure to meet you," said Russ, a bit taken aback. He was not sure what to expect before he met her, but imagined more of a plain looking female with a tomboyish demeanor, not that he was disappointed. She had an athletic quality, but her looks were too stunning to be described as a tomboy.

"Same here, Russ. Luke has great things to say about you."

"Luke's a great guy and a fine young attorney—works hard, that guy."

Baxter was immediately impressed with how she carried herself, even though she dressed casually. They entered the Hamburger Shack and chose a padded booth over a table with wooden lattice-back chairs. There were no frills on the inside of the restaurant—only its homey décor and food made it appealing. Old signs from the fifties and sixties hung on the walls around three sides of the restaurant. ESSO, TEXACO, COCA-COLA, ALKA-SELTZER, and more, in colorful, but aging metal signs had been foraged from antique stores and chosen to enhance the oldies atmosphere. A tall wooden Native American brave stood in one corner overseeing the dining room.

After seating themselves and exchanging niceties, Baxter reached into his zipped black leather portfolio retrieving a manila folder containing Paula's resume. He placed it on the table, and then his keys on top of it, as if to secure it for a moment.

"We need to go to the counter to order, or would you prefer me to order for you?" said Baxter.

"Thanks just the same, but I'll go up there with you. I've been here once before, so I want to get a closer look at the menu first." To Paula, Baxter seemed like a nice man, down to earth, non-pretentious, as Luke indicated.

"Great, let's go. We'll go over your resume when we get back."

She glanced at the menu hanging above the counter offering multiple combinations for the giant burgers. The cashier sat on her stool smacking her chewing gum behind an old timey register. With a pencil in hand and small pad on the counter to write their order, she waited for the pair to decide.

"What y'all gonna have today?"

"You first," said Baxter, politely, standing by his new prospect.

"I'll have the pimento burger with pickles only, and a sweet tea," said Paula.

"Fries with that ma'am?" asked the cashier.

"No thanks, no fries for me. I'll take the potato chips."

"And what do you want to drink, ma'am?"

"Sweet tea will be fine."

"Good choice, Paula," Baxter interjected.

"And for you, sir, what can I get you today?"

"I'll have the cheeseburger with bacon, ma'am, a side of jalapenos, chips, and a sweet tea, also," he said.

The cashier bellowed the order to the cooks, who seemed not to hear her, as they continued to flip the burgers, patting them with their spatula. Methodically, the cashier walked over next to the large flat grill and hung the slip of paper on a clip in line with previous orders. Russ and Paula turned, winding their way through the customers back to their booth with their ice-teas in hand.

The windows in the old restaurant were too high to see outside, but the bright sunlight streamed through the red-plaid, partially drawn curtains. The lunch crowd began to fill the restaurant with chatter, as they enjoyed the quaint atmosphere and the homemade fare. Paula noticed the Mason jars with handles filled with ice and soft beverages on the other tables, reminding her of a small restaurant back home in Georgetown where she ate with her family as a child. At the end of the dining area, a patron dropped four quarters in a large jukebox to get the maximum of five songs for a dollar. Soon the air was filled with the sounds of the oldies from the fifties and sixties. Everything from the Beach Boys to Motown sounds were cycling through from selections by the patrons. The aroma of grilled burgers permeated the air making its own statement for preeminence over the music.

Baxter scanned her resume once again. "Everything looks great, Paula, but I'm curious. Let me ask you a couple of questions."

"Sure Russ, that's what I'm here for."

"Why do you want to work for a detective agency?" he asked, bluntly.

"As you can see on my resume, I have worked in this line of work before, and frankly, I enjoy it. It is exhilarating and rewarding. Yes I know some of it can be humdrum, but isn't every job?"

"Indeed," said Baxter. He continued viewing her resume then looked at her. "Tell me about your last job working for the attorney in Georgetown, Denby, I believe is his name. I know about the Judge Parks incident, so we will not need to cover that. Just tell me what you did in terms of private investigative work."

"Okay, sure. I stopped the normal paralegal work, and started doing investigations during the end of my second year. My employer assigned me to some of the divorce cases to verify accusations of infidelity. I really didn't do too many stakeouts, though I was not a stranger to them. I usually worked with a P.I. who used a camera, and went to happy hours, here and there, to find out what I could from spouses who our clients thought were cheating," she said.

"That's one thing we do a lot of, Paula."

"What, go to happy hours?" she replied.

"No," said Baxter, with a chuckle, "handle divorce cases. It seems to never end. Anything else you can think of that would translate to investigative work?"

"We also investigated business partners for misdeeds, you know, when they were breaking up," said Paula. "I preferred those cases over divorces, but we did what we had to for our clients and the firm."

"I agree, Paula. I will say this in light of what you said. I do not take cases from just anybody. I screen them as best I can by using the ole gut-check method. I also gauge it by whether I know anything about their reputation. I prefer to help out the person getting dumped on, and not the other way around."

"I'm glad to hear that, Russ. I can relate to that."

"Really, how's that?" he asked, the statement arousing his curiosity.

"I don't know. Call it my need for social justice. I don't mean to get personal, but I was in a bad marriage in the past. The dead-beat father of my two girls still doesn't pay child support."

Without showing surprise, Baxter responded. "Oh, I thought Luke said you were married."

"Yes, I'm happily married for a little over a year to the most wonderful man I've ever met," she said, beaming.

"Awesome, Paula, that's very important in our line of work. Okay, let me get down to the job duties. Most times we'll be busy with investigative work, but I'm sure you don't mind handling phone calls and filing as needed do you?"

"Oh no, whatever it takes to get the job done, but I don't view myself as a secretary. I know it may sound negative, but I do get bored easily with repetitive routines."

"No, it doesn't. I'm bored easily, as well. I think it's a sign of an intelligent mind. I see here on your resume that you have experience working for Charlie Satterfield down in Savannah. He's a well-known investigator in the Southeast."

"Yeah, Uncle Charlie got me interested in the world of investigations when I lived there attending technical college. He taught me quite a bit. I tried to get away from it, but it seems to be calling my name again. I was thinking that I would continue working as a paralegal after our move to Charleston, but right now that doesn't seem to be my lot. I hope that doesn't sound bad."

"No, it doesn't sound bad at all. You're just being open and honest; I prefer you to be that way going in, so that there are no surprises. Wow, so Satterfield is your uncle? What did you do for him?"

"Yes, he's my uncle on my mother's side. With Uncle Charlie, we occasionally had to track somebody down, or catch a cheating spouse. I enjoyed it a lot."

"Well, let me tell you what I need. Right now, my business is growing, and most of the clerical work is covered. I've lucked into the best college co-ed I could possibly want for that part of the business. I need help on the front end interviewing potential clients, and I need help with investigations. I can guarantee that you won't get bored. We will do background checks, fraud cases, marital infidelity, and more. Are you licensed to carry a weapon, or do you have any experience with a handgun by any chance?"

"Yes sir, I got my license a long time ago when working with Uncle Charlie. I have maintained my skills at shooting galleries after my initial training at the Savannah Police Academy. I carry a concealed weapon with me everywhere I go."

"I do, as well, but I don't ever mention it to my clients. It's with me for protection, a tool of the trade for self-defense, or the defense of innocents."

"Absolutely, that's the way it should be."

"Paula, I must admit you seem to be the right fit for the job, if you are interested?"

"Yes I am," said his eager applicant.

"Good, well, I can offer you twelve dollars per hour when you are not handling a case, and a percentage of the cases you handle, or a straight salary. What would be your preference? I took in ninety-one cases last year netting a pretty decent income by anyone's standards, but it's more than I can properly handle now. Because of the overload, I'm turning cases away that I really would like to take."

"Hmm, would you please explain how the percentage thing works?"

"I'll give you sixty-five percent of each case you bring in, or that I assign to you, and the hourly rate I mentioned when you are not on a case. We can split some of them down the middle and other cases we'll divide according to time spent. I'll also pay one-half of your health insurance, and allow one week's vacation after six months, two weeks after a year's employment."

"That sounds very generous, Russ. Let me talk it over with my husband before I officially commit. How long do I have to decide?"

"Take as much time as you need. I didn't have the position advertised, except by word of mouth. In fact, it was over a burger at this same restaurant that I told Luke to keep an ear out for me. I've worked several cases for him," said Baxter.

"Yeah, that's what he said. Great, then I'll get back to you within a week, or sooner, if I have an answer before then," she said.

"That'll work. I'll be waiting."

As they shook hands completing their tentative agreement, the sound of their names resonated across the diner. "Burger baskets for Russ and Paula, burger baskets are on the counter," the worker bellowed.

Baxter went to the counter to retrieve their order. Leaving off business discussions, they enjoyed the old timey burgers while sharing small talk about each other's family.

"That was delicious, and I hate to run, but it's almost 2:30 PM. It's time for me to be back at work," said Baxter.

"No problem, I've got to pick up my girls from school soon. Thank you for your time."

"The pleasure's all mine," he said.

The beginning of a partnership was forged. Baxter left a tip on the table and they made their way to the front of the restaurant. He reached around Paula to open the door.

"Thanks again for coming, Paula. I'll wait to hear from you."

"Thank you, and thanks for lunch, Russ. I'll be in touch soon."

"No problem. Have a nice day!"

"And you, as well," she said.

Four

⚜

Mark Jennings drove down a narrow dirt road bordered by tall pine trees, an occasional oak, or dogwood scattered about, within the predominantly long-leaf pine forest, to a darkened, secluded cove on Johns Island. At precisely three in the morning, he was to meet a fishing boat, which made its way to Johns Island from the Caribbean. Exactly where in the Caribbean the boat came from, Jennings did not have a clue. The only thing he knew was that he got the best prices and purest product for cocaine distribution from this particular supplier since he had become financier over the past year and a half. Jennings' supplier also brought him a pound or two of pot whenever he requested it, but he did not much like handling it because it was too hard to conceal. If he copped the weed from time to time, he did it for his trusted coke distributor, who smoked it regularly, and distributed the rest to several of his pot-smoking friends.

Paula Roberts P.I. - Johns Island

Anna Leigh Jennings had found white powder residue on the bathroom counter once when he was careless, but her husband explained it away as baby powder that he used on his feet. She did not think to taste it, not that she would know what it was, and he was never that careless again. As a banker, he led a double-life and kept his contact with drug users to a minimum. The community knew him as an upstanding citizen and family man. Obviously, he preferred to keep it that way. Jennings dearly loved his children and knew that he needed to turn from his egregiously destructive habit, but seemed unable to break the chains of bondage, which held him unmercifully in his dark, personal dungeon.

His closest friend, Jimmy Snyder, and his girlfriend, Carol, knew about his habit, but only Snyder knew of his dealing. Snyder ran the distribution to the lower level dealers and to a few select users, who were his friends. Jennings remembered the scene at his best friend's house watching football one night, when his friend surprised him while they were drinking, and his inhibitions suppressed.

Snyder made a comment on the game then retrieved a small glass vial from his jeans pocket. He proceeded to pour the off-white powder gently tapping the side of the vial with his finger. Jennings watched while his friend rolled a crisp twenty-dollar bill into the shape of a straw.

Snyder leaned over snorting up the cocaine, and then handed the rolled currency to him.

"Do you want to try it, Mark? It gives you a great rush. You will feel like you can do anything."

"Cocaine?" asked Jennings.

"Yeah, man. I've been messing around with it for a while now, but didn't know if I should tell you."

"How long does it last? And, what the heck do I do, Jimmy?"

"Just do what I did," said Snyder.

"You mean I'm to snort this chemical up my nose with a twenty dollar bill?"

Snyder tilted the vial and tapped the side pouring another line of coke on the glass coffee table. "Yeah, man. Go ahead. There's nothing to it."

Hesitantly, Jennings leaned over following his friend's example. The cocaine went to work fast making him feel special, powerful, as if he were invincible. Jennings had never felt an artificial exhilaration like that in all his life. He had read enough to know that it was dangerous, but with his marriage on the rocks, he did not much care anymore.

Snyder had been using for some time, and dealing on a minor basis to his friends, but he did not have the resources to finance large shipments. The small deals that he transacted kept him in the drugs without tying up money he needed for bills, but he knew that Jennings had the money to finance large deals upon which he could make extra cash. Soon after Snyder turned his old friend on, Jennings asked questions regarding the price the cocaine sold for, and other details on how they might go into business with each other. Snyder's hopes materialized as his long time friend contemplated the drug from the business angle. Not being content just to make enough to feed his habit, Jennings figured that he could make some easy money on the drug, as well as support his extra-marital affair. At least, that was one justification that he rationalized in his mind. Never mind the illegality, or the cops. He knew most of them well, and figured that they would never suspect him of being a drug dealer.

The boat's owner, Captain Greg, steered the vessel into the cove and guided it to an old dilapidated dock, portions of the wooden structure covered with green algae. A large willow tree stood on the edge of the bank, branches draping over the dock like an octopus's tentacles reaching to claim its prey.

The first mate, Davie, tossed a rope to the waiting Jennings who caught it with one hand and helped pull the boat into place against the aging rubber bumpers, cracked and worn. Davie jumped off the boat long enough to secure it, and then hopped back on the deck standing watch in a crouching position near the bow.

Jennings boarded the boat behind Davie, briefcase in hand, and climbed down a ladder below the deck to a cabin area near the boat's midsection to meet Captain Greg who was busy getting his shipment ready for inspection. They had met each other on several occasions and the meeting had almost become routine, except for the normal heightened anxieties of handling large amount of money and cocaine.

"How's it going this morning, Captain?" said Jennings. "Did you have a good trip up from the islands?"

"Yeah, man, it was fine. Only thing is, we made a run past a couple of Coast Guard cutters on the way into the waterway. That wasn't too cool, but there seems to be more of them out on the ocean nowadays. Sit down. Make yourself at home." The captain glanced up from the little fold-down table where he sat with a worn, brown leather satchel next to him.

"I'm sure there is," said Jennings, as he took his place at the table. "The Coast Guard has to justify their budget by intercepting what they can when they can. I'm glad they left you alone."

"So far they have," said the captain.

Jennings watched the captain unzip the old satchel and reach inside pulling out two large zip-lock plastic bags filled with uncut cocaine.

"There you go man, your two kilos of cocaine," said Captain Greg. He separated the seals on the oversize, heavy-duty freezer bags then gestured with his head and hand for his buyer to inspect the product, as he spoke. "Go ahead, check it out."

Jennings moved closer and pulled out his Swiss Army knife that he used primarily for this purpose. Opening the knife, he slid the dull blade with a squared-end under the off-white powder then lifted enough to sample with the tip of his tongue. "Tastes pure enough," said Jennings.

"Oh, it's pure alright," said the captain.

Jennings nodded approvingly then dipped the blade in the powder again, scooping a larger amount. He turned his head away for a moment and exhaled all of his breath. Carefully, he positioned the blade to his nostrils and snorted the cocaine with Hoover-like suction. Without saying another word, he waited for a moment, looking away from the captain at nothing in particular. Captain Greg waited patiently for the drug to take effect, tapping his fingers of one hand on the table, his other armed crossed in front of him resting on the table, as well.

Jennings concentrated on how the cocaine affected him while the power in the back of his throat melted and oozed slowly down the walls of his esophagus. Suddenly, the drug gave him the familiar rush that he knew all too well, sending his brain into overdrive. Confident that the product was a pure form, he opened his hard-shell briefcase that he brought with him, and faced it where the captain could count the money. Jennings thought about how his regular customers would clamor to get the purest stuff he had ever ingested.

"Here's the money, Captain, fifty thousand big ones, laid out the way you like it, not hard to count."

"Very nice, mate. Just gimme a minute to verify," Captain Greg retorted in his Bahamian brogue.

The captain thumbed through one stack of hundreds counting the precise number, and then counted the remaining stacks while flipping quickly through them like a deck of cards to insure the money's authenticity. It might have seemed that the captain was too trusting and could be deceived by counterfeit, but his experience as a money counter at a Casino in Nassau gave him all the knowledge that he needed to recognize authentic American currency. Just the touch and smell was enough for him, although he knew a couple of other methods for verification.

"Okay man, it's all here. You have your product, and I have my payment. Are you satisfied?" said Captain Greg.

"Yeah, it's the real deal," said Jennings.

Jennings lifted the stacks of money from his briefcase to the table. Captain Greg scaled the bags of cocaine and pushed them toward Jennings then quickly stacked the money from Jennings into his satchel, zipping it.

"We hate to rush, but we need to shove off. A rolling stone gathers no moss, and all that jazz, mate. You know how to reach us when you need more. Remember to use a different pay phone and calling card each time you call."

"I always do," said Jennings, a little irritated that the captain reminded him of the same process every time. Jennings grabbed the sealed bags of cocaine, and placed them carefully side by side in his briefcase then turned the combination lock. The men slipped out from the folding table and stood to their feet.

The captain rapped on the side of the hull twice to signal to Davie, who in turn untied the ropes, and prepared to shove off as soon as their customer stepped off the boat. Jennings moved quickly across the deck and stepped down from the boat to the dock. He trotted over to the back of his car and opened the hatch, securing the briefcase in a compartment that he had made to conceal the contraband. Slamming the hatch, he jumped behind the wheel, leaving the secluded cove on his way back to the main road.

Captain Greg resumed his spot at the helm, preparing to launch out to sea. The fishing boat, named the *Bahamian Recluse*, powered by two rugged, efficient diesel motors, stirred the gurgling water below. He let the engine idle while he waited for his first mate to shove off. Davie pushed the boat out from the dock, and instantly, Captain Greg engaged the twin motors in reverse backing the boat from the dock and turning it, bow facing the sea. Engaging forward throttle the captain made his way out to the Atlantic Ocean and charted course for his destination.

Anna Leigh Jennings had a fitful night's sleep because of the news that Baxter had given her. Her husband was out again to the wee hours of the morning. She rolled over when she heard the garage door opening. Letting out an exasperated sigh, she smacked her pillow with her fist and flipped it over. She pushed her head down into the pillow and hid herself under the covers. Anna Leigh chose to pretend that she was sound asleep so that her husband would not attempt to arouse her. She lay there in the dark beneath her silk, womb-like fort, hearing the sounds of her own breath. Soon she picked up the sound of her husband closing his car door entering the home. She could hear him in the kitchen talking on the phone to someone.

"Yeah, I got the shipment. You can call me tomorrow at work, and we'll arrange a time and place to meet. Okay, okay, don't worry. I'll cover you until you can bring in some money."

Anna Leigh heard him hang up the phone, and sit down at the kitchen table. The chairs always squeaked, but she could never part with them because her grandmother had given her the dining room set when she was admitted to a nursing home. After his conversation ended, she heard her husband slide the chair against the table and walk to the bedroom. He opened the bathroom door and flipped on the light.

"Thud," one shoe dropped to the tile floor, and then the other shoe. In his sock-feet, Jennings slipped quietly out of the bathroom. Anna Leigh turned away from the center of the bed so that her husband would not face her when he got in.

Thinking his wife was fast asleep, Jennings carefully pulled the covers back just far enough to slip in and lay down beside her. He checked his alarm to ensure it was set for 7 AM. Anna Leigh was so angry with him that she chose silence over getting into an argument, which she knew would end like the other ones. She preferred to have divorce papers served and let it go at that. She remembered one of her mother's sayings, "revenge is best when served cold", and decided to keep her new revelation of his infidelity secret, just as he had been doing to her.

She had gone to great lengths to talk to her husband in the past to no avail. He dropped out of counseling when they got into an argument because he would not keep the appointments on time, despite the fact that she was paying for the sessions. She suspected, as did the psychiatrist that he had come to the sessions high on a few occasions. Furthermore, his problems were primarily what the psychiatrist was addressing. *Not this time, turnabout is fair play,* she thought. She forced herself to go back to sleep. In a few hours, she would awaken their children for school. Regardless of their domestic problems, she maintained a routine for the emotional stability of their children.

Five

⚜

Paula arrived in time at Low Country Middle School to pick up her children. Her daughters exited the front entrance behind a group of rowdy boys who had pushed their way down the halls into their afternoon freedom. The heavy-gauge, green metal doors swung open forcefully, smacking the doorstops with such force that the tops of the doors hit the brick exterior walls to the schoolhouse. Rachel and Christine giggled with each other about the rambunctious boys who bolted out ahead of them. The boys were a little older than they were, but knew they lived in the neighborhood, were cute, and came from good families.

"That's Tommy Brown, and Billy Langston," said Christine.

"They're just showing off," said Rachel. "Don't pay any attention to them, Christine. You will encourage them."

Christine giggled, skipping the last couple of yards to the vehicle and hopped in. Paula waited with the engine running at the curb, as did most of the other parents. Rachel shuffled behind her little sister a couple of steps, then tossed her book bag on the floor of the car and plopped down in the back seat next to Christine.

"Hey Mom, we have ten more days until summer," said Rachel.

"Yeah, I know, honey. It'll be great to be out of school for the summer, won't it?"

"Sure will, Mom. We'll get to sleep in. Won't we, Christine?"

"Uh huh." said Christine.

Rachel and Christine continued to talk with each other about who had the most homework and what their teachers and friends did that day. Paula envied her kids growing up in this time of innocence that she could no longer fully remember, but smiled, happy that they enjoyed themselves and were into their academics. She took in tidbits of what they were saying, but was deep in thought about accepting the job that Russell Baxter had offered to her over lunch. She worried that Jim would be upset, but she wanted to escape a bad case of cabin fever, as well as contribute to the family income.

After a short ride home, Paula turned in their driveway, and the girls raced each other to get the spare key hidden in the garage. Rachel won as usual and opened the door for them. As they entered their home, the telephone rang, and Christine ran toward the phone.

"No, Chrissie, I've got it," said Paula. Putting her purse on the table, she lifted the handset from its cradle. "Hello."

"Hey, honey," said Jim. "Did you just walk in from school with the girls? You sound like you are in a huff."

"Yes, and no, I'm not in a huff, Jim…just normal stuff with two young teens."

"Good, I'm glad you're day is going well. Mine is, too. Listen, I know you're busy with them, but I couldn't wait to share the good news."

"What's that, honey?"

"I found a suitable place to move the business to in Charleston. The only kicker is that the rent will be twice what I am paying now, but I feel sure that the business increase will more than justify the move. It's over on East Bay one block from the old City Market."

"That's fantastic, Jim! I am excited for you. That's what you wanted…well, what we wanted. We knew the overhead would be higher, but look at the area. It's booming, and the interest in antiques is big here."

"That's right, and once we build up our regular clientele in Charleston, not to mention benefitting from the tourist traffic, I'm thinking it could be huge for the future."

"That's my hubby! I knew something would pop for you soon, dear. You're such a hard worker." Paula's mind began to swirl as she looked for an opening to break the news of her employment opportunity to Jim.

"Thank you, sweetheart. That means a lot coming from you."

"Well, it's true, Jim. I'm so proud of you. Do you think some of your regulars who buy from you at the Georgetown location will drive to Charleston?"

"Oh yes, I've received several commitments from current customers to stick with me and to continue to refer business my way."

"That's great, Jim. Listen, honey, since we're in the news breaking mode, I have something to tell you too." She cringed a little because she figured he would not like what she would tell him next.

"What's that, Paula?"

"I interviewed with Russell Baxter today at lunch about that job at the Crescent Moon Investigations."

"Oh yeah, that's right. How did that go?"

"It went very well. This man pleasantly surprised me. He didn't seem like a private investigator. He acted more like a normal businessman, but dressed down, very nice."

"What's that suppose to mean, Paula?"

"Well, you know... he was down to earth, not shady looking at all. I told him about my work at the Denby Law Firm. He already knew about the Judge Parks' blackmail case and did not hold anything against me, which was a huge relief. Of course, he had talked to Luke already, so that helped immensely."

Jim fidgeted, as he listened, not liking where this conversation was heading. Departing from his normal disposition, he blurted out, "Okay, so you had the interview, and you are asking me if I approve of you taking the job."

"Well, yeah, that would be nice. I am leaning heavily in that direction and your support means a lot. If it turns out to be anything too dangerous, I'll resign."

"Paula, you're asking me if I want you to work as a private investigator, and the answer is, no, not really, but if you feel that you must work right now, and are willing to walk away should it become dangerous, then I'll go along with it. Maybe that's not the answer you want to hear, but that's the best I can do, considering what happened with your last employment putting you in the hospital."

Paula had hoped for more of a positive response from her husband, but she knew his hesitation was because he loved her. "Thank you, Jim. I knew you would understand. Besides, with your moving the business at this time, it will help us to stay on our plan to lay aside college funds for our kids each month, in spite of our bills, don't you agree?"

"Yes, dear, I agree. When do you start?"

"I haven't told him that I would work for him yet. I wanted your approval first."

"Well, I'm glad you did, Paula. I love you, and I will see you at home for dinner. I may be a little late because I'm going to run by the new location to meet with the landlord to finalize details on improvements of the building, and sign the contract."

"Okay, hon, I want to hear all the details over dinner. Love you, too," she said.

"See you later," he said.

Jim was bolstered by her supportive tone for the move, yet concerned about her new employment. He hung up and tried not to think about anything but what he had to do. Paula hung up relieved at her husband's response, and happy that things were moving fast for him in relocating his antique business. She hoped the move might take his mind off of her new business venture.

No time to waste, Paula thought, *I'll call Russ Baxter to accept the job.* First, she called out to her daughters to make sure they were on track. "Girls, let's get the homework out of the way."

"Mom, we just got in. We want to wait a while before doing more schoolwork," said Rachel.

"Alright then, one hour. At 4:30, both of you need to get with the studies. We'll talk about your homework at the dinner table."

"Okay thanks, and Mom?" said Rachel.

"Yes dear?"

"We love you," both girls shouted from upstairs, giggling.

Paula laughed at her girls, shaking her head, yet admiring their negotiating skills, which were developing rapidly. Almost four o'clock in the afternoon now, Paula lifted the cordless phone from its base, and walked out onto the patio for privacy. She knew the girls listened to her conversations when they had the chance. They always did. Feeling the excitement of landing a new job with the potential for a good income and interesting work, Paula's mindset took a positive turn now that she would be contributing to the family financially, again.

She felt like a grown-up kid in a candy store, as she dialed the number for Crescent Moon Investigations. Flipping back her silky brown hair, she pressed the phone to her ear. The light from the sun poured over the patio refracting through the screen lighting up her emerald green eyes. A light breeze periodically lifted her hair, the suns' rays warming her face.

"Crescent Moon Investigations, how can I help you?" said Carla.

"May I speak to Russ Baxter, please?"

"Sure thing, may I say who is calling?"

"Yes, tell him it's Paula Roberts."

"Hold, please, Mrs. Roberts." Carla pressed the hold button. "Mr. Baxter, a Paula Roberts is on line one for you. Should I transfer the call?"

"Yes, Carla, that will be fine. Put her through." Baxter dropped a manila folder on his desk then pressed the button for line one. "Paula, hi, how's it going?"

"Awesome, thanks. I bet you didn't expect to hear from me so soon."

"No, I really didn't. Did I leave something out in the interview today?"

"Oh no, not at all, I've already talked to my husband, and he's fine with me working for you. I'm ready to take on my new job duties, and look forward to the opportunity. Your offer was very generous, as I said earlier."

"That's great to hear. I know a good applicant when I see one, Paula. I believe the agency can grow leaps and bounds with the three of us working together as a team. When do you want to start?"

"What about next week, Mr. Baxter?"

"There you go again with that Mister stuff."

"I can't help it. It's the way my mother raised me. It might take me a little while to get used to calling you by your first name."

"It's alright, Paula, I understand. I'm just picking at you. Come in to the office on Monday morning at nine o'clock. Do you know where we are located?"

"Yes sir, Luke told me. You're at 26 King Street, right?"

"That is correct. Listen, just so you know… we are going to hit the ground running. There's a case I'm on right now that we'll be serving papers first thing Monday, so I can use your help right away on this one."

"That's good to hear. I like to stay busy. I will see you next week. Have a great weekend. Good-bye now, and thanks again, Russ," she said, careful to address him as he requested.

"My pleasure, Paula, I'll see you then. Good bye."

Six

❧

Captain Greg steered his fishing vessel out into the open waters and had a good run until the break of day. The giant yellow ball of fire rose in the sky casting its radiant warmth on the ocean calling the rich wildlife beneath to energize and begin its daily routine. A little after sun up, the *Bahamian Recluse* cruised through a large school of herring switching directions simultaneously, like synchronized swimmers on the ocean's surface, as they fed voraciously on plankton. Nearby a pod of bottlenose dolphin bobbed up and down effortlessly creating their high-pitched noises as if laughing for the pure delight of swimming free in the vast expanse of the Atlantic.

"Captain, there's a Coast Guard Cutter. I repeat, a Coast Guard Cutter up ahead, two-hundred yards on the starboard side!" shouted Davie, above the sounds of waves and the twin engines.

"I hear you loud and clear, Davie. I'm turning portside forty-five degrees and proceeding straight ahead. Turn that reggae music off, and we'll try to slide on by these bad boys without attracting too much attention."

"Aye aye, Captain, it's done."

The only sounds now heard onboard the *Recluse* was the sound of the diesel engines humming, and the bow of the boat sloshing against the waves of the blue-green ocean. Captain Greg set the throttle steady at a medium-fast speed not to appear to be running from anything.

On board the *Durango*, the Coast Guard Cutter assigned to waters off the South Carolina coast, Captain Neeley received word that a suspicious looking fishing boat was approaching, and was veering off its previous course. The captain read from a report that a similar boat was reported in the area earlier before the sun came up. The *Durango's* crew was well experienced at interdiction because their primary mission was to eradicate drug trafficking on the Southeast coast.

With the fishing vessel in its sights, the captain of the *Durango* conferred with his officers and decided to confront the vessel. Approaching the *Bahamian Recluse* at a reduced rate of speed, Captain Neeley followed protocol precisely.

"Steady as she goes, men," he calmly spoke to his crew. "This is Captain Neeley speaking. Attention, all crewmembers. Begin preparations for interdiction. We have a fishing vessel moving past us on the leeward side. We will board the vessel immediately. Boarding crew, prepare your craft and launch immediately. Crew members prepare for the unknown party, possibly armed, over."

The boarding party commenced preparation in double time while the remainder of the crew simultaneously followed protocol for support. Designated members manned their guns and trained their sights on the target. The boarding party donned their bulletproof vests, and armed themselves with their weapons and ammunition clips. The support crew on deck readied the Deployable Pursuit Boat (DPB). The captain maneuvered the USCG *Durango* directly in the path of the fishing boat.

"Oh great, Captain Greg, it looks like the Americans are closing in to intercept us."

"Stay calm, Davie, we're gonna make a run for it. We'll find out in a few minutes what their intentions are."

Captain Greg pushed the throttle forward revving up the twin diesels to the highest RPMs they could muster, moving the seventy-five footer at twenty-five knots on an angle away from the *Durango*. The cutter was within distance to broadcast to the fishing vessel over a loud speaker. The *Bahamian Recluse* felt the wake of the larger vessel bearing down on it. The Coast Guard captain knew the boarding might be uneventful, but he also knew it could be very dangerous. He pulled his microphone from its cradle, and blew for a quick test at the highest volume.

"This is Captain Neeley of the United States Coast Guard," he began. "By authority of the United States government, I order you to slow your vessel to a halt, and drop anchor. We will be boarding to inspect your documents immediately, over."

Although Captain Greg heard the warning, he had no plans to comply. He looked straight into the great expanse of the ocean in front of him and continued to steer toward the Caribbean Sea. Peripherally, he could see the outline of the huge Coast Guard cutter closing. At best, Captain Greg still hoped that they would observe his vessel only, take pictures, and allow him to pass, but the warning sounded ominous.

Captain Neeley perceived that the men on the fishing vessel were ignoring his order. He had seen a similar reaction many times when a boat was running drugs, or up to something dubious. He put his microphone to his mouth again.

"I repeat, this is Captain Neeley of the United States Coast Guard *Durango*, I am ordering you to bring vessel to a halt for an inspection. If you choose to ignore this order, we will fire shots into your boat. Do you understand this warning, over?"

The gunners aboard the Coast Guard Cutter loaded their fifty-millimeter guns upon the captain's command. Captain Greg continued to ignore the order, as the *Recluse* bounced up and down on the high seas spraying ocean mist and cutting through the waves.

"Fire ahead of the boat, men," Captain Neeley shouted.

A barrage of bullets sprayed the water fifty yards ahead of the *Recluse*. The fishing vessel continued to slice through the waves with its best effort to outrun the *Durango*. Upon the captain's order, shots rang out again, landing twenty yards ahead of the *Recluse*, and still no response from Captain Greg. For a third time, in rapid succession, the Coast Guard captain ordered a round of shots. The fifty caliber bullets hit the bow of the fishing vessel this time. Black smoke billowed upwards from the damaged boat.

"Damn it! Captain Greg," said the first mate. "The sons of bitches hit us, and if we don't stop, they will sink us.

"Davie, they can't get anything on us. They're going to board, so let me do all the talking."

"Aye, Captain, will do. If they ask me anything, I don't know crap," said Davie, as he prepared to drop anchor.

From the pattern of fifty millimeter shots hitting the bow, Captain Greg knew the amidships and stern would be next. He had no choice now, but to stop, or risk another round of fire, which could ultimately sink his boat, possibly killing him or his first mate. He pulled back on the throttle to slow the vessel then slid the gear into neutral. Shifting into reverse briefly, the captain brought the boat to a complete stop then dropped anchor, only the waves of the ocean rocking the boat up and down, side to side, like a the bobber on a fisherman's rod.

Captain Greg picked up his microphone broadcasting to the captain of the *Durango*. "This is the Captain Greg of the *Bahamian Recluse*, for what reason do you demand to board our boat, over."

"Captain Greg, as you should know, the United States Coastguard has a right to search any suspicious vessel in these waters in accordance with our country's drug policies and laws, over."

"I can assure the good captain that we are clean. There is nothing suspicious about our vessel. We are a Bahamian fishing vessel, and on the way back to our port, over."

"We understand your assertion Captain Greg; nevertheless, we have information from the Bahamian Government which indicates your vessel may be carrying contraband. We will be boarding shortly, please prepare accordingly. If you have weapons aboard, we advise that you disarm yourselves immediately and lay them on the deck in plain sight so that no one gets hurt, over."

"Captain Neeley, I acknowledge your demands and will cooperate, but under duress, over."

The *Durango* launched a thirty-eight foot DPB transporting the landing party to board the fishing vessel. After Captain Greg produced his documents, which indicated ownership of the boat, for Lieutenant Jones as the landing party spread out to search the fishing vessel. The party searched the cabinets in the captain's quarters, and adjacent cabins without finding contraband. A drug dog, Swimmer by name, that accompanied them, began barking when the party went below amidships. Lieutenant Jones was intrigued by the German shepherd's actions as he continued to bark, bounding up and down, his paws scratching against a section of wooden paneling. The lieutenant had seen it a hundred times, the same as he does when he sniffs out drugs. The search party from the DPB surmised that the scent of the cocaine, or marijuana, was present, and that the drugs were likely hidden well.

After thirty additional minutes of plundering through cabinets and storage spaces, Lieutenant Jones spoke into the microphone on a radio attached to his shoulder, "Captain Neeley, Swimmer is giving us positive signs for contraband, but we have not located anything yet, over."

"Roger that, Lieutenant, inform Captain Greg that his vessel will be towed into port for a thorough search, over."

"Affirmative, Captain. We will make it so."

"Captain Greg, I'm pretty sure that you heard Captain Neeley's order, but in case you didn't, the good captain is ordering that your boat be towed into port for a thorough search."

"Yes, Lieutenant Jones, I heard your captain, and we will comply. We have no drugs, and we have no choice but to cooperate. I request to contact my government as soon as possible. May I speak to your captain?"

"Be my guest" Jones said, as he passed his radio to the perturbed captain of the *Recluse.*

"Captain Neeley, this is Captain Greg of the *Bahamian Recluse*. I can assure you that our only mission is sport fishing, and assisting an occasional private passenger. Our trip to your coast was to bring a passenger who hired me after missing his cruise ship back to Charleston. Do you really think it's necessary to detain us any further? Your men have disturbed us and rifled through our entire vessel finding nothing. We do not possess any contraband, over."

"Captain Greg, I will take that under advisement; nevertheless, we are towing your vessel into port, as I indicated. Please cooperate to your fullest, or I will have to place you and your crew in cuffs. Until our search is completed, your boat and your weapons have been seized by the United States Coast Guard."

"There are only two in my crew, my first mate and me, Captain Neeley. As I stated, we will cooperate, but under duress. I intend to file a complaint with the Bahamian government as soon as we port."

"Thank you, Captain Greg. You and your first mate will be fairly treated, and you will have that opportunity after the search is completed."

Captain Greg hoped that his hiding place for the cash would hold up. After leaving the cove, he put it in the safest hiding place that he had on his boat. Remaining calm, he attempted to portray a sense of confidence, and hoped that the search in the harbor would not be successful. His fear was that the Coast Guard would do a systematic, thorough search, and find the satchel containing the fifty thousand dollars where he had stowed it away.

Shortly after towing the *Bahamian Recluse* to harbor, the Coast Guard search team doubled in size and a meticulous effort was well under way. The team of specialists began to tear out the urethane coated, pine panels of the cabin walls. Being detained and held on board, the captain of the fishing vessel stood by as a new officer approached him.

"Captain Greg, I'm Lieutenant Fielding Moore, team leader. Now, I am going to ask you one time, where did you hide the drugs? And don't give me that crap about "you don't know what I'm talking about." I'm not a very patient man."

"Lieutenant Moore, it's like I've said already to the previous officer, all we do is fish, and occasionally transport a passenger to the States. We do not, and have not ever transported contraband."

"Then tell me why our drug dog has been barking off the chain, Captain!"

"I guess your dog is mistaken, or maybe he does not like us. I don't know."

"We will find whatever it is that's causing his excitement, Captain Greg, if that is your real name. You can be sure of it. I don't care if we have to take your boat apart piece by piece."

"That's my name, Officer Moore, and from the way you are treating us, I don't think you like us either."

Moore directed his attention toward his crew. "Men, go ahead, tear out the panels where Swimmer is sniffing."

The search team began at the center of one wall in the captain's quarters tearing out the pine panels one by one. They had ripped out a few panels with a flat crowbar when one man hit something other than insulation.

"There's something here, Lieutenant," one of the men said. When he pulled the panel down halfway, a leather satchel was visible.

"Get it out of there, Petty Officer. Let's see what's in it."

"Aye aye, sir," said the officer.

Upon Lieutenant Moore's command, he lifted the satchel completely out from the hidden compartment. The petty officer opened the soft briefcase revealing the wrapped stacks of American currency.

"It's a satchel full of money, Lieutenant."

"Good job, Petty Officer, good job."

"Interesting, Captain Greg, you must be on the backside of your delivery. No drugs, but you do have money. You want to tell us more about it?" said Lieutenant Moore.

"I don't know how that got there, or anything about it."

"Like hell, you don't," replied Moore.

"There's no law saying I can't have money, and there's no proof that this has anything to do with my trip to the US," said Captain Greg.

As the men spoke, another member of the search party pulled a small brass pipe and a bag of pot from behind another panel. He reached up again and pulled out a small bag of cocaine, the personal stash of the small boat crew.

"Lieutenant, look at this. It came from behind a panel near where we found the money," said the enlisted man.

"Ah, lookie here, Captain. You and your deckhand are possessing contraband to boot," said Lieutenant Moore. "You are both under arrest."

"You can't do that," protested the captain.

"Tell that to your attorney, Captain Greg. I believe we have probable cause enough. Besides, it is not just the money now. You are in possession of drugs on this boat. Men, search their persons and cuff them."

Moore's men searched them, uncovering one knife that the boarding team missed, and then placed them in shiny silver handcuffs, cinching them tightly, pinching their wrists. Lieutenant Moore, accompanied by two armed sailors, brought the suitcase and other contraband to Captain Neeley upon their return to the *Durango*. Captain Neeley, who was in close contact with the Drug Enforcement Agency (DEA), apprised them of the current situation. The DEA advised Neeley to port in the Charleston Harbor until the money was turned over to the United States Treasury Department, who in turn would examine the bills by serial number to trace them to the last bank location. The two Bahamians were incarcerated in the Charleston County Jail.

After careful scrutiny at a lab at the Treasury Department, the bills were traced to a bank in Richmond, Va., and then to the bank in Charleston where Mark Jennings worked. The fingerprinting was inconclusive. It appeared that the money was handled with gloves, and numerous other parties, except for when the captain, thumbed through it for verification, and there was not enough of a print to lift anything other than Captain Greg's fingerprint.

The agents pressured Captain Greg, later identified as Gregory Anderson, to reveal his international supplier and American buyer, but with little success. Davie, the first mate remained loyal to his captain playing the ignorant shipmate hired to help navigate the vessel only.

Seven

Monday could not come soon enough as Paula, who was anxious to get to work, arrived for her new job at nine in the morning. She entered the rear door, as instructed, and walked down a short hallway to find Russell Baxter in his office shuffling through papers, and reading messages from small, perforated sheets that Carla had written and left on his desk. Like any new job, she was wide-eyed, excited, and ready to take on any task requested of her.

"Good morning, Paula. Glad to see you," said Baxter. He glanced up from his desk then back down at the last message he gripped in his hand. After reading it, he stood and shook her hand. "Please, have a seat at the desk that I cleaned off, and make yourself at home." He motioned to the workstation he had prepared for her. "I need to get a handle on what's going on here with the messages that came in over the weekend. I'll be right with you."

"No problem, Russ," she said. Paula stepped into her work area separated from Baxter's by decorative dividers, which allowed for some, but not total privacy. It was as if Baxter wanted to know what she was doing, and she was fine with that. She was new after all.

Carla turned from her desk, positioned in front of the new hire's, and cut her eyes at Paula, surprised that she was calling Russell Baxter by his nickname. *I still call him Mr. Baxter most of the time,* she thought.

Paula placed her purse on the army green metal desk. A large, plain monthly planner, a penholder, in the form of a US Navy coffee cup, and a three-tiered letter tray imperfectly positioned lay scattered on her desk. Hanging her green cardigan on a coat rack, she sat down to test the comfort of her chair. *Seems good enough,* she thought, *but I will have to do something about this ugly desk.*

She leaned back for a moment, and then glanced at the hand-painted sign on the glass window of the storefront. It read "Crescent Moon Investigations", backwards, from her view. He did not seem extremely organized, although she tried not to prejudge. *I hope Baxter's ways are not backwards like the sign I am reading. After all, Jim's nephew referred me. I'm gonna make the best of it, and see where this goes,* Paula thought, reassuring herself, more out of it being the first day on the job, than doubting she had done the right thing.

She noticed that Baxter's office was decorated with a mixture of furniture—old and new. His desk was an antique roll-top, behemoth, which had been given to him as payment for his services on a small business case. One partner was embezzling from the small company and when Baxter got the goods on him, the other partner, the client, could not pay in full and arranged to barter for his services.

Baxter's chair squeaked as he stood. He shuffled passed Paula to Carla's desk. "Okay Carla, if you will return these two calls and find out everything you can. You know what to do; screen them as best you can, and take notes on what they say. Make no promises, and I'll call them back this afternoon."

"Yes sir, Mr. Baxter."

Baxter had acquired Carla from a staffing agency that usually sent him students from the College of Charleston, political science or criminal justice majors. She had worked out longer and better than others before her.

Walking back to Paula's desk, Baxter greeted her, this time with a smile and much more relaxed.

"Good morning, again, Paula. I am very sorry that I was so preoccupied. How are you today?"

"I'm great, Russ. I'm ready to get to work, and yourself?"

"That's good to hear. I'm doing well, also, thanks. Well down to business, we need you trained in all the office duties that Carla does, as we can fit it in. I'm sure that will be a breeze for you. Right now though, there is a flurry of activity, and as I mentioned on the phone the other day, I'm going to put you right to work on a couple of cases. I'm sure you can handle it because you've done it in your past jobs," he said.

"I expect no less, and am prepared for pretty much anything. Whatcha got for me?"

"I need for you to go by the courthouse and pick up divorce papers that Luke Bradley filed on behalf of his client, Anna Leigh Jennings. Her husband has been cheating on her for some time, and I finally nabbed him the other night."

"Oh joy, this will be fun. What type person is this Jennings man, other than an adulterer?"

"He's a banker at Citizens Federal Bank on the corner of King and George Streets. He's been there for some time, a guy in his early forties—a loan officer with a very respectable job and salary."

"So, you want the papers picked up and for me to serve him at work, right?"

"Yes ma'am, you can handle that for us?"

"Without a problem," said Paula. "I can't wait to see his face when he's served."

When Paula arrived at the bank, she noticed a few more law enforcement cars in the parking lot than normal. *Strange*, she thought, *what the heck is going on here? Is it payday for law enforcement?* She got out of her vehicle, and fed the meter with a couple of quarters. Walking into the bank, she noticed a man in a starched, white, button-down shirt and distinguished necktie standing to the left of the main counter by an office. He was shaking hands with two men in charcoal suits, subdued ties, and well-shined shoes. Paula had seen how Feds dress many times, and it did not deviate much. She overheard them speaking to the man that she pegged for Mark Jennings.

"Yes, Mr. Jennings, well, I don't think you want us questioning you at your workplace, do you? one agent said.

"No, it would be best if we were someplace else," said Jennings.

"If you want to get your coat, we'll need for you to come with us."

Jennings stepped into his office as one agent followed him to his office door. "What will this involve?" he asked.

"A fishing boat from the Caribbean and information that a Captain Greg gave us, if that rings a bell," the man in a dark suit said.

"Maybe I don't need to go with you guys. I don't know what you are talking about, or a Captain Greg."

"We would not come here, Mr. Jennings unless we had reasonable cause."

"Your office is downtown near Broad Street, isn't it?

"Yes sir, it is," said Agent Black. "It will be easier if you come with us voluntarily, and much less embarrassing."

Jennings slipped his sport jacket from the corner coat rack in his office.

Paula observing what was transpiring realized that she was going to miss her opportunity to serve him if she did not move quickly. She darted forward sidestepping the men who were standing near the entrance to Mark Jennings' office. Quickly she ducked her head in the office and rapped on the opened door.

"Mark Alexander Jennings?"

Jennings looked up as he grabbed his keys off the desk. "That would be me."

"Sorry if I'm adding to your problems today, but these papers are for you, sir," said Paula, as she handed him the divorce papers.

Taken by surprise, Jennings had the papers in his hands before he knew what hit him then looked up at the striking female intruder. "What's this?" He unfolded the papers and read for a few seconds, his head moving back and forth quickly like a typewriter carriage. "My wife is filing for divorce? Are you serious? My day has to get better from here."

"It's what you choose to make it, sir. Have a nice day."

Jennings cut his eyes at Paula with disdain, not appreciating her comment, as she turned and walked away briskly. The men from the Drug Enforcement Agency overheard the conversation between Paula and Jennings.

"He just got served," one said to the other.

"His day's not going too well, eh?"

Jennings walked out of his office with a sheepish look on his face knowing that the men probably overheard the conversation. His house of cards was falling in and he knew it. *Beating the drug investigation is my first priority, and then I'll deal with my wife serving me,* Jennings thought.

"Mind if I follow you men in my car?" asked Jennings.

"I'm afraid you will need to ride with us, Mr. Jennings. We won't put you in cuffs since you are coming with us voluntarily, but that's the best we can do," said Agent Black.

The men escorted Jennings to the back seat of a black sedan with a cage separating it from the front seat. A two-car caravan returned to their offices at the judicial center, Jennings riding in the lead car. Parking in the back of the building, the agents led him through a private entrance to the DEA office for questioning.

Paula returned to Crescent Moon Investigations to continue her first day on the job. When she opened the back door to the office, she saw Baxter sitting at his desk talking on the phone. Coincidentally, it was Anna Leigh Jennings on the line.

"Yes, Mrs. Jennings, we served your husband today. My assistant is walking in now. Let me confirm with her that everything went as planned, and I'll call you right back, if that's okay?"

"Sure, that's fine, Mr. Baxter."

Baxter hung up and looked up at his new prized employee. "How did it go, Paula? I was just on the phone with Mrs. Jennings."

"It went well, except for the fact the DEA was shaking him down as I arrived. I did get the papers served before he went with them, but it appears that Mr. Jennings got a double whammy today. What the heck do you think that was all about?"

"His wife told me that she suspects he's using cocaine. It looks like she's right and that he is into some other things that are coming to light now."

"Yeah, I'd say that's highly likely. The DEA doesn't show up on your doorstep unless they suspect something is going on in a big way."

"That is correct, Paula. If they are taking him down to their offices then it is something serious. I wouldn't have thought that Jennings would be involved in trafficking drugs, but he may very well be."

"Neither would I from the looks of him, but one can never tell by the outward appearance these days, as you well know, Russ."

"I've got a friend at the FBI. I will see if he can find out exactly what is going on. Jennings' poor wife doesn't need any more surprises, especially from the news media. They'll be all over this before another sun rises, if he is charged with anything. He's a prominent banker in this town".

"Yeah, so I've heard. Well, what's next for today?"

"Just hang out with Carla for the rest of the day, Paula, and learn what she's doing, if you will. You can answer the phone some, and she can show you the system. It will free her up to pay bills. I'll get back to you as soon as I can. If you don't hear from me before five, I'll see you tomorrow morning."

"Alright, Russ, will do. I'll be here."

Baxter made a quick call to his friend, Mike Atkins, at the FBI explaining the situation. Agent Atkins invited him to come down to his office, which was located on the same floor as the DEA. Fifteen minutes later, Baxter walked down the granite hallway at the Federal Judicial Center to the agent's office, eager to find out more information on Jennings. The large muscular agent opened the door as he heard the buzzer.

"How ya doing, Russ? Come in and sit down a minute," said Agent Atkins, leading the way to his desk.

"I'm well, Mike. How are you and the family doing?"

"The wife is doing great, and the kids are a challenge to both of us, as usual. Thanks for asking. How's your family, Russ?"

"The kids are growing like weeds, Mike. Everybody is good. My wife stays busy keeping us all happy."

"I am glad to hear it. Well, you didn't come by here to exchange niceties. You want to know about the Jennings case, right?"

"Well, yeah, his wife is my client," said Baxter. We served divorce papers on him this morning for fooling around on her. If there is anything I could let her know before she finds out in the newspaper, I am sure she would appreciate it; besides, I feel sorry for the poor woman. She's been through so much with him, and doesn't deserve any of it, from what I've learned."

"Russ, I'll get right to it. Word is that he may be smuggling cocaine in fairly large quantities for distribution."

"I was afraid of that. I hate to hear it. We only knew that he was likely a recreational user."

"No, no, much bigger…what I'm hearing is he's buying kilos of the mess. The DEA guys think he met a boat for a shipment, and provided a drug runner fifty grand for two kilos of cocaine."

"Not good news for his wife, Mike, but at least I can let Mrs. Jennings know what is going on so she won't be blindsided. I owe you one."

"No problem, man, and as always, what we talked about, or how you know this information, is strictly between us."

"That goes without saying. I don't even know you people over here," said Baxter, as he stood to leave.

"See you later, Russ."

"Thanks again, talk to you later, Mike."

Baxter winked, shaking his friend's hand and exited out the door and down the hall, a ball cap cupped over his forehead. Leaving out the side door, he hustled back to his office to catch up with his new assistant, while he thought about another assignment to give her. *She is lightning fast and unafraid,* Baxter mused.

Eight

Paula listened to her younger cohort explain telephone procedures and how Russell Baxter liked things done. He did not seem to have too many rules, but there was a protocol in place and he expected it followed. Six years spent in the Navy instilled within him a need for a routine that he could count on, and his business model verified that military structure helped more than hurt. The routine he had set in place got the job done, and yet, there was room for flexibility when a given situation demanded a change for expediency's sake.

"And as far as the files go, Paula, they're all alphabetized, and are located there by the wall in those tall metal filing cabinets where any of us can get to them easily. The bills come in at all times of the month, and I will handle those, unless Mr. Baxter tells us differently. Basically, I pay all of them five days before the due date because that's the way he likes it done."

"Gotcha," said Paula, "always good to pay the bills early."

The able young college student continued, "Our billing is done once per month by the fifteenth, with the due date being the first of the following month. If people have not paid by the 15th of each month, we add a 5% surcharge as a late fee. I keep a running balance for each case in Excel on this PC, which can be accessed from either of the two other computers in the office."

"I like the setup, Carla. It seems very efficient."

"Thanks. I'll use the same process on your cases, so he may have you using a Dictaphone, as well, or if not, you can use email. We don't rely much on verbal because it gets too confusing, and it is hard to remember everything."

"That makes sense. It looks like a system we used at my former job at a law firm. I'm sure it will be easy to follow," said Paula.

"We like it. Mr. Baxter records his activity on each case in a hand-held digital recorder twice per day. He keeps notes on cases that he scrawls on a pad attached to his dashboard. All I have to do is listen and create billing for whatever he dictates."

"So, you don't want any written notes," said Paula.

"I really don't, unless it's an emergency. Email gives me a record. Papers get lost and are not secure. You can keep notes in the field, but if you do, then you will need to transcribe them to email, or digital recorder, in order for me to follow the cases and bill properly. Whenever written notes are used, Mr. Baxter emphasizes that anything written on paper must be recycled in our shredder, which you can see over there is located next to the filing cabinets."

"Not a problem," said Paula. "That makes perfect sense to me. I know better than most about not leaving paper trails, believe me."

In the middle of the training, Baxter bolted into the office in a rather forceful manner, the backdoor banging the inside wall. The expression on his face, driven and concerned, marked with lines. Carla noticed it more so than Paula, who was still learning her new boss's facial expressions, although his hurried entrance took her aback.

"Paula, can I talk to you in my office, please?" said Baxter, abruptly.

Eager to please her new boss, she jumped from her chair, and hustled back to his office, wondering what was going on as she went. Baxter plopped down in his brown leather office chair. He stretched briefly, leaning back then landed with both feet firmly on the floor. Hunching his shoulders forward, he looked at Paula with a file in both hands, and spoke with a little hesitation.

"I know you just started, but I need you to go to Anna Leigh Jennings' house for a face-to-face. I feel that it would be better for you to go than me. She needs a woman to talk to, not only to break the news concerning her husband, but also to console her. I anticipate that she could break down very easily when you share what she needs to know, and frankly, I'm not nearly as good at that as I think you will be," said Baxter.

Paula was elated to get out in the field, but also concerned for Anna Leigh Jennings. "Hmm, sounds pretty serious. She already knows about him cheating on her and about us serving him the papers. What else do we need to tell her, Russ?"

"As you already know, Mrs. Jennings suspects her husband uses cocaine, but it's far more severe than that. It seems that her husband is in serious trouble with the law. Of course, you're aware of the visit by DEA agents to his bank, since you were there when it happened."

"Yes, of course, Russ."

"Well, he is suspected of delivering fifty thousand dollars to two Bahamian smugglers for two kilos of cocaine. The Bahamians are in lock-up at the Charleston County Jail, and they are talking."

"Oh my gosh, Russ! How did you find that out?"

"Let's just say that's the latest word from a reliable inside source I have."

"I can't say I'm surprised at this, but I can imagine how Mrs. Jennings will feel. My ex was not into trafficking drugs, but he was into using, which didn't sit well with me. What do you want me to tell her?" She scribbled notes on her pad, as Baxter spoke.

"Only what we know at this point. Let her know that it is best if she does not mention anything to her husband about the DEA investigation, unless he brings it up. If Mark Jennings happens to come home while you are there, wrap it up, and get out of there. He was still at the DEA offices when I left the building a few minutes ago. I really don't know how long they will detain him."

"I can do that, Russ," she said, confidently.

"Here's the address," said Baxter. He handed her a yellow sticky with the information he had scribbled.

"Okay, I'm outta here. I should be back in an hour or so." Paula took the sticky and reached into her purse, sticking it against a leather flap, which concealed her weapon. She trotted quickly back to her desk, grabbed her sweater, and darted by Russ on the way out the back door.

"Thanks, Paula, I'll give her a quick call and let her know you're heading over for a brief visit to tell her what we didn't want to share over the phone. Sorry to spring this on you."

"It's my job, Russ," she said, as she darted by his office giving him a quick salute.

Driving her vehicle, Paula turned the corner at a four-way stop heading down a primary street into an upper middle-class neighborhood. The abundant tree branches sprouted their tender, new leaves with various shades of green. Camellia bushes were budding with their deep red flowers. Pink and red azaleas, and dogwood trees with their white, symbolic flowers, decorated a park's perimeter as she drove deeper into the neighborhood. *This isn't far from where I take my daughters to school*, she thought.

Coming up to the next stop sign, she yielded for a horse-drawn carriage as she watched the driver sitting sideways turn back and forth speaking to his load of tourists. He held the reigns loosely in his hands while he educated the riders on the history of the streets, homes, and some of the residents who lived there in previous centuries. She could not hear what he said, but she had been on the buggy rides several times, and knew the drivers' monologues well enough to repeat much of the refrain verbatim. She remembered the colorful drivers stating that most of the homes were built one-hundred and fifty to two hundred years before. The driver stopped his carriage briefly on the side of the road to point out one particular home where a wealthy merchant lived in the pre-civil war era.

"Folks, this mansion, formerly owned by the wealthy and infamous pirate, Blackbeard, has interesting markings that I want you to notice. You can see the ship rope carvings around the door and windows created by the master carpenters, which indicated the owner's trade, and love of the sea. It is believed that he buried the bulk of his treasures and booty on Fripp Island, south of us down the coast, before he was hanged for his atrocities. It is said that he had a good lawyer, but apparently not good enough." The tourists howled with laughter as the driver maneuvered the carriage to the next point of interest to entertain them with his colorful dialogue.

Paula drove slowly around the carriage drawn by the magnificent Belgian Draft horses who did not so much as acknowledge her vehicle. The horses were accustomed to cars passing by, as long as the drivers did not do anything stupid to alarm them, like some tourists who honked their horns. Even this did not usually bring anything but an annoyed snort from the great horses. She remembered her nephew working for the carriage company for a couple of years when he had dropped out of college to find himself. Hearing him tell stories of the horses and how they endured their work dutifully, despite the heat and cold, gave her a special respect for these animals.

"Twenty-four Rutledge Avenue," Paula muttered, as she looked at the numbers on the homes. "Ah, there it is." She turned in behind Mrs. Jennings' white Volvo station wagon. *I wonder how she's going to take this news. She seems like a trouper. Well, we'll find out soon enough,* she thought.

Paula bounced out of her SUV and walked briskly up the sidewalk to the lovely two story grey stucco home. She opened the false front door and rang the doorbell at the second front door on the piazza. Peering inside from the porch, she could see Anna Leigh Jennings drying her hands with a kitchen towel. Paula straightened up so that she would not see her looking in. Anna tossed the blue plaid dishtowel on the counter and walked through the den to the foyer. She peeked though the security hole in the door and saw Paula standing back a few feet, then opened the door.

"Yes, may I help you?" Anna Leigh stood at eye level with her visitor. Paula was impressed with her perfect, statuesque features, naturally blonde hair, and blue eyes, the color of a rare sapphire.

"Hi, are you Anna Leigh Jennings?" Paula inquired, needing to be sure before she divulged sensitive, private information.

"That's me, although sometimes I wish it weren't," she said, in a playful manner.

Her pleasant Southern accent and spontaneous laugh caused people to like her instantly. These endearing ways were common to this region of the country and passed down from generation to generation among gracious Southern women. In fact, women trained in this art were so adept at this display of congeniality that it was difficult to tell when it was genuine, or staged.

"Hi, Mrs. Jennings, I'm Paula Roberts of Crescent Moon Investigations."

"Hi, Mrs. Roberts, yes, I just spoke with Mr. Baxter, and was expecting you. Come on in."

"Thank you, Mrs. Jennings," said Paula, as she crossed over the threshold.

"Call me Anna Leigh, or just Anna is fine, Mrs. Roberts."

"Thanks for that Anna Leigh, please call me Paula."

"Let's go to the living room, Paula. We'll sit in there and talk," she said, motioning to her guest with her arms, as she walked a little ahead of her visitor.

A prominent, gold-embossed mirror covered a portion of a wall behind a long formal sofa. A matching chair and ottoman on one side of the sofa, and a Queen Anne chair on the other, blended perfectly. Several sizable streetscapes of the Charleston area hung on adjacent walls giving an atmosphere of warmth and distinction to the living room. A ten by fourteen Oriental rug brought gravity to the room in a subtle, yet unique way, with its intricately woven patterns of burgundy, gold, green, and black. The women took a seat, Anna on the cream-colored sofa, and Paula on the burgundy Queen Anne chair. The gorgeous Southern Belles completed the beautifully furnished room.

"Could I get you an iced tea or lemonade before you tell me whatever it is you came to tell me?"

"No, thank you Anna Leigh, I appreciate it though. Listen, I do not like to be the bearer of bad news, but it seems to be my lot lately. I'll cut to the chase because things are changing very rapidly. Additionally, your husband could come home at anytime."

"You have my full attention, Paula. Please, go ahead." Anna Leigh folded her hands in her lap.

"Your husband was taken for questioning today while working at his bank by agents from the Drug Enforcement Agency. Mr. Baxter didn't want you blindsided later on, if anything were to appear in the news."

"Why am I not surprised? I knew he was up to something no good. I just could not put my finger on what it was. He does not spend a lot of time at home lately, other than sleeping. What do you think the DEA wants with Mark?"

"I don't know how to be gentle with this, Anna Leigh, so I'll just say it. Mark is a suspect in delivering fifty-thousand dollars to two Bahamian men in exchange for a shipment of cocaine. The Coast Guard seized their boat off the coast of Charleston on its way back to the Bahamas. They discovered the money, but no drugs. The men are in jail, but so far deny they know how the money came to be stored on their boat. The US Treasury traced the money back to your husband's bank."

"My God!" exclaimed Mrs. Jennings. "What on earth will happen next?"

Snatching a tissue from a decorative box on a side table, Anna Leigh reached deeply within herself to find the resolve to regain composure. She dabbed the tears from her eyes and cheeks with a tissue, sighed deeply, and then leaned forward with her arms on her lap clasping her hands and looking away to a window. Paula waited for Mrs. Jennings as she pulled herself together.

"I can and will get through this. I'm just worried about how it will affect the children," said Anna Leigh.

"You can do it. I know it may not be of much comfort to you, Anna Leigh, but do you remember hearing about Judge Parks who was killed about a year ago?"

"Yes, I do," she replied, turning to face Paula.

"May I share a personal experience about that particular incident?"

"Sure, go ahead. Anything supportive I could hear right now couldn't hurt," she said, her eyes still welling with water.

"I was hospitalized from the shock seeing Judge Parks killed, and from a grazing bullet, which nearly took my life. My kids were ostracized and belittled at school. I was caught up in the middle of a blackmail and murder investigation, and somehow I got through it. I have a good husband now, though my ex is a pothead who does not support his children. I know what it's like to go through tough times, and to be mistreated by someone you love."

Anna Leigh looked at Paula with a new sense of respect. "My goodness, Paula, I don't know what to say, except, I appreciate you sharing. That's quite an ordeal that you have been through."

"One more thing Anna Leigh, Mr. Baxter asked me to tell you is that it's best if you don't say anything to your husband about this investigation unless he says something to you. If it's spilled in the news, it can't be helped. We understand that, but you don't want to stir a hornet's nest while things are fluid."

"I understand. I will not say a word, Paula, although I would love to give him a piece of my mind. I will call my attorney as soon as you leave. I want Mark out of this house as soon as possible."

"That's understandable, Anna Leigh." Paula stood to her feet to leave. "I apologize again for being the harbinger of bad news. Will you be okay?"

"You can't help that, Paula. Thank you, I'll be fine. My faith is strong and I have a good family to confide in for support. I will call you, if I need to talk to anyone outside of my family," Anna Leigh said, as she stood to her feet, as well.

The ladies walked to the foyer. "I'm glad we met today. I feel a kinship with you somehow," said Paula.

"I feel the same way," Anna Leigh replied.

The two women hugged each other, their shared experiences bonding them together, as if they were long-time friends that had reacquainted.

"We'll be in touch, Anna Leigh, and say...you might want to keep your door locked since possible drug trafficking is in the picture now. People trafficking drugs do some of the strangest things. I'll give you my cell number and you can call me anytime you want to talk."

"Yes, I will lock it now, and thanks for your number, Paula. I really appreciate it."

Paula's heart went out to Mrs. Jennings. She remembered how her ex-husband remained behind long after their marriage fell apart, until she forced him out of the house because of his constant drug usage, and verbal abuse. Paula tried to hold her family together because of her firm belief, that in most cases no one could raise children better than the biological parents. Finally, though, she realized that if one of the parents would not do what is best for the relationship and the children, then it was better to move on. Her belief was that an extremely dysfunctional marriage will damage children much more than being in a healthy single parent home.

Daniel Easterling

Nine

⚜

At the four-story Federal building, DEA agents completed their task of grilling Mark Jennings who continued to deny any involvement with drug trafficking. Jennings had no idea exactly what type of evidence the DEA might have on him, but when they could produce nothing specific, his decision to hold firm with denials remained intact. The Feds had the money traced from the Richmond Federal Reserve, but fortunately for him, the record of the cash leaving Jennings' bank was missing because of a mysterious computer glitch. They tried coercion with threats, but finally he requested an attorney before answering any more questions. Getting nowhere, the agents stood as they were forced to release him. They escorted Jennings to their vehicle and returned him to the bank where he worked. He was never so happy to leave an office in his life than he was that day. The agents released him from the black sedan at the bank parking lot. Agent Black got out of the vehicle, as well, to give Mr. Jennings a final warning.

"Mr. Jennings, you can go for now, but do not leave Charleston until you hear from us otherwise. Is that clear? said the agent.

"It's crystal clear, Agent Black. As I stated before, those guys you talked to from that boat must have mistaken me for someone else. I don't know anything more than what I have already told you."

"Well, it's like we said earlier, Mr. Jennings, we know for sure the money was traced to your bank, so this case is far from over."

"Take care, Agent Black," said Jennings. "No offense, but I hope I don't see you, or your men again."

"I have a feeling that we will be seeing more of each other down the road, Mr. Jennings. Have a good day."

Jennings got in his car, heart pounding, hands trembling, hoping his denial would hold up. He imagined the worst that could happen to him. *Prison time and separation from my family would be a disaster*, he thought. He also knew he would have to face his boss, and his wife, regardless. He figured it was only a matter of time until the media came snooping around hoping to find juicy morsels for the daily news. *Search warrants may be imminent, as well*, he surmised. He was relieved that the DEA did not get a warrant before they paid him a visit at the bank. He wondered if they made a blunder, or merely a strategy that they employed to catch him off-guard. He thought about where he could store his personal cocaine stash, and when to contact Jimmy Snyder to apprise him of the situation.

Jennings pulled his cell phone from his jacket pocket and called his boss to beg off from working the rest of the day then went home. An undercover cop followed him, just in case he had contact with anyone else who might be involved. Parking in his garage, Jennings paused as he opened a door to the kitchen entrance. Anna Leigh was out to pick up the kids from school. He looked to his right and saw a black unmarked sedan drive by. The square-jawed man wearing sunglasses glanced in his direction then quickly back to the road ahead. Jennings tried to act nonchalant, as if he did not notice the cop.

Once inside, Jennings hurried to his closet and pulled down a locked metal box that he kept on the top shelf, hidden behind his sweaters. Quickly, he located a small key on his key ring and opened it. He pulled out his sandwich size zip lock bag of coke. With his Swiss Army knife, he scooped up enough of the drug to line the edge of the blade. He positioned the dull edge of the large blade against his philtrum and snorted the white powder with one long, energized sniff. The head rush was almost instantaneous as he felt the back of his throat go numb. Tinkling took over his whole head, with feelings of false confidence rising to the fore. Euphoria mushroomed in his brain like an atomic explosion of ecstasy, or so he thought. Never mind the abundant research which indicated cocaine, whether pure or not, could without warning cause the brain to seizure commanding the heart to stop beating. Funeral directors across America knew that many families disguise these heart attacks as natural occurrences when they lose loved ones who are hooked on the insidious drug.

After putting his stash back in place, he went to his favorite place in the garage. With the garage door pulled down, he grabbed his well-worn canvas director's chair, and folded it out to relax for a while. He slid over next to his wooden worktable to reach the PLAY button on his CD player. Pushing it, he cranked the music and plugged in his earphones, his form of relaxation and escape. As he listened to classic rock music, he pondered what would likely happen next. *If I stay here, the DEA, the FBI, and other local law enforcement personnel may come with a warrant.* He imagined how the house might look after a search, if law enforcement were to rifle through it. *They could embarrass the hell out of my family and me, only to find the small amount of drugs that I have for personal use,* he thought. A major head rush caused his brain to drift like an unfettered boat across a stormy ocean. Managing to get a grip on reality, Jennings dialed his close friend.

"Jimmy, ole buddy, what's going on?" he asked, barely able to focus.

"Same ole thing, but prettier with white snow on it, if you get my drift," said Snyder.

"Yeah, I hear ya. I am as high as a kite right now too. Listen, man, we have serious trouble on our trail. I was able to stall it, but it's very possible that it won't be long until the law is searching my place."

"What? Do not be messing with me like that man. News like that is bad on my heart."

Jennings stood to his feet and began pacing back and forth, as he brainstormed about what to do next. Adrenalin kicked in enough to help him think more rationally.

"I wish I was kidding, but the DEA took me in for questioning today," said Jennings. They got the runners from the Bahamas, and I think agents know more than they are letting on. I denied everything, claiming the two men are confusing me with someone else. I was wearing gloves when I handled the money, so they will not be able to lift my fingerprints. My guess is they are obtaining search warrants as we speak, so you might want to let your people know to lay low for a while."

"Okay, thanks man. I have a place to store the stuff that they won't find, and will do as you suggested." Jimmy slowly grasped the reality of what he was hearing. "This is a scary trip!" said Snyder.

"Jimmy, now listen to me, I might disappear for a while, but if I do, I'll stay in touch. Let me call you instead, for a while, unless I say otherwise, okay?"

"Yeah, alright, I can do that. You didn't say nothing about me did ya?"

"Hell no, man. You know me better than that. It is just as I said. I denied everything, and they don't have anything on me."

"Okay, I thought so. I just need the reassurance. All this crap has got me paranoid I guess," said Snyder.

"I understand. You don't think I'm not shaken to the core? I am. It's not easy for me either."

"Okay then, Mark, you take care, and let me know how to get some money to you next time you call. I'll set it aside like normal as I make some deals."

"Yeah, I'll do that. Listen, I'm going to discontinue the cell carrier I have and open another account using my middle name, so tapping will be more confusing, if the Feds try that. Also, after this conversation, let's be more careful what we say. They haven't had time to get a wire tap yet, but they could soon," said Jennings.

"I hear ya, man. Good thinking."

"I try. Later, Jimmy. I have to go now."

"Later, Mark."

Jennings went to his bedroom and packed a bag. He had made his decision to get out of town for a couple of days. After calling his boss and asking for a few days off for personal leave, he walked to the kitchen table and wrote Anna Leigh a note, then jumped back in his tan Nissan 300-Z. Leaving town without informing her first was not the usual way he interacted with his wife, despite the fact that their marriage was on the rocks.

He headed out Highway 17, and then took a turn on I-26 travelling west and did not talk to anyone about where he was going. He drove up I-26 until he reached I-95 and turned left heading south–his destination, Miami. Tuning his radio to 104.1 to his favorite classic rock station, he cranked the volume and lit a cigarette to calm his nerves. He exhaled a puff of smoke while winding through the gears, and shifted the smooth running machine into overdrive. He set the cruise control on seventy mph, disengaging only if he had to brake.

Jennings had decided it was best to be absent from the area for a while, and possibly avoid a search of his premises until he could sort out exactly what to do. He pushed the button to the electric sunroof, which slid into position. Fresh air blowing through his hair now he put on his sunglasses as he sniffed up the coke drainage from the back of his throat. He loathed himself for his cocaine habit, wishing for a better life than to what he had foolishly succumbed. Lost in the rock music, he tried to forget his troubles for the time being. Ten hours later, he reached the outskirts of Miami.

Jennings' brother had lived in Miami since graduating from the University of South Florida with a degree in business. His younger brother, Matt, had followed his brother's footsteps in the banking business right out of college, but he rose up faster in a bigger venue than his older brother did in a small city. Matt did not mind a little drinking, or having fun legally, but that was where it stopped. He always saw his brother as a family member who had great potential, but did not fully reach it because of his drug habit. Matt would not have known about his brother's habit, but once after drinking together, Jennings had tried to turn him on. Afterwards, Matt gave his elder brother a tongue-lashing not soon forgotten. The lecture from his little brother sent Jennings into a year-long hiatus from even contacting Matt. Now though, they had gotten past that event, and Jennings needed his little brother.

He did not bother to explain to Matt why he was coming down for visit, except to say that he and Anna Leigh were having problems, and that he needed a break from Charleston. He turned on the exit that led him down to a posh section of Miami. Palm trees graced the boulevard, looking like a scene out of Burn Notice. The street led him to an entrance of the subdivision where his brother lived. He was not sure why his little brother never married by the age of thirty-seven, and he would not consider the possibility that his brother might be gay.

Jennings pulled into his brother's driveway with a bump on the underside of his low riding car. He saw a porch light on as his brother had stated. Already he knew where to find the spare key to the Spanish style home with red tile roof. Arriving at 1 AM, he let himself in, and then found his way to the den where he planned to sack out for the night. Dropping his duffle bag on the floor by the sofa, he slipped out of his jeans and shirt, and into a pair of scrubs that he wore when sleeping. Matt heard his big brother in the den getting settled, but instead rolled over and went back to sleep, choosing to greet him in the morning.

Once stretched out on the long sofa, Jennings flipped the remote, channel surfing through the various stations, never landing on one for too long. The Spanish speaking stations were a novelty to him as he perused. He found a couple of senoritas chit chatting on one Hispanic station that he liked and tried to follow their fluent conversation from the smattering of high school Spanish he recollected. It did not work very well, but the senoritas were easy on his eyes.

The strange environment, with so much more Hispanic influence than he was accustomed to, caused him to feel as though he was in a foreign land. His body was tired from the drive but his mind was still churning from the events of the past seventy-two hours, making his connection with Captain Greg, getting a visit by the DEA, and from Paula who served the divorce papers from his wife. He set the TV sleep timer on thirty minutes, and flipped the channel to ESPN. Listening to the latest in sports news relaxed him, and his eyes began to blink as he fought to hear the latest NFL news. Yielding to sleep with his mind still fighting to engage his thoughts, his twitching eyelids finally closed. The television switched off shortly after Jennings began to snore.

Ten

A few days passed for Captain Greg and Davie, still incarcerated, but they maintained their story as to how the fifty thousand dollars was likely planted in their fishing vessel. Their statements were the same; that they did not know, except that a passenger they transported a couple of months back had a briefcase which looked like the one that was discovered behind the paneling amidships. Although the DEA had separated the men immediately after their arrest, hoping to gain a contradiction in their testimony, they could not break them. Jennings had told the DEA that he did not know these men, and while they suspected someone was lying, they could not make a definitive case based on the evidence they had.

Davie contacted his father, a government minister in the Bahamas, who made calls to the Bahamian ambassador in Washington, D.C. who applied diplomatic pressure on officials in the State Department. A federal official, of undisclosed origin, in turn, made a call to the local authorities in Charleston demanding Davie and Captain Greg's release if hard evidence had not been obtained linking the money to drugs. Possession of the small amount of drugs they had for personal use did not constitute trafficking. After the local government and the DEA could not pin anything on the two men, they released them to return to the Bahamas without the money. The US Treasury insisted on keeping the money to complete testing before a decision was reached to retain or to return the money.

After a few days passed, Jennings heard the news that there may be no arrest. He received no calls requesting him for questioning, and thought about heading home to be near his family. He phoned Anna Leigh, hoping that she had cooled down a little, but she informed him that he had three days to vacate their home with his possessions, courtesy of a court order citing physical cruelty, and pending divorce. He tried to convince her not to go through with it, but did not prevail. He had bruised her arms her months earlier when he grabbed her in an explosive rage after she confronted him about him keeping late hours.

He promised that he would never manhandle her again, but when she saw that his patterns remained the same, she finally pulled the trigger on the legal separation. The memory of the wild look on his face, and of his hands squeezing her arms like a vice grip was fresh in her mind. She was smarter this time, and took pictures of the bruises. In addition, she made a visit to her family doctor who recorded the incident in her records. To finalize the decision, the discovery of his infidelity gave her all the impetus she needed to put him out, and seek a divorce.

Depressed that he had to leave his home and missing his kids, Jennings said his goodbyes to his brother the following morning before he left for work. Driving straight through ten hours from Miami to Charleston, he arrived in the afternoon when his wife was out of the house picking up the kids from school and running errands. Seething in anger and realizing that his marriage was falling apart, he wanted to take it out on someone, anyone he perceived as responsible, but himself.

With his family absent, he took the opportunity to access his stash for a quick snort. After putting the paraphernalia away, he decided he would drive to Folly Beach to visit Jimmy Snyder and pick up any monies he had coming. He grabbed the bedroom phone as he switched out some clothes from his travel bag. A business card on the bedside table sticking out from beneath the phone base caught his attention. He slid it out for close examination. "Crescent Moon Investigations" it read, "Background Investigations, Domestic and General Investigations, Business Investigations", neatly printed on the card. *So, these are the guys that tailed me to Carol's house,* he thought. *Maybe I'll pay them back for costing me my family and job.*

"Hello, Snyder Painting, how can I help you?"

"Jimmy, it's Mark, I need to come over."

"Oh, you're back. I thought you were in Miami."

"I was, but I hear things are cooling off, so I came back since my wife is demanding that I move my things out."

"Seriously? Sure man, come on over. I'll be here. You can tell me all about it."

"I'll be there in about fifteen or twenty minutes."

"You got it, man. I'll be here chillin'."

Jennings stuffed the business card in his shirt pocket and drove to Folly Beach via Highway 17 South to visit his friend. Jimmy owned a small beach house a block and a half from the beachfront property. He worked as a painter during the day picking up whatever contracts he could from the many businesses that needed renovations, or new construction. It always kept him busy enough that he really did not need to deal cocaine. Nevertheless, it was his vice. He loved the drug, and enjoyed sharing it with his friends, while making money and using without paying.

Jennings pulled in his friend's driveway, his tires crunching over the crushed shells and sand used often at the beach for inexpensive faux pavement driveways. The small wood-framed house needed a paint job, odd since Snyder was a full-time painter. Jennings could tell by the flickering light that Snyder likely had candles burning. He started towards the small two-step concrete porch lit with a yellow bug light. Opening the screen door, he rapped on the white wooden door with three small glass panes staggered at the top. He could hear the music that his friend was playing, hard driving rock 'n roll. Again, Jennings knocked on the door, this time loud enough to be heard above the music. Hearing the knocks above the din, Snyder peered outside through the closed blinds. Seeing his friend's sports car in his driveway, he opened the front door.

"Dude, come on in. I've been waiting for you. Man, you looked stressed out. Grab a chair and spill your guts."

"I appreciate it, Jimmy. My life is falling apart and somebody is going to pay. Do you know anything about the people who work at this private dick's agency?" He held the business card between his middle and index finger extending it to his friend.

Snyder took the card for a moment and reading, said, "As a matter of fact, I do. I did a paint job for them about a month ago. He is a guy we went to school with, but a little older. I think we were freshmen when he was a senior."

"That's right. I thought I recognized that name. What else do you know about him?"

"The way I hear it, Mark, he went overseas with the Navy, and fought in Dessert Storm," said Snyder. "He's some sort of Gulf War hero. He had a referral written down for me when I dropped by a week ago to pick up the last payment, a very nice man. He's got two women working there. It's a small agency, but I hear he stays busy."

"Well now, it's a small world. Yeah, he stays busy alright," said Jennings. "He tailed me to Carol's house, and evidently recorded us in her bedroom. Anna Leigh has filed for divorce, and I have three days to get out of the house. She took photos of a couple of bruises and saved them from a spat we had months ago."

"Man, that stinks," said Snyder, lighting up a cigarette.

"What did the women look like, Jimmy, do you remember?" Jennings' jaw clinched in anger, as he evaluated how much being caught in adultery was costing him. He would not accept the blame. It was still fresh, and his emotions ruled his actions. Too much was happening too fast.

"Well, let's see...there was one young woman, looked like a college girl, maybe. There was another female, also. She was a gorgeous woman with brown hair and green eyes that sparkled, a real looker. She looked to be in her mid to late-thirties. I remember speaking to her because Baxter was out of the office. They had the check ready for me, and both of them were very polite and professional."

"The older one sounds like the lady who served me divorce papers. Did you get her name by chance?"

"She gave me one of the agency cards and wrote her name down on the back...said something about not having her cards yet. I know she's new because she wasn't there when I first met the owner and started the job. When she found out that I painted houses she said that she might want to get some spring painting done."

"Can you put your hands on that card, Jimmy?"

"Sure, I think so. Want me to get it?"

"Yes, would you do that? I need to find out who these people are for sure."

"Hang loose, man. I'll be right back."

Snyder went to the kitchen to retrieve the card from his planner where he kept information for potential customers. Jennings leaned back to relax on the worn, tufted-leather chair with wooden arms and black cigarette burns scattered about. He noticed a half-burned joint lying in an ashtray. Picking it up, he lit it, and took a hit to mellow his coke rush. Snyder came back to the den with the card and dropped it on the end table. Jennings handed the half-joint to his friend.

"No, go ahead, and hit it, Mark. I'm wasted from toking on that thing before you arrived. It's good stuff man... Jamaican, I think."

"Damn, the Caribbean! I don't want to hear about that place for a while," said Jennings. He took a deep drag and held it for a while letting it out slowly as he drifted off into a world where not much mattered, his face slightly reddened.

"Yeah, dude, that's some crazy situation. What's going on with them getting busted?"

"There's bad news mixed with some good, at least," said Jennings. "The cops can't pin anything on me. I delivered the money to the men on the boat, same as I've done several times before. The Coast Guard seized their boat about three miles off the coast on its way back to the Bahamas. The bad news is that I was busted by that private eye while stepping out on my wife. I made a mistake with that girl, Carol. I knew it was the wrong thing, but she was hot and I caved in. What can I say?"

"Man, that's heavy. You're like... blowing me away. I need to hide the stash that I've got, and you might not want to drop by here again for a while, in case you are being tailed. Were you watching over your shoulder when you came here today?" asked Snyder.

"Yeah, you know I was. You are right, though. You probably need to meet me somewhere the next few times until we know that things have cooled off," said Jennings.

"What are you going to do now?"

"I'm going to have to find a place to stay fast. Also, about the money, I don't know what will happen next. The Bahamians are out fifty grand, and I'm sure they aren't too happy about it. They must have gotten out on bail. I got a call from Captain Greg, but I didn't answer it. I don't want any contact with those guys, but he's putting pressure on me. He left me a message on voicemail. Can you believe the dude wants me to split the loss with him? I'm not the one whose boat got seized!"

"That's right, Mark. It's not your damn fault."

Changing his mind about taking another toke, Snyder took the small joint from Jennings and inhaled, and after a moment of holding it in, he blew the marijuana smoke across the room. He floated for a moment into a daze. Then, coming back to reality, he reached into a drawer in the side table and pulled out a metal box. Snyder opened it and pulled out the money he had collected from the cocaine deals then handed it to Jennings.

"Thanks, man. I may need this for my defense fund. Did you get your cut?"

"Yeah, I'm good. I took it out already."

Jennings counted the pile of hundreds, fifties, and twenties then placed them in neat stacks on the side table. "Forty-two thousand and five hundred dollars, is that what you figured, Jimmy?" Jennings asked. He slipped the cash into a blue vinyl zippered bank pouch that he confiscated from work.

"Yeah, that's it. I've got a big buyer lined up for ten grand's worth later on tonight, and two other people for five each tomorrow."

"No sweat, buddy. I appreciate it. When do you think that you will have it all distributed?"

"By next weekend, I would say to be safe. We'll end up with eighty-five thousand out of it and the usual we keep for ourselves—the way I figure it."

"Alright man, that's damn good," said Jennings. He took a last toke from what was now a roach, burning his index finger and thumb as he inhaled, squeezing the last bit of THC from the weed. "I'm gonna get that detective for serving me."

"Mark, I wouldn't do that if I were you. You're in deep enough now. Why not let sleeping dogs lie?"

"I hate to say it, but I don't give a crap anymore, Jimmy. I'm pissed right now," said Jennings, as he stood to leave. "I'll be in touch later, and if anything hot comes up, give me a call; otherwise, we'll lay low like we said."

"You got it, dude," his faithful friend replied. "I'll catch you later."

"I'll call you mid-week, Jimmy."

As they stood, they shook hands, giving each other a brotherly handshake, using a different than normal grip to seal the agreement and confirm their long-time friendship. Jennings exited the front door feeling much more relaxed than when he had come in. His combination high, which he knew would not last long, at least provided a temporary relief. His experience was that the effect from the cocaine superseded the marijuana high in about thirty minutes.

Driving back to Charleston, he flipped open his cell to call his wife. As he put the phone to his ear, he noticed an older vehicle behind him. It followed him for some distance, but he pretended not to notice as he limited his head movement to quick glances in the rear view mirror. It appeared to be an Oldsmobile Delta 88. He knew the shape of the body style well because his mother owned one when he was a teen.

"Anna Leigh, hi, it's Mark. Listen, I'm going to comply with the court order for me to get out, and I don't know how you want to do it. I can come by now to get a few things, if that's convenient with you?"

"Yes, Mark, you can come and get what you need for now, but that's it. You'll need to arrange to get all of your things when the kids are in school. They are here and I don't want them to see you packing. Also, I don't want to argue. We don't need to upset them anymore than they have been already."

"I completely agree, Anna Leigh. We won't argue in front of them. In fact, I don't want to argue at all anymore."

"I hope you mean that, Mark. I'll also need your keys when you leave," she said.

"Sounds like you've thought of everything, Anna."

"Somebody has to, Mark."

"I'm leaving Folly Beach now, and will be there in a few minutes," said Jennings. "I want to see my children."

"Mark, wait...." Anna Leigh hung up exasperated.

A short twenty-minute ride and Jennings arrived at what was soon to be his former home. The garage door rose with the touch of the remote that he carried in his console. He parked in the driveway and reached over to his glove box depositing the bank bag loaded with cash, then locked it with a key. He put Visine in his eyes that he carried to disguise his marijuana high and dabbed cologne from a travel-size bottle before entering his home.

Anna Leigh heard Mark arriving, but continued her routine of getting their kids in bed. She really didn't know what to expect when he arrived since this was new ground for each of them, but she didn't feel like hearing him plead for forgiveness, or make false promises like he had done a dozen times before. A knock at the door and before she could answer it, her husband had let himself in.

"It's just me, Anna Leigh."

"Mark, you could have let me answer the door."

"Sorry, could I please sleep on the sofa tonight? That way I can speak to Nathan and Samantha, and see them off to school in the morning. I'll get all my things out after you take them to school."

"I don't like this short notice type stuff, Mark, but for the kid's sake, alright. Make sure everything is locked up," she responded. She glanced at him then retreated to her bedroom.

With that short exchange, both of them retired for the evening. Jennings went in to each of the kids' bedrooms and kissed them goodnight. Thirty minutes later, as he was watching television in the den, a slow moving car passed by in front of the home, and then circled back through the neighborhood. Stretched out on the sofa in the den, and without a view of the front, Jennings could not notice anything unusual occurring in his neighborhood.

"We can get in the house tomorrow morning if they both leave," said the passenger, dropping his binoculars to his lap as they drove slowly down the street. "I'm thinking we might find where he hides his money and be out of there in less than an hour."

"If he stashes it in the home, you mean. How do you know he won't take it with him when he leaves?" the driver replied.

"I don't know. That's just the chance we might have to take. We need get out of here. You know this neighborhood might be on a crime watch of some kind with the banker under suspicion. We can come back later," said the passenger.

Eleven

Paula continued to hone her skills each day as an investigator and found it exhilarating to be working with a man of integrity. Baxter's mannerisms and character reminded her of her renowned uncle in Savannah. As far as Paula was concerned, everything that Baxter did with his agency was above board, albeit her experience there was brief. Did he have to slip around at times, ignoring a few details of the law, to help his clients? Of course, but the means always justified the end and she was fine with that. He never did anything, which she considered over the line, as her former boss would do to accomplish his goals.

She arrived home around five in the afternoon after completing her first two weeks on the job. So far, things had gone off without a hitch, except for her daughters having to ride in a car pool with their friends, instead of with her. She wasn't crazy about the lag time between when the girls got home, and when either she, or Jim arrived. On the positive side, it was usually only an hour and a half, and the neighborhood where they lived was historically safe. She had taught Rachel and Christine how to be careful. Additionally her neighbor, Emily, who was in the group carpool, said she would keep a watchful eye on the house and the girls until one of them arrived. Most neighbors in the neighborhood did, in fact, watch out for everyone who lived there. Crime watch signs posted in the neighborhood, and meetings several times per year were strategies that homeowners followed to deter crime, and keep the neighborhood safe.

    Jim closed the antique store at 6 PM, and got home about 7 PM. He was in the process of moving his merchandise to the new location in North Charleston. Supervising the relocation of the furniture was stressful because some of his help did not always understand that antiques were most valuable when kept in the best possible original condition. As a result, he had to closely oversee its handling to prevent damaging the antiquities, and some of the small delicate pieces he moved by himself.

    Jim put his opposition to Paula working as a private detective on the back burner because his life was too busy with his own affairs. Also, she seemed happier working and contributing financially to the family's well being. That was good enough for him when it got right down to it, though he valued his wife beyond measure and was always concerned about her well-being. He placed her happiness and desire to contribute above what he thought about the possible perils of her job, having seen her handle herself well in adverse and dangerous situations, which amazed him on many levels.

Today, not unlike any other weekday, Rachel and Christine were working on homework at the kitchen table from the time they got home until their mom came in from work. Paula greeted them with kisses and hugs, and then plunged immediately into conversation with her daughters about their day at school. The phone rang as she finished reviewing Christine's homework. Russ Baxter had not called Paula at home since she started working for him, but she knew that it came with the territory when necessary.

"Paula, this is Russ."

"Hey Russ, yeah, I recognized your number. What's going on?"

"I know you just got in, Carla said you just left the office, but I talked to Anna Leigh Jennings tonight. She called me late, which she never does. Did you know that her husband has just a few days to move out per court order?"

"Yeah, Russ, I remember her telling me that she was going to get a court order for him to vacate, and I can't say I blame her."

"Well, he came by their house this afternoon and Anna Leigh says that she heard him talking on the phone to someone about getting revenge on people, possibly at our agency. She said that she let him sleep on the sofa last night so that he could see the kids, and that he is moving his things out tomorrow morning. She thinks he is using cocaine heavily right now, from the signs that she can glean. I'm thinking we might need to be proactive. What do you think?"

"Russ, you're the expert, but I absolutely am in agreement with that. What do you have in mind?"

"I'd like to tail him, but I need you with me. If we follow him to a location, I may need to get on foot suddenly. This way you can get behind the wheel, and pick me up… that sort of thing."

"Plus, you'll have back-up if the situation gets dicey," she replied.

"Exactly, Paula, you know how it goes."

"Yep, Russ, I do. Things were getting kinda boring at the office answering the phone and filing," she said, with a chuckle.

"From what Mrs. Jennings said, Mark hung around most of the day today making some phone calls from the garage. She overhead him as she went in and out saying something about depositing the money tomorrow. Afterwards, she heard him say he was going downtown. Why don't we follow him?"

"Sounds like a plan. We'll beat him to the punch, I like that. We might get him on camera depositing large sums of money, or snooping around our office."

"There ya go. Maybe we can kill two birds with one stone. I've got buddies in law enforcement that would love to trace his deposits."

"When do we start?" she asked, eagerly.

"How 'bout let's meet at the office early...say 7:00 AM tomorrow morning. We'll be in his neighborhood before he starts out to the bank. That's why I have the old work van just for occasions like this. You may have seen it parked behind the office," he said.

"Do you mean that dark blue van with the ladder on top?"

"Yeah, that's the one, the good looking one, ha-ha," said Baxter. "Say, Paula, could you put your hair up in a pony tail, wear a baseball cap, and slip on an old sweat shirt and jeans?"

"Ah, I like it. Of course I will. We're going on my first undercover mission with Crescent Moon Investigations. I can look like a slim, shorter man very easily. I love dressing in disguise...not the first time I've done this," she said with a laugh.

"I'll be the guy with the paint spattered jumpsuit and ball cap, as well. I guess you could call it under cover, but I wouldn't call it deep cover."

"No, of course not, but I'm down for all of it. In fact, I'll work that way everyday if you like. I like running around in jeans, sweatshirt, and a pony tail."

"Ha ha, a comedian too, I hit a gold mine," said Baxter, "but don't push it."

"I'll see you there, boss man."

"See you then, Paula."

Baxter was amazed that his new hire was so flexible and positive. He drew from her energy and felt a bond growing with his new co-worker, something he had had not experienced since Desert Storm with his fellow military buddies. He was used to having the reigns, but working with her was going to be easy, and he didn't mind sharing control with her because she was incredibly gifted and smart. *She fits in, is upbeat, and very capable for everything I need,* he thought. *She reminds me of Lieutenant Johnson,* a buddy in his platoon, who was extremely intelligent, but broke the monotony of day to day routines when in Kuwait with his humor.

Twelve

The two men in the green Olds sedan, who had followed Jennings the day before, continued their surveillance of his home, watching and waiting for him to make a move. With Anna Leigh's ultimatum hanging over his head, he reluctantly gathered his necessary belongings to move out. He packed what he could in his car, and rented a small storage unit not far away for the rest of his belongings. Things like his tools, hunting and fishing gear, and extra clothes, he organized for easy pickup for when he could borrow a friend's truck. Jennings' life was in turmoil through his own doing, and the seething anger he felt was pure displacement for the deep sadness he felt because his world was crumbling around him.

The dubious duo in the Olds waited inconspicuously in the neighborhood park for Jennings' car to drive by. They believed he had not yet deposited the proceeds from the drug deals, and that they could take him in broad daylight by surprise. They figured they could rip him off and be out of Charleston before Jennings knew what hit him.

Paula pulled up next to Russ's Jeep behind the office sipping her venti caramel macchiato. Shifting the gear stick in park, she glanced up through a large magnolia tree, which grew up from the ground close to the building. An orange sun rose higher above the eastern horizon transforming into a blinding bright yellow ball through the branches of a large tree. She rolled the window down to enjoy the fresh cool air and took a few moments to listen to songbirds fill the morning with their melodious tunes. She knew Russ would be early, so she finished off her beverage and exited her vehicle.

Upon entering the back door, she saw her boss seated at his desk inserting then snapping a loaded clip into his Glock. Baxter slid the .45 caliber pistol in the leather shoulder holster beneath his jacket. Paula thought for a moment about what kind of man would this proficient with his weapon. He made it look like second nature, something he had done a thousand times or more. Baxter had told her of his six years in the Navy, but she did not know the details of his missions in Iraq and Kuwait, which he was reluctant to disclose to anyone. She could tell from the way he handled the weapon that he was not a casual shooter, but one who was well-trained and experienced.

Baxter had already asked her about her concealed weapons permit and he knew she would be prepared. She had shown him her pearl-handled .38 caliber Smith and Wesson in the first week on the job. In time, he figured he would have her upgrade, but for now, her trusty little snub-nosed revolver would do the trick. There really was not anything negative for Russ to be concerned about regarding his new assistant. He looked for weaknesses, but so far, he had found none. He was thrilled with the prospects of her working with him for some time to come.

"I see you're about ready," said Paula.

"Five minutes, and I'll be really to roll."

Paula stepped close to Russ's desk as he gathered his things. "Have you seen many purses like this?" She opened it showing him the inside where she had a customized pocket sewn into a holster. He saw her revolver on one side, and another pocket on the opposite side with a spare clip.

"Heck no, I can't say I have. I like it. How did you come up with that?"

"I got tired of getting make-up on my revolver and the revolver smashing delicate items that I carry in my bag. It's a good way to carry when I'm not wearing a jacket to cover the belt clip on my back."

"That's smart thinking, Paula. Okay, I'm ready, if you are."

"Waiting on you," she replied.

"We need to gas up the van. You never know how far our trip will take us on something like this," said Baxter.

Paula followed Russ, who took the lead exiting the back door. She turned the lock from the inside, pulled the backdoor shut, and then turned the deadbolt with a key. The determined twosome hopped in the old blue van and drove around the corner to a convenience store. Russ filled the tank, grabbed a coffee to go, and with Paula behind the wheel, they cruised, looking like a couple of repairmen. Magnetic signs attached to the sides of the van advertising *Handyman Remodeling* completed their disguise.

"You said Mrs. Jennings leaves to take her kids to school around 7:50 AM, Russ?"

"Yeah, that's what she said. Naturally, she wants us to let her get out of the way if we approach her husband. She's going to do some volunteer work today at the school, and should be there most of the day."

"That's smart," Paula replied. "I'm glad you called her. We're right on schedule then."

Driving by the park, Russ and Paula noticed the green Olds sitting with the engine running, exhaust fumes drifting up from the tailpipe. The men's heads were barely visible, their bodies sunken down in the seats.

"Did you see that, Paula?"

"Yes, I surely did. The two men in the car at the park we just passed...they're wearing toboggans and sitting low in their seats. It's not that cold out here."

"Exactly, I was thinking the same thing. It definitely looks fishy to me. Let's be on the lookout for them and get a tag number, when we see them again."

"You got it, Russ." Adrenaline pumped briskly through her body, aiding her caffeinated circulatory and nervous systems.

Driving by the Jennings' home on a first pass, they saw a light on in the kitchen, and Mark Jennings' 300-Z parked on one side of the driveway. The sleuths noticed the tail end of Anna Leigh's Volvo Wagon from the opened garage, fumes drifting up from the tailpipe, vibrating as the engine idled. Baxter got a glimpse of Mark Jennings downing a cup of coffee as he walked through the kitchen and paused by the window above the sink.

"Keep driving. Paula. Anna is leaving shortly, and Mark is probably not far behind."

"I will. I'm going to make the block and hopefully we can come in behind him when he leaves."

Anna Leigh backed out of the driveway, her station wagon loaded with her son and daughter, as she made a beeline to their school. The detectives turned at the corner and circled back around the block to make another pass. Baxter fit the persona of a painter, his hat pulled down over his brow, while Paula looked more like a young man driving her employer to a work site. They turned the corner at the perfect time to see Jennings' Nissan backing up then driving away. Twenty-five yards more and Jennings passed the park where the men in the Olds were waiting. Slowly the men pulled out between the Nissan and the work van. Baxter and Paula had waited and kept an appropriate distance not to arouse suspicion.

Jennings did not notice that anyone was following because he was focused on getting to Summerville to deposit the proceeds from the drug deals. Jennings rolled up slowly to the last four way stop before exiting his neighborhood. Suddenly, the Olds closed in on his bumper and rocked forward in a sudden stop, tires skidded a few feet. One man, ski mask on his face, jumped out with a pistol in his hand held low by his side. Jennings, though taken by surprise, caught a view of the man from his rear-view and reacted quickly. He hit the accelerator and sped off as the man tried to grab his door handle. The would-be assailant ran back to the Olds and jumped in the shotgun side, as the driver spun his tires in pursuit. Screeching sounds of burning rubber made an unwelcome disturbance to the quiet subdivision.

"I know you saw that, Russ. My God! These two men are trying to rob, or kill Mark."

"I did, Paula. Hit it!"

He no sooner got the words out of his mouth than gravity threw Baxter against his seat by the sudden lunge forward. The van was not much to look at, but the V-8 engine responded well enough to send them barreling in pursuit through the residential section at a surprising velocity.

Jennings got a good head start on his pursuers and knew the city streets much better than they did, but the men following managed to keep his sports car in sight. Suddenly up ahead, the flashing lights of a train crossing appeared. The black and white arms of the train's crossing gates fell, in jerking motions, as the freight train engineer laid down a long blast of his air horn. Jennings, forced to make a split-second decision, pressed the accelerator to the floor, not knowing if his car would clear the crossing gates, or not. He swerved to the middle of the road where the two arms met, avoiding them, and scooting through the intersection just in the nick of time.

Amazed at the action that unfolded before their eyes, following from the rear of the three vehicle caravan, Paula and Baxter watched the Olds sedan speed up. The driver, apparently, was going to cross before the freight train rolled by, as well. The train let another blast from its horn. Realizing he could not make it, the driver of the green sedan slammed on his brakes, sliding through a closed crossing gate, and stopping only two feet from the speeding train, which rumbled down the tracks without mercy for anything in its way.

"Who the hell is that tailing Jennings?" Baxter exclaimed

"No clue, Russ. What do you want to do?"

"I'm not sure, but we are going to find out one way, or the other."

Baxter, aggravated by what had just occurred, wanted to take the matter into his own hands, but thinking better of it, restrained himself. He grabbed his cell and made a call to the Charleston police, where he had instant credibility from a good relationship and reputation with local law enforcement, and reported the incident. After giving the dispatcher the tag number, description of the vehicle, and what he could of the men, three patrol cars were dispatched to the scene. Instead of waiting on the train, Paula and Russ circled back and found an alternate route out of the neighborhood.

"Glad you made that call, rather than take on those two guys, Russ," said Paula.

"My mother didn't raise a fool, Paula. Besides, we don't need to reveal our identities to them. We could run into them later on, who knows. We'll sit back and let the police do their job. That was the morning train, usually a hundred cars or more. The police should apprehend them soon. We'll see if we get lucky and catch up to Jennings. If not, we'll go back to the office."

"Sounds good, Russ, but it looks like we lost Jennings for the time being. I bet he's going to a bank to deposit the drug proceeds."

"That would be my guess, also" said Baxter. "Do you think we could get his wife to help us look through his personal belongings for his account number?"

"Russ, I think we're a little late for that. He's moved out now with his personal belongings. Plus, I just don't know if we want to involve her to that extent right now. She's kicking him out, but she may not want to assist in busting him. He's still her husband and the father of her children."

"Know what, you're right. I really appreciate your input. You're a woman, and naturally you would know more about the female psyche than I do. That's what my wife keeps telling me anyway."

"You're wife is a very smart woman, Russ. Seriously though, we're sort of walking a tight wire in this situation with the Jennings couple."

"You're exactly right, partner."

The train passed and as the Olds started to pull away, the driver saw circling blue lights in their rear view mirror. Two additional police cars arrived from the front sealing off any possible escape. Making a smart choice, the two men did not attempt to flee or resist. The police officers cuffed the men and took them into custody without further incident. Two handguns were confiscated, as well.

So far, no one had indentified the private detectives, except the dispatcher who had sent the patrol cars, and she was sweet on Russ, so recorded him as an anonymous caller at his request. Paula drove a parallel route with Jennings then turned back to the road that he was on earlier.

"I think he might be heading to the interstate. Who knows, we could get lucky," said Paula.

"I agree. There're only a few routes that he could have taken," said Baxter.

As they drove down the street, Paula spotted the orange Nissan 300-Z pulling in a service station twenty-five yards in front of them. Russ noticed the car simultaneously.

"You have an uncanny ability, Paula. Your hunch was correct. Isn't that him up ahead?"

"That's Jennings, alright. He's pulling into the gas station on the corner by the entrance to the interstate."

"Alright! That's great. We'll keep on tracking the son of a gun and find out where he's headed. Are you sure it was him?"

"I'm very sure, Russ." Paula slowed the van as they approached the store, moving into the center lane for a left turn. "That's him coming out of the store slapping a pack of cigarettes against his hand."

Russ narrowed his focus to the parking lot by the door where Jennings paused to light a cigarette.

"So it is, partner, so it is," said Baxter.

Paula slowed the van to a crawl pulling into the far end of the parking lot of the convenience store. She liked the sound of Russ's new nickname for her, *partner*.

"Watch him like a hawk, Paula. I'm gonna walk around the van as if I'm checking our tires."

"I'm on it, Russ. Do your thing. I've got this—I'll open and slam my door when he cranks his car."

"Ten-four," said Baxter, as he opened his door to exit.

Russ got out, and bent over by the first tire feigning a pressure check. Paula observed Jennings making a call from his cell. She watched carefully from her side mirror as Jennings took a couple of drags in rapid succession then crushed the cigarette under the sole of his foot with a twist of his ankle. He shut down his cell phone with a quick snap and moved toward his car. Paula opened and closed her door with a thud, and Russ hearing the signal, hopped back in. They waited a moment until Jennings pulled back out on the street, and then followed him keeping a car between them for cover.

Jennings made a left at the next street to the entrance to I-26 to Summerville. After a short twenty-minute drive, he exited the freeway in route to downtown.

A few blocks into Summerville, he turned into the United Bank and went inside. Reaching the counter, he slipped his hand inside his coat pocket, pulling out an envelope filled with nine thousand and fifty dollars and deposited it in his savings account. Accepting the receipt from the teller, he withdrew another envelope from an inside jacket pocket, nine thousand and seventy-five dollars and deposited it into his checking account.

Paula circled around the block so that Russ, who had gotten out on her first pass, could put eyes on his subject. Entering the bank from another entrance, Russ picked a pamphlet from a plastic stand on a coffee table and sat in a waiting area. He pretended to wait for a loan officer while he observed Jennings. With the pamphlet, pulled close to his face, he sneaked glances over the top observing his target. He felt his phone vibrate in his shirt pocket. Lifting his cell to his ear, he answered his partner.

"Russ, what's going on?"

"It's just as we suspected," he said, standing up and walking about in the lobby. "He is definitely making multiple deposits. We'll watch him until he leaves Summerville for Charleston, or elsewhere."

"Wonder how much money he's unloading?"

"I don't know for sure, but I'm guessing fifty grand, or more."

Jennings tucked his receipts in his shirt pocket and left the bank, pushing open the heavy glass doors. He appeared to be returning to Charleston, but instead, turned onto a street before reaching the entrance ramp to I-26 East. The shrewd banker repeated the process with two more accounts, and kept the remainder of the money. Afterwards, he got back on the main street out of Summerville, and then turned right at the entrance ramp to I-26. For a second time since being followed, he noticed the old blue van behind him. Knowing it was not likely law enforcement, he managed to observe it without letting on that he was aware of the sleuths tailing him.

Arriving in Charleston, Jennings turned onto Highway 17 South to Folly Beach. He decided to vary his speeds as he drove to Folly Beach, hoping to lose his tail. He decided that he would look into a short-term lease, instead of snooping around downtown to seek revenge on Crescent Moon Investigations, for now at least. Jennings figured that he could do that another day when he had time, and when he was not being tailed.

"Paula, let's head back to the office. It's apparent that he's going elsewhere. I'll have a tip for my man at the FBI concerning the bank deposits."

"Are you going to let the agent know right away?"

"I don't know. What do you have in mind?" he asked.

"I was just thinking that we might consider watching him ourselves for a while," said Paula. "We can see how everything plays out... that type of thing. We can let law enforcement do their thing and we'll do ours. If Jennings keeps dealing drugs, then we have no choice but to turn him in. If he decides to straighten up, then maybe we can look the other way for the sake of Anna Leigh and the children."

"Hmm, I like that. Good thinking, Paula. I'll hold off contacting my man with the information for now."

"Thanks, Russ. I think this family will be better off for us doing so."

Thirteen

❦

Captain Greg had taken the time to make a few phone calls to his local contacts before he left town to ensure his directive was carried out. Jennings had received a message on voice mail from Captain Greg that he should not ignore him. The captain and Davie flew out of Charleston to Miami, and then back to Freeport, Bahamas as directed by the DEA. However unfair it seemed, the fifty thousand dollars that he lost in the drug deal had to be reconciled before the captain would leave Jennings alone. He hoped his local hired hands could pull off the theft, or some type of coercion effort to force the money out of Jennings.

Arnie Jones and Bobby Spires were released from jail, but did not leave the area because the man who hired them instructed them to stay on the job until they got his money, one way or the other. Jones and Spires stopped to gas up their vehicle, buy cigarettes, and regroup. They were not bright enough to cut their losses and run.

Reading the handwriting on the wall, for them, was like an amateur explorer attempting to read hieroglyphics. Ignorantly, they figured they could make some fast, easy money and get away with it. They had done it for quite some time selling weed, so why not this, they surmised.

"Arnie, I think we should grab one of the Jennings' kids, and use 'em for ransom money," said Spires.

"You mean, kidnap one of their children?"

"Yeah, we can get a cheap paint job on this car, and switch the tags. Then we grab one of the children while they are playing in the yard, or something. I bet Jennings will want to give up the fifty grand then."

"Good thinking, Bobby. I like that idea, although it's illegal as hell," said Jones.

"Don't worry, we'll get the car painted at that same-day paint shop that we saw around the corner, you know the one advertising the specials. After we get the car painted, we'll go back to the neighborhood and snatch one of the kids. I'll call the captain and let him know what's going on to make sure he approves," said Spires.

Jennings spent the night with his schoolmate, Jimmy Snyder. He woke up the next morning on the worn leather sofa, and as usual, got high on cocaine, then went out searching for a condominium to rent. After signing a short-term lease on one that suited his needs, and still bitter from his experience with Crescent Moon Investigations, he drove to downtown Charleston. Parking about a block away from Crescent Moon, he put on a pair of shades and a gray tweed hat then walked towards the detectives' office.

Paula and Carla were both in the office working files, while Baxter was in the field meeting with a new client. Jennings walked by the glass office-front glancing inside a couple of times as he passed. He recognized the woman in the back as the one who served his divorce papers. His blood began to boil as he thought about all the trouble he was going through. *What can I do to get even with these people?* he thought.

Passing the window, Jennings loped down half the block, and ducked into an alley where he found his way behind the storefronts. Knowing that most employees parked in the back to avoid the meters, and entered their places of business from the rear, he walked near the back entrance to Crescent Moon Investigations. There he spotted a car, an SUV, and an old van. Jennings figured the Honda Accord with a College of Charleston sticker belonged to the student worker. He recognized the blue van as the vehicle that was tailing him, and thought it had to be Baxter's. *No woman would drive anything so hideous*, he thought. The late model SUV, he correctly pegged as belonging to Paula.

With his heart pounding in his chest, he pulled out a sturdy three-inch pocketknife from his pants. He looked both ways then flipped it open. Bending down out of sight, Jennings punctured two tires on the van. The air swooshed forcefully from the van tires, as he duck-walked quickly to Paula's SUV and punctured her two front tires. Satisfied that he could exact some measure of retribution, he skipped over the student's car, not holding her as culpable, then hurried back to his vehicle before his luck ran out.

Captain Greg was no longer satisfied to get half of the money that he initially demanded, since Jennings avoided him. He knew how much the street value of the last shipment was when distributed, so he decided that Jennings would have to come up with all of the money. Once Bobby Spires explained his proposed plan, the captain was all in.

A day passed when Bobby Spires and Arnie Jones got the Olds out of the paint shop on the quick turnaround they were promised. The Oldsmobile was now a dark brown color, nothing that would attract attention. They had the paint manager use a satin finish as well to soften the sheen. With a different look and tags, they drove by the school where Jennings children attended. Noticing that school had let out, they continued on to their neighborhood.

It was a warm sunny day, the kind of day when kids love to play outside. The neighborhood where the Jennings family lived was on the exclusive side, upper middle, and considered safe. Anna Leigh did not worry about her kids playing in their yard. The lawn was comprised of lush green Bermuda grass as thick as shag carpet. She checked on them frequently, as any good mother would.

Nathan Jennings was only eleven years old, but strong and rather large for his age. He was chasing his sister, Samantha, whom everyone called Sam, in the front yard when the Olds sedan suddenly appeared like a bear stalking its prey. The driver, Bobby Spires, glided the vehicle to the edge of the Jennings property, two tires rolling up on the edge of the lush green grass next to a dogwood tree in full bloom. As soon as the car stopped Arnie Jones jumped out of the car, and ran to where the kids were playing, scooping Nathan up with one strong arm. Carrying him like a sack of potatoes, the young boy kicked and yelled at the top of his lungs. Mr. B, the family dog, a larger than normal Pomeranian, barked furiously and nipped at Jones' ankles as he loped back to his car.

Sam turned around to witness what was happening. Horrified, she froze, watching as her brother kicked the tall, angular man anywhere he could. Nathan managed to bite Jones' arm, but he was too strong. Before her brother could put up much of a struggle, the brawny redneck, from the backwoods on a nearby island, thrust Nathan in the backseat of the sedan. Sam's heart leaped into her throat as she saw her big brother being forced into the car. She could see through the tinted windows as Jones muzzled Nathan with a wide strip of duct tape then popped him on the head a couple of times because he was resisting.

"Mama, Mama!" screamed Samantha.

She ran around the edge of the house and into the garage. Shoving the kitchen door open with a bang, Sam ran frantically to find her mother. Not seeing her mom in the kitchen, she ran into the den. Anna Leigh had started dinner, and was watching the early news when her daughter came crying hysterically—tears leaping out from her eyes onto the floor like the beginning of a rain shower.

"What? What is it, Sam?" her mother asked. She sprang off the sofa to console her daughter, her adrenaline kicking into overdrive. She knelt down on one knee and wiped the tears from her daughter's eyes, then held her by the shoulders, looking directly in her eyes. She knew that Samantha did not act this way unless something was terribly wrong.

"Mama, two men in a brown car took Nathan." She was speaking so fast that she could barely pronounce her words.

Anna Leigh brushed the hair back out of Samantha's face. "What, honey? Slow down. Tell mama again what you just said."

"Two mean men threw Nathan in their car and took him away. Nathan was fighting with the man and trying to escape. He hit him on the head, Mama, and put tape on his mouth. I saw it! I saw it!"

"Oh my God, Sam, no, this can't be happening."

Anna Leigh stood to her feet and ran outside to the front yard hoping to get a glimpse of the tail end of the car, Sam following close behind despite her mother's plea to stay inside. To Anna Leigh's dismay, the kidnappers' vehicle was out of sight. Her heart sank like a rock in water as she bent down, mother and daughter clutching each other in the front yard. They were in shock that

Nathan was gone so fast, and that the serenity of their neighborhood was so brutally assaulted. Samantha sobbed uncontrollably, as her mom attempted to comfort her.

"Mama, they've got Nathan. They've got Nathan," the child blubbered.

Sam's nose was running, tears streaming down her face like tiny rivers rushing from a late winter's snow. She felt the warmth of her mother's bosom finding some solace. Anna Leigh remained strong for the moment, although she needed comforting as well.

"It's going to be alright, Sam. We will get Nathan back."

Her words seemed to help a little, as Sam continued to sniffle, trying to gain control of her emotions.

"Listen, honey, did you see anything else that will help the police find Nathan?"

"Mama, one man drove the car and one man grabbed Nathan and put him in the backseat. They had ski masks on, but I saw the man's hands. They were big and hairy, and he was a white man."

Anna Leigh Jennings jumped up from her daughter's embrace, shaking, and ran up the sidewalk to the next-door neighbor's home screaming. "Nathan! Where are you? Nathan! Answer me!"

Nathan settled down shortly after the kidnapper pulled a small burlap sack over his head and threatened to beat him. Jones secured the boy's hands and feet with a rope, but after wriggling his wrists and ankles, Nathan managed to loosen the restraints. He figured he had nothing to lose, so with one last burst of energy before they were completely out of his neighborhood, Nathan leaned over and grabbed the door handle on his side of the car. He tried to jerk it open, but it would not budge because of the locked child safety mechanism. In an instant, Nathan saw the problem and kicked the release to the open position so the door would open on his next try, if he got the chance.

"You can't git outta this car, boy. His captor jerked him upright with brutish force then popped him on his head again with his open hand. Sit still and don't try that crap again," demanded Jones. Nathan feigned cooperation, as he did the time before, remaining calm and still.

Both men, after being distracted briefly from Nathan's attempted escape, focused again on getting to their hiding place. Thinking that Nathan was securely bound, the men chatted and watched the road ahead. Nathan grabbed the door handle once more giving it one ferocious jerk. This time the door of the moving vehicle flung open. He leaned over pointing his sack-covered head and shoulders toward the cool air he felt from the outside. Nathan's reflexes were lightning fast as he attempted to jump out of the car. He pushed up with his legs, trying blindly to dive to the ground then roll as he had hundreds of times. Only this time, he did not know what he would land on, or how. He figured that it would be pavement, or at best, the side of the road. An adrenaline rush surged through the young boy as he lifted up into the air. For a second he thought that he would make it, but the strong hands of the kidnapper snagged him by the back of his collar.

"Let me go!" shouted Nathan. "Let me go!"

"Shut up, boy! I told you not to try anything again."

Jones forced Nathan with both hands against the backseat, pushing the breath out of him. He gave him another pop on the head with his open hand, this time harder, stunning the struggling young boy, and bringing him back into full submission.

"Now shut that mouth of yours, and be still, or I'll really clobber you one. You got that?" shouted Jones.

Nathan sat slumped over in the car seat crying softly, his jaw clinched and defiant. Spires and Jones drove out of the neighborhood and on to Johns Island where they lived. Shrimpers by trade, when the season was in, but neither of them earned a sufficient living in their only legitimate occupation. Both of them used pot and cocaine for recreational purposes, but after they met Jimmy Snyder and Captain Greg, they began to distribute the bulky marijuana that the cocaine dealers did not want to handle. It worked for them as a supplement to their regular jobs, and kept them in weed to get high.

Terrified and in shock that Nathan had been kidnapped, Anna Leigh called 911 and relayed the information her daughter gave her, along with other pertinent data to identify her son. Immediately afterwards, she called Russ Baxter.

"Hello, Crescent Moon Investigations, can I help you?"

"Russ, this is Anna Leigh Jennings. Something terrible has happened to Nathan. Samantha said two men in a brown car drove to our front yard and grabbed him. He's been kidnapped!"

Russ Baxter had been through just about every kind of scenario imaginable since opening his business ten years prior. Practiced at the art of consolation and calming the nerves of a desperate client, he softly spoke, albeit his mind was in overdrive.

"Anna Leigh, I know this is tough right now, try taking a deep breath. I need you to listen to me carefully," said Baxter, in a firm, but soothing voice.

"Okay, I'll try, but why the hell would they take my son? What have I ever done to anyone?"

"This is not about you. It's about your husband. This will likely be followed up by a phone call with an offer to return your son for a sum of money. We suspect that Mark was involved in trafficking cocaine. We believe the dealers gave him the drugs, and he paid them the money, but the cash has been confiscated by the DEA. We also believe that the dealer may not get his money back from the government for a long time, even if the DEA cannot prove it is drug money. So now, the dealer wants your husband to pay, even though it was not him that lost the money."

"How do you know this? Are you serious, Russ? This is crazy."

"I can't share everything I know right now and I could be wrong, but that is my educated guess derived from sources I have, Mrs. Jennings. I've seen it happen before. The worst thing that can ever happen to a parent is that a child be kidnapped, and while every parent knows it is a possibility, there is nothing that can prepare a person for such a horrific event."

"What do I need to do?" she asked.

"You called the police, right?"

"Yes, right before I called you."

"Just sit tight, and wait on the police. Tell them everything you can, and cooperate with them in every way. The only thing I am asking you to do, if you want us to help, is to keep us informed, but do not let the police know you are including us. They won't like private investigators encroaching on their territory."

"I'll do whatever you say, Russ, I just want my son back."

Anna Leigh broke into tears again, her voice trembling. After giving him a description of the vehicle and the men precisely the way Samantha described them, she hung up. A similar car in the same neighborhood, but now a different color puzzled the investigator; still he considered it a possible match. Baxter began formulating a plan to find the boy.

Anna Leigh dialed her husband to break the news of Nathan's kidnapping. Seeing her number on his cell, Mark Jennings answered "Yes, Anna. What's going on?"

"Mark, I hate to tell you this, but someone took Nathan from our front yard about fifteen minutes ago. Two men in an older brown four-door car, Sam said. Nathan and Sam were playing like they always do and it happened so fast."

"What? Are you serious? Tell me you're messing with me," he said. He jerked the steering wheel of the car from the shock of the bad news, almost swerving out of his lane. Reacting quickly to recover, Jennings gripped the black leather wheel, steering the car back to the center of his lane.

"I wish it was a bad joke, Mark, but you know I would never kid about a thing like this."

"I'll kill the bastard," Jennings said. "Did you call the police?"

"Yes, Mark, I called 911 immediately, and then called Russ Baxter."

"Well, I am going to try and find him, too. Are you sure the car wasn't dark green? Two men who tried to jump me the other day at a four-way stop were driving a green Oldsmobile."

"Samantha said it was brown. Mark, listen, law enforcement is on the move. Why don't you let them do their jobs? You don't know anything about this type of thing."

"I know more than you think, Anna. He's our son, and nobody cares about him as much as we do."

"Yes, I know you're right about that, but I'm talking about experience dealing with thugs who may be armed."

"I can handle myself, Anna, but thanks for thinking of me. I don't deserve that I know. I've got to go now."

"Mark, wait, listen...."

Jennings hung up without allowing his wife to finish her sentence. Trembling inside, he pulled onto the shoulder and switched off his car. The emptiness and desperation he felt inside was the greatest he had ever known in his life. The bravado he portrayed, propped up by his cocaine habit, came crashing down like an avalanche in the Sierra Nevada Mountains during a horrendous blizzard. He slumped over on the steering wheel, with a hole the size of the Grand Canyon in his heart. Lifting up his thoughts to God in prayer, he remembered the lessons his Sunday school teacher shared when he was a child. Like a blinking neon sign, a couple of times in his life flashed in his mind where in earnest he prayed, and always seemed to get an answer. Reaching out in faith, he offered up supplication for his son, his life, and his family.

"Dear God in Heaven, forgive me of my sins. I have fallen to a new low. Cleanse me from this horrible feeling, and get me off this drug. Please bring my son home safely. And, Lord, if it's not too much to ask, restore my family, in the name of your Son, Jesus. Amen."

Jennings lifted his head up after a moment of meditation, sensing that something within him had changed, but he was not sure of what it was. He cranked his vehicle and began driving again, not conscious of time, turning blindly down one road after another looking for a brown Oldsmobile with two men, and most importantly, his son.

Paula, busy digging through notes she had kept, consolidated her activity into an email for Carla when her phone rang, "Hello, Paula Roberts, how can I help you?"

"Paula, the worst possible thing happened to the Jennings family," said Russ Baxter.

She stopped flipping through her notes, giving him her complete attention. "What's happened, Russ?"

"Nathan Jennings has been kidnapped from their front yard."

"I can't believe this crap is happening!" She smacked her legal pad down on the desk.

"I've never heard you so upset. You're usually Miss Cool," said Baxter.

"I know but it's a freaking nightmare to have a child kidnapped."

"I know it is, Paula. Listen, I need a huge favor."

"What's that, Russ?"

"Would you be willing to go to the Jennings' home right now? You might even need to stay with Mrs. Jennings tonight, if necessary."

"Of course, I will. She must be going crazy. I'll get over there right away. If she needs me to spend the night, I can work it out. Jim will understand."

"Thank you, Paula. Money can't repay you for the way you've come in here and dedicated yourself like you have in such a short time."

"Russ, one thing you will find out about me is when I work at something, I give it my all. If it's not worth giving it my all, then I don't need to do it."

"Yeah, I'm finding that out. It's a rare thing to see these days, and I appreciate it. I'll talk to you later on, when you can give me an update."

"Sure thing, I'll be in touch should anything come up. Later on, call me if you have not heard from me, please."

"Will do, partner." Baxter hung up.

Paula picked up her purse, checking the contents briefly, applied lip-gloss, and grabbing her jacket from the coat rack, out the back door she trotted.

Fourteen

"Bobby, where're we gonna hide the kid?" said Jones.

"We'll have to take him down to the old homeplace in the marsh, Arnie. This kid is a handful. You saw the way he tried to jump out of the car," said Spires, the leader of the two.

"Yeah, I know. I had to hold him back from diving headfirst on the pavement. That boy has guts not to give a crap about hurting himself, while trying to get away. So, what are we going to do once we get him there?" asked Jones.

"We're gonna keep him until that Jennings man comes up with the money," said Spires.

"That sounds good, Bobby."

"I'll leave once y'all get settled, and get us some supplies. You will need to watch the boy close, Arnie. I'll make a call to Jennings while I'm out and demand the money."

The kidnappers continued on their route from Charleston to Johns Island. Looking down, as they travelled over the connecting bridge to the island, Arnie could see a pair of white egrets high stepping in the shallow marsh water foraging for small fish. The sky was blue with cumulus clouds gathering above, resembling giant mounds of popcorn. Once on Johns Island, they drove down a two-lane road then turned onto a side road. After a short trek through a heavily wooded area, they turned on to a dirt road on the marshland.

The Olds bounced a little side to side on its loose suspension down the dirt road, yet the sturdy vehicle performed like a tank as it pushed its way deeper into the woods. The wooded area consisted of numerous large pines and oaks dotted by palm trees and dogwoods throughout in the thicket. The closer they got to the hideout the trees thinned out and the foliage peculiar to the marshlands were dominant.

The dilapidated old house, built in the early fifties, was situated not far from the waterway. The place where Bobby Spires grew up as a kid was full of memories, some good, and some bad. The Spires family abandoned it ten years earlier and moved to the other side of a stand of trees, not as close to the water. The aging homeplace was a small six room wooden frame house with a foundation consisting of short brick columns. The exterior was once painted white, was dingy, faded, and peeling. Blown off by strong coastal winds, several old shingles from the roof littered the front yard. Birds flew in and out through broken glass panes, using the hideout for shelter from the elements. The green shutters in front were loose and crooked. One seemed to be hanging by one last eight-penny nail.

    A huge orange ball of fire slowly made its descent on the western horizon just above the trees to the west. From this part of the expansive marsh on Johns Island, fishing and shrimp boats accessed the Atlantic Ocean, which was the livelihood of many of the native islanders. The brown vehicle continued its jostle, side to side, and up and down on the dirt road, reaching the opening where the hideout lay behind the cover of the marsh. The bouncy backseat awakened Nathan out of a deep sleep, but Nathan kept quiet as Bobby Spires slowed to a stop and shifted into park. Suddenly, Nathan felt the strong grip of a man's hand around his bicep as Arnie pulled him out of the car. Practically dragging Nathan up the walkway, lined by large, unkempt clumps of monkey grass, it was nothing like the manicured lawns that Nathan was used to in his neighborhood.

    "Come on boy, stand up, and walk. I know you're awake," said Jones.

    Spires, leading the way, pushed the front door open. Arnie dragged the stumbling Nathan behind him into the hideout. Once inside, Jones pulled the burlap sack off the boy's head and dusted the top of his head with several sideways slaps of his hand, much harder than anyone who cared about him would have done. Nathan spat out fragments of the burlap sack that clung to his mouth. He looked around quickly, as he shook his head like a dog shaking water, slinging the remnants from his hair.

Cobwebs lined the corners of the ceiling, which overlooked the four walls where abandoned, cheap prints of seascapes hanged crooked in their tired weathered frames. Mrs. Spires, Bobby's mom, did not take the prints to her new home, figuring that those who came to fish would enjoy them. The fishing was seldom since Bobby's dad died, and his mother was homebound with diabetes mellitus that resulted in her having an amputation of one leg above the knee.

An old cast iron potbelly stove sat stoically at the middle of one living room wall on a metal tray, which caught the stray embers when the fire crackled and popped. A circular metal pipe from the wood stove ran up the wall and out the roof. Except for its haggard looks, the old contraption was still functional. A pine table and four wooden chairs with straw-latch backs, dusty and worn from years of use, stood in an adjacent kitchen.

Nathan coughed a few times, followed by a loud sneeze. He studied the two men carefully when they were not looking at him. Wanting to test them again to get their reaction, he gained enough boldness to address them.

"Y'all aren't going to get away with this. You know that, right?" protested Nathan.

"Shut up kid!" Jones fired back. "We can be easy on you, or make it real hard for you, boy. Take your pick, cuz I don't much care myself."

Jones moved closer to the young man, eyeing him with an evil glare that caused Nathan to recoil, raising his arms in a defensive posture to protect his head. He still felt the sting from the last time Arnie popped him across the side of his head.

Bobby Spires watched the interaction between his subordinate and Nathan. *It's getting late in the afternoon, I should get supplies for a few days,* Bobby thought.

"That's the way to keep him in line, Arnie. Listen, if you need me to help get him settled before I go get supplies, I will, but I do need to run to the convenience store. I'll be back in an hour or so," said Spires, as he twirled his keys in his hand.

"No need to worry, Bobby, I know how to handle this kid. Hey, would you bring some cold beer? I've worked up a thirst messing with this youngun."

"Yeah Arnie, I'll bring some beer, but you need plug in that old refrigerator in the kitchen. It should work; at least it did the last time we hung out here. You remember, that weekend we pulled a drunk for three days?"

"Yeah, I remember that," said Jones. "How could I forget? We had a good time with those two Yankee women that wanted to see the marsh up close."

"Oh yeah, a mighty fine time it was, too. I won't ever forget that weekend. Listen, I'll be back in a little while. You watch that kid good now, you hear me," said Spires.

"I will, Bobby. You see how I got him under control."

Mark Jennings dropped by his workplace to inform his boss of what had transpired, and to ask for more time off. As he walked in, he met the vice-president who demanded that he submit to a random drug screen. He refused, and being abruptly dismissed from his job, he left undaunted, unconcerned about losing his job. He had one mission now, to get his son back by any means necessary. He stopped by the condominium that he just rented to grab a beer to settle his nerves. He thought about what action he would take next while he lit a cigarette and downed a cold beer. Deciding to get back on the road, he was determined to find the two men who had taken his son. He trekked his way from Folly Beach to his neighborhood and from there, began to work his way around Charleston, his eyes peeled for any vehicle that fit the description his wife had given him.

As he drove, he thought that if this nightmare would end, he would relocate somewhere and start over since his wife had forced him out of the house. He was heading for divorce court anyway. He knew from her disposition that she was serious, and that he had used up all his chances. Acceptance sinking in, he thought that a new location, like Miami, a much larger city would be more forgiving than his smaller community of Charleston. Everyone in the banking industry seemed to know each other around home, and in light of his dismissal from the bank, he knew it would be difficult to find work around home.

Paula rounded the corner turning into the Jennings' neighborhood. She wished that she had time to inform her girls and husband in person about working late, but did not, as she rushed to Anna Leigh Jennings' home. Dialing Jim's cell she called to explain the situation. Although he did not say so, she could tell from his tone that he was not too happy hearing that after only three weeks on the job, his wife might be spending the night outside the home in a potentially dangerous situation.

Nevertheless, Jim did not object and went straight home after work to supervise his stepdaughters' homework and prepare dinner. Rachel and Christine found it easy to bond with Jim because of his understanding nature. Paula was lucky to have him and she knew it because he not only loved her, but also accepted her daughters as his own. He missed not raising children, and since he could not have his boys from his first marriage with him all the time, this was the next best thing for him to fulfill his parental instincts. With summer just around the corner, Jim's sons were scheduled for a visit, He yearned to soak up time with them like a dried sponge washed ashore on the beach and baked by a Carolina summer's heat.

Spires arrived at the small grocery store on the island to buy beer, cigarettes, bread, bologna, and cheese, but his chief mission was to make a phone call. He stepped out of the car and shuffled over to a phone booth situated on the front corner of the off-white cinder block building. Inserting the handful of quarters at the prompt, Spires dialed Mark Jennings' number. Jennings, busy driving in a poorer area of residential Charleston where he figured the low life who took his son might be more apt to live, heard his phone ring. He viewed the LED on his cell, "UNKNOWN", it read on the display. He hated answering anonymous numbers, but with Nathan kidnapped, he did not take a chance.

"Hello."

"Yeah, this is the man you need to talk to," said Spires. "I've got your boy. Nathan is his name, I believe. Are you Mark Jennings?"

Jennings quickly pulled over to the shoulder of the road to avoid driving recklessly. "Yes, this is Mark Jennings Who the hell is this?"

"Never mind who it is. You might want to listen instead of running your mouth. I'll do the talking here."

"Look, I don't know who you are, but you had better release my son immediately."

"I wouldn't talk so tough if I were you, Mr. Jennings. We know who you are and what you've been into. I ain't seen your car around your house in a while, but you can be sure that we know where your family lives. If you want your son back alive, you're gonna need to cough up some money."

"What are you talking about?"

"Captain Greg wants his money back, all of it, fifty thousand dollars."

"Hey man, it's not my fault that he got busted. I don't owe him a thing!"

"You sure as hell do, according to him, that is, if you want to get your boy back," said Spires. "You got forty-eight hours to get the money to me, and I'll see that your son is returned safe and sound. You might not know this, but the captain is well connected, and I don't think you can afford to ignore him."

"First of all, whoever you are, if I do cooperate with you, I'll need to confirm you have my son, and secondly, how do I know you won't rip me off?"

"That's easy, I can arrange for you to hear your son on the phone. And to your second concern, you will have to trust a little."

"Why should I trust you?"

"You really don't have any choice now, do you, Mr. Jennings?"

"How do I get back in touch with you? You called me from an unknown number," Jennings said, hoping to get more information from the man.

"Never mind that, I'll be calling you again soon, and you had best be answering your phone. You got that, Mr. Jennings?"

"Yeah, I understand, but you better not hurt my son. I expect you to let me talk to him the next time we talk to verify he's okay. After that we can arrange to meet and swap the money for my son."

"I'll let you hear your boy's voice, but don't try anything funny with the cops, if you want him back alive."

As unexpectedly as he called, Spires hung up. Mark Jennings sensed anger so intense that he wanted to kill the man holding his son. He gritted his teeth, and threw his cell phone on the floorboard with such force that the battery bounced out. *"If I can get my hands on this heartless bastard, I'll choke him to death with my bare hands,"* he thought.

Fifteen

Paula wheeled her SUV into the Jennings' driveway for the second time in the same week, this time under more horrific circumstances than before. She imagined how she would feel if someone were to kidnap one of her daughters. The thought was unbearable, making her sad for the Jennings, and viciously angry with the kidnappers. Anna Leigh heard Paula's vehicle turn into her drive. She ran to the kitchen window and peek through to see who it was. Opening the front door before the doorbell rang, she lunged at Paula and clutched her in her arms. Anna Leigh pulled back from the much needed the embrace, as she sobbed uncontrollably with her hands to her face. Paula consoled her as they walked to the den to sit down, her arm wrapped around the distraught Southern belle. They found a seat next to each other on the living room sofa.

"I'm sorry, Paula, I can't seem to keep it together for very long without breaking down."

"Anna Leigh, listen to me," said Paula. "We will get Nathan back. I know this is hard, but try not to worry. Whoever has him is most likely having a problem with your husband over drugs, or something of that nature. When we find out what the problem is, we'll solve it."

"I know this is terrible to ask, but you don't think Mark could be involved in the kidnapping, do you?" she replied.

"I don't know for sure, but that's not what I'm feeling here. I may as well tell you this. When Russ and I were tailing your husband earlier, we observed two men following him. One of the men got out at a stop sign with a gun in his hand, and approached your husband from the rear. Mark was able to get a handle on what was happening, and sped off. We called the incident in, and the police apprehended the two men, but I don't know how quickly they were released from custody. Since they couldn't get to your husband, my guess is that they are the ones who kidnapped Nathan."

"I guess that does make sense," said Anna Leigh.

"Where is Mark now, do you know?"

"He's around Charleston somewhere. I called him a little while ago to tell him about the kidnapping. He's furious and says he will be driving around looking for Nathan on his own. I tried to convince him not to, but you know how a hard-headed, stubborn man can be."

"Yes, I do," said Paula. "I'm thankful that I have a good man now who is flexible, but it hasn't always been that way."

Just as Paula completed her answer, Anna Leigh's phone rang.

"Mark said he would be in touch. That could be him. Excuse me, Paula." Jumping up and making her way to the kitchen, Anna grabbed the yellow wall-phone. "Hello."

"Anna Leigh, it's me."

"Yeah, Mark, what's going on?" She walked through the doorway, stretching the lengthy cord within a few feet of Paula so that she could hear the conversation with her husband.

"I just received a call from one of the men who has Nathan. We need to come up with fifty thousand dollars fast to get Nathan back." Jennings nervously took a last drag from his cigarette, his hand shaking from anger. He dropped the butt then crushed it beneath his foot.

"Mark, call the police and let them handle it," she pleaded.

"Anna, damn it all, we can do this. Besides, the police are already looking for Nathan. This man, whoever he is, warned me that if I try anything, such as contacting the police, we would not get our son back alive. I know the accent. He sounds like a local, probably a shrimper, or a construction worker."

"Mark, for God's sake! What are you going to do?" Anna Leigh asked, waving her free arm in the air.

"I'm going to do what he wants me to do, get the money to him, and get our son back."

"Suppose they don't come through; or worse yet, suppose you and Nathan get hurt. Besides, you are not trained in dealing with this type of thing."

"I may not be, Anna, but we don't have any choice."

Paula, sitting not more than a few feet from Anna Leigh, overheard enough of the conversation to get the gist, and motioned for her to put her hand over the phone.

"Mark, hold on, someone wants to speak to you," said Anna Leigh, as she passed the phone to Paula.

"Mr. Jennings, this is Paula Roberts. I work for Crescent Moon Investigations, and I..." she began.

"Yeah Mrs. Roberts, I know who you are. How can I help you? I thought our speaking days were over when you served me my divorce papers," said Jennings.

"Mr. Jennings, I was only doing my job. I am sorry we had to meet under those circumstances, but now is not the time for us to bicker. I could talk about my tires getting slashed, if you prefer me to," she said.

"What do you want, Mrs. Roberts?"

"My partner, Russ Baxter, and I, are committed to helping you and Mrs. Jennings get your son back. We would like you to work with us since we are attempting to do the same thing. You will be an integral part of the team. Russ is very experienced with all sorts of situations, having been a Seal in Desert Storm. I can handle myself pretty well, also."

"That may be so, Mrs. Roberts, but the man told me not to contact the police." Jennings inhaled then exhaled a long stream of smoke after lighting another cigarette to calm his nerves.

"Exactly, Mr. Jennings, the police won't know we are involved, either. If they did, they would order us to stay out of their way. Time is our best ally, or our worst enemy, in cases like this. It is imperative, for Nathan's sake, that we get him back as fast as we can. I don't know how much you know about kidnappings, but statistics are terrible the longer a child is held ransom."

"Well yeah, but what are you saying, Mrs. Roberts?"

"I'm saying, let us partner with you to get your son back. You won't be going it alone, and you haven't broken your word to the kidnappers not to contact the police. Do you think you can do that?"

"I guess I could. It's probably the best option I have, although I'm still pissed at you people right now," said Jennings. He inhaled another puff of his cigarette then blew out the smoke forcefully.

"I understand that, but we are on your side, as well, this time. Would you give me your cell number?"

"It's 844-771-9474, but may I ask why you and Baxter want to help us get our son back?"

"We were working for your wife when all this happened," said Paula. "Russ and I have children, too. It's not about just a case anymore. It is about getting your son back safely. We feel that if we were to wait on the police that it could be too late, and none of us want that."

"No, of course not, what do you want me to do?" he asked.

"First of all, let me get a hold of Russ. I will give him your number and one of us will call you with a place to meet. Did you agree with the kidnappers to do anything specific so far?" she asked.

"I agreed to deliver fifty thousand dollars in exchange for my son. The man demanded that I keep my ear out for the phone to ring. He said when he calls again that he's going to give me instructions on where and when to deliver the money. He said he would let me talk to Nathan to verify he's okay," said Jennings.

"Did he say anything yet about the location where you will meet?" Paula paced back and forth. As she talked, her juices began to flow with anxiousness to get on the hunt for Nathan.

"No, not yet, but I think that he's not far from here. I could hear the ocean in the background from where he was calling. He had to be outside somewhere not far from a beach."

"That could be anywhere up and down the South Carolina coast, but like you said, probably not far away since you were contacted so soon after the abduction."

"That's what I'm thinking, Mrs. Roberts."

"Did he say when to expect his call, Mr. Jennings?"

"No, he didn't, and it's driving me crazy. He only said to be listening out for his call."

"Alright, Mr. Jennings, listen…"

"Please, call me, Mark."

"Okay, Mark, I'll relay all this to Russ. If the man calls, would you commit to call me immediately?"

"Yes, I will. Thanks for your help, Mrs. Roberts."

"Just call me, Paula. We can leave off with the formalities."

"Okay, Paula, I'll be in touch as soon as I hear anything from the man," said Jennings.

Paula Roberts P.I. - Johns Island

Jennings was weary of driving the streets without finding a car that remotely resembled the Oldsmobile, and his nerves were nearly shot. Deciding to get off the road for a while, he called Jimmy Snyder who was busy making appointments to deliver cocaine. He managed to catch Snyder at home before he ran out to make connections at three designated spots downtown within walking distance of the Market.

"Jimmy, it's Mark. I've got some very bad news."

"Oh, man, not again. What's up now?" said Jimmy. He took a toke from a joint waiting to hear what his friend would say.

"My son has been kidnapped by a couple of thugs demanding money. Captain Greg orchestrated it. I know he did. He wants me to reimburse him for the fifty-grand which was confiscated when he got busted," said Jennings.

"You have got to be kidding me. This is way too heavy, man," said Snyder.

"I wish I was. My guess is that he can't pay his supplier, so he wants me to cough up the money so he can settle-up. The captain called a couple of times and left messages. When I wouldn't return his calls, he paid these guys to kidnap my son for ransom."

"Dude, I can't believe this crap!" said Snyder.

"Yeah, me either, but it is real. Listen, I'm extremely upset, and would like to drop by if that's cool with you."

"Yeah, come on by, man. I don't have any more money yet, but I have some hook-ups later on tonight."

"I'm not concerned about the money right now, Jimmy. I need something to calm my nerves. You got any weed?"

"Yeah, sure… you know I do. Good stuff, too. Come on over, man. It's cool," said Snyder. Relieved that Jennings did not want more money now, Jimmy put out the remainder of the roach, leaving it in a pile with the rest that collected in a colorful, oversized, hand-blown glass ash tray.

"I'm on my way," said Jennings. He pressed the accelerator to make haste to his friend's house, gravity pushing his back against the bucket seat.

Upon Jennings arrival, they lit up a newly rolled joint, which sent him floating in a high that calmed his nerves. As soon as he relaxed enough, Jennings opened up telling Jimmy the details of his son's kidnapping from his front-yard and of the ransom call.

"The man said he was speaking for Captain Greg, and that he wanted fifty thousand dollars for me to get my son back safely. That's exactly what I bought the two kilos for," said Jennings.

"Well, hell, Mark, it's got to be someone one knows the captain and who lives around here. We might even know the son of a bitch. Could you tell what model and color the Oldsmobile was?" said Snyder.

"I could have sworn it was dark green one day, and then it appeared on another day in my neighborhood with a fresh coat of brown paint," said Jennings. "I think it's a nineteen eighty-five Oldsmobile sedan, something in that range. It had a certain classic shape. Do you know the model I'm talking about, Jimmy?"

"Yes I do, as a matter of fact, and I have a customer that buys weed who fits the description. He lives over on Johns Island where you make your connection. He drives a Delta Eighty-Eight, and if it's the vehicle I'm picturing in my head, then I think I know who it is. He has a buddy that hangs out with him all the time."

"That's interesting. It sounds as if he could be the one. You know I'm a peaceful man, but when it comes to my children, I'll kill the bastards, if they harm Nathan," said Jennings.

Jennings' blood began to boil again despite the marijuana-high. Instead of the peaceful frame of mind he hoped to attain, he felt more like one of Pancho Villa's men back in time out, to exact revenge by raiding pioneering Texans who settled in the Rio Grande Valley.

"I hear you, Mark, but listen to me for a second...these guys are local fishermen, potheads, said Snyder. They aren't too smart, but they can handle themselves pretty well. They hunt and fish, when they're not shrimping. You're going to need some help, if you try to take 'em."

"I'm working on something, Jimmy, but thanks for the tip. Listen, I need to go. I can't sit around here anymore with my son missing."

"Where are you going, dude?"

"Where would you go if you were me?"

"I would be heading to Johns Island," said Snyder.

"You hit the nail on the head, Jimmy. Guess no more."

"I'll go with you, man."

"Nah, Jimmy, I appreciate it," said Jennings. You do what you need to do. I want to be alone for this. If I am apprehended by police, or taken captive by these thugs, you don't need to be in the middle of it. I brought some protection along, two friends rolled into one, Smith and Wesson." Jennings drew a deep breath, satisfied that he was not afraid to confront the men who had taken his son.

"That helps, but I still think you still need someone with you," said Snyder.

"I'll be alright, bud. I do have someone else helping me. Don't say anything to anyone, but I struck a deal with the devil, you might say."

"What do you mean, Mark?"

"Well, you know the private investigators who were working for my wife?"

"Yeah, sure, the ones we talked about last time you were here...that Baxter guy and his female partner from Crescent Moon Investigations," said Snyder.

"Yeah, those are the ones," said Jennings. Well, he and his assistant, that Roberts woman, or whatever her name is, who served me divorce papers, offered their help to track these men and get Nathan back, pro bono, too."

"I would take the help, too, if it happened to me."

"I suppose they are good people after all. I let my pride get in the way in dealing with these people after they served me divorce papers. I slashed their tires, like an idiot," said Jennings. He looked down at the floor for a moment, embarrassed at his actions.

Before Jennings left, he and Snyder each took a snort of cocaine for a pick up. Both of them had a job to do and wanted their heads jacked up, rather than to be in a daze with a "pot-high" that yielded sensory deprivation. Jennings left Folly Beach driving in the direction of Johns Island. He thought of the sincere prayer he had made, and felt ashamed of himself for succumbing to drugs again. The high, seemed empty now, not like before. He vowed within himself that this would be the last time he would ever alter his mind with illegal drugs. Jennings continued his course hoping he would get a call from the kidnapper.

From the information that Anna Leigh Jennings gave the police, the authorities searched all the body shops within a fifty-mile radius, which may have painted a green Olds sedan within the past three week. At Jaako Paint, the assistant manager gave incorrect information to the police because the men gave him an extra three hundred in cash to keep quiet, if anyone were to come by asking questions.

Russ Baxter was right, the information needed to recover Nathan Jennings would probably come to surface quicker on the streets than through the police. Only, he did not figure that Mark Jennings would find out faster than anyone else would. Jennings had been a paperboy growing up where he learned how to canvas a neighborhood, talking to everybody. These skills gave him adeptness like an investigator, but the fact that his son's life was at stake gave him an extra-ordinary edge.

As soon as she was able to help calm Anna Leigh's nerves to a manageable state, Paula phoned her boss. Baxter was busy chasing down a couple of people that he thought might know something about the two men when his cell phone rang. Turning a corner to stop in a bar where locals gathered to play poker in a back room, he opened his phone while rolling forward into an over-sized parallel parking spot.

"Paula, I'm glad to hear from you. What's new?

"Russ, things are developing rather fast. Nathan's kidnappers have made contact with Mark Jennings. He called his wife to bring her up to speed and told her that he was instructed to bring fifty-thousand dollars to a location, yet to be specified, and he will get his son back alive and unharmed."

"Not too surprising. Does he know anything else?"

"He said the men sounded like locals, and from what I gathered, he sounded pretty intent on doing whatever he is told to get his son back."

"Well, you can't blame him for that. Is there anything else?"

"No, except one little thing, and it was something I said."

"What's that, Paula?"

Paula cringed before she delivered the news of committing their help without asking her partner. "I told him to call me before going to meet them alone, and that we would assist him. "Was I out of line to say that?"

"No, that's good, Paula. Where are you now?"

Paula breathed a sigh of relief. "I'm with Mrs. Jennings. She says she's okay if I leave. She mentioned possibly going to her parents."

"That sounds like a good idea. Reinforce that. Tell her I suggest the same thing, will you?"

"Sure, thing, Russ."

"Listen, we need to pick up a few things there so we can be ready on a moment's notice when we get the call. Let's you and I meet downtown at the office to get prepared," said Baxter.

"I'm down for that, Russ. When a child's life is on the line, if I get a shot at a kidnapper, it will be target practice. I'll be there in ten minutes."

"See you there, partner," he said.

After meeting and setting strategy, the two sleuths agreed that each would be "on call" until this case was completed. Since no call had come and nightfall was approaching, they each headed home for the evening, not knowing what to expect, or when.

Sixteen

⚜

Bobby Spires returned to his old homeplace and found his partner and Nathan napping. The big red sun had dipped below the trees, seemingly into the swamp, not far from where the kidnappers held Nathan. The formerly bright, blue skies scattered with cumulus and cirrus clouds turned a shadowy gray. The horizon painted with swaths of pink, purple, and orange strokes across the darkening blue sky from an incomparable artist, Mother Nature, gave way to nightfall.

The screen door banged with a loud noise as its spring recoiled, pulling it back against the doorjamb when Bobby walked in. His boots clomped heavily on the wooden plank floor, intentionally heavier than normal, to awaken his inept cohort. A lone kerosene lamp flickered, shadows of furniture resembling aliens and wild animals danced on the walls.

"Arnie, wake up man! I'm back with supplies. I got cigarettes, beer, and stuff for sandwiches."

Jones' eyes fluttered, struggling to open, still in a dreamy, almost comatose state. Spires approached Jones kicking the soles of his boots hard enough to make him jerk, causing him to nearly lose his balance from his chair, which leaned against the wall.

"Wake up, I said! How the hell are you going to keep this boy from running away with you sleeping like a fat alligator?"

"Oh my God, Bobby, you scared the crap outta me! What are you trying to do, give me a heart attack?"

"Arnie, you've got about as much sense as a fiddler crab. I told you not to be sleeping, you numbskull."

"The kid is asleep, Bobby, lighten up," Jones replied, glancing over at Nathan.

"I'm not worried as much about him as I am about someone looking for him, Arnie. You should know they're doing everything in their power to find him. You're such an idiot." Arnie looked up sheepishly at the dominant one of the pair, as if he had just been caught red-handed in his mother's cookie jar.

Nathan awakened with Bobby's entrance, but feigned sleep so the men would think he did not hear what they said. He thought about the possibility of trying to escape, if Arnie Jones were to fall soundly asleep again. He wondered how close he was to Charleston. Nathan knew from looking out the windows of the old house that the surroundings were definitely similar to local islands he had seen many times. The more he looked, the more he realized that he was not very far from home. He heard the sounds of seagulls making their familiar cawing sounds, and could periodically see them through the windows swirling in the sky.

Spires lit an additional kerosene lamp that sat opposite the other one in the small living room. Jones got up and put the groceries away while his partner went back to the car to retrieve a few more items. Nathan coughed, and then opened his eyes, pretending to wake up at that instant. When Spires walked in again with another plastic bag of supplies, he noticed that Nathan was alert and sitting upright in his chair.

"Sorry we have to do this to ya, kid, but if your dad had listened to us then you wouldn't be here right now," said Spires.

"Go to hell!" replied Nathan. "If my dad finds you, you will get what's coming to you."

"Your dad can't do squat to us, boy. Now, shut up before I pop you on the head again," said Jones. He stood up and moved quickly towards the boy, pulling his arm back, as if to strike him.

Nathan remained defiant, though the threat quieted him for the moment. While the men were busy making sandwiches, he looked out the window again and saw a worn path, overgrown with weeds that led down an incline to a dock at the water's edge. His mind churned as he observed a fourteen-foot aluminum Jon boat with a small outboard motor attached. Thoughts of commandeering the little boat bounced through Nathan's mind like a pinball in the machine of a skilled player. He remembered how his dad had taught him to drive a Jon boat just like this one when he was only six years old. Nathan rehearsed the steps to prep and crank the motor.

He pictured himself squeezing the black rubber bulb to get the gas flowing in the engine before pulling the rope. He wondered how many pulls it would take to crank the small outboard engine, if he could make it to the boat. There was no telling how long it had been since the motor was last cranked, but at this point, Nathan did not care anymore. He wanted to escape and nothing was going to stop him from attempting it. What did he have to lose? The men had not done too much to seriously hurt him thus far, but he was not sure how long he would be safe.

Spires finished his beer and sandwich while Jones continued chomping on his second sandwich and sloshed down another beer. It was obvious to Nathan that Jones's appetite was more insatiable than his partner's was. Jones puffy paunch plainly indicated his malady. Nathan refused to eat, but did accept a soda, which he had difficulty drinking with his hands bound, but managed to get it down. Finishing his third beer, Jones burped long and loud, as if he was in a contest of some kind.

"Ah, that felt good," said Jones. "I'm gonna get one more, Bobby. How 'bout you…can I get you one?"

"Nah, I'm good, Arnie. We better get some sleep, I don't think I'm gonna get a call from the captain tonight. He's probably tied up."

"Yeah, I guess so," said Jones. "I'm sleeping on the couch, I reckon. Where's the boy gonna sleep?"

"Put him in the back bedroom on that single cot. I'm going to my house to spend the night. It will be better not to have the car parked outside. I'll come back early in the morning."

"Alright, boss man. We'll be here waiting."

Jones guided Nathan to a twin bed with a stained mattress, and a smelly, worn pillow with feathers protruding. The bed looked like it had been wet and dried one too many times for use. The stench was horrific, but Nathan had no choice, as the strong man led him by his arm to the metal framed bed. After shoving Nathan onto the bed, Jones spread an old, green, moth-eaten Army blanket over the boy, whose legs and hands were still restrained. The heavy wool blanket, even though old and full of holes, rebuffed the chilly night air, which drifted through the broken windowpanes.

Arnie returned to the living area and turned on the TV until he fell asleep watching the Andy Griffith Show. He never knew why he loved the show so much, but subconsciously he identified with Barney Fife, and Bobby Spires was Andy Griffith. "Nip it in the bud, Andy", were the last words that ran through his mind as he drifted off to sleep on the sofa in a drunken stupor, numb from the alcohol.

The next day, Bobby arrived early as promised. The sounds and smells of the marsh were alive with all manner of fish, fowl, and crustacean. His entry awakened both Arnie and Nathan, as it did the previous evening. There was not much to do around the homeplace, but wait. An uneventful day passed while Spires waited on a final word from Captain Greg to move forward with the plan that he proposed to Mark Jennings.

The men drank beer, ate snacks, and watched a small portable TV that Spires had left at the shack for times when he came there, until sunset came again. Nathan sat watching television with the men. Spires, bored with the process, stood up and paced the floor. Clearing his throat, he looked at his watch.

"Damn it all, I can't stand this waiting around anymore," said Spires. "Wonder what the hell the holdup is. If we don't go ahead with the plan pretty soon, the law is bound to catch up with us."

"I'm with you on that man. This is crazy. I don't like just sitting around here with this boy either. It's too dangerous," said Jones.

"I'm gonna ride over to Jakes Landing where I know I can get a signal for this stupid cell phone. I need to give that Jennings man a call. I'm running later than I wanted to, anyway."

"Alright, Bobby, that sounds good. Are you gonna pin him down about the money?"

"Of course, I am, stupid! You just keep a tight rein on this boy, and after that beer, how bout you stop drinking so you'll be alert enough to stay awake this time?"

"I can do that Bobby...not saying I want to, but I can do it."

Jones let out another long burp that could win a contest at a county fair. His lackadaisical attitude got under Spires' skin, who promptly stood up and moved toward Jones, shaking his fist and gritting his teeth.

"Let me make this clear, Arnie, you're near the end of a deal that's gonna make you more money than you've ever seen at one time, so you had best stop drinking, and keep a damned good eye on that boy. If you can't do that, then you ain't no good to me," he said.

"I know, Bobby. I'm just messing with ya. Go make your call, man, and hurry back," said Jones.

"I'll be back after awhile," said Spires, as he opened the screen door letting it bounce, and shut behind him.

"Alright boy, do you want anything before I get comfortable on the couch?" Jones asked.

"No, I don't need anything, except for you to let me go," said Nathan defiantly.

"Now, you know I can't do that boy. You are valuable property to us. You just sit there and watch TV, and behave yourself, like I told you. Your daddy will come get you soon."

Nathan sat sunken in a soft, putrid green, vinyl cushioned seat, split from wear, the chair arms made of silver stainless tubing with matching padded armrests. He did not know whether to believe the crusty ole shrimpers, or not. The men had kept him two days now and he had not heard them talking to anyone on the phone that would indicate a deal being struck. He kept waiting for an opportunity to escape, still hoping that his rescuers would come. Determined not to pass over another chance to escape, he looked down at the rope, which secured his legs. He felt the burn around his ankles, especially on the inside where he had wiggled his feet to loosen its hold. When Jones was not watching, Nathan continued to wiggle his hands and feet hoping to get the restraints loose enough that his feet and hands would be able to slip out when he was able to make an escape attempt.

Seventeen

Mark Jennings crossed the two-lane bridge from the mainland to Johns Island. An image of the type of car that he saw trolling through his neighborhood was fixed in his brain. He pulled into the local convenience store from where Bobby Spires phoned him earlier. He shut off his lights and sat in the parking lot for a minute before going in, reminiscing about happier days when he played with his kids in his yard, or in one of the many city parks in Charleston. He remembered times when he took his family to watch Nathan play Little League baseball. Samantha would dress up in her cheerleader outfit and bring her pom-poms to root on her big brother. Anna Leigh packed sandwiches for the family outing and her presence made everything complete. He wished things could return to the blissful times that he had taken for granted.

Anger welled up inside him, like an aggressive tumor, as he thought about these two men taking his son.

He knew he had done things, which had indirectly contributed to the kidnapping, but they did not have to involve his kids. *What are they doing with Nathan right now? If those men do anything to hurt him, I'll kill the sons of bitches,* he thought.

Jennings got out of his car, slamming his door and entered the corner convenience store. The exterior, made of wooden siding with light green paint had faded from the sun and was beginning to peel. The building stood crooked from years of wear on its original foundation, and shifting sand beneath. Jennings perused the store a moment then helped himself to the hot dog station. He grabbed the set of stainless tongs, inserting a wiener between a soft white-flour bun. Squeezing a generous bead of mustard from its yellow, plastic dispenser he carefully zigzagged the length of the wiener with the spicy condiment. After adding a spoonful of chopped onion, he topped it off with a small ladle of home-made, heated chili. Loading a Styrofoam cup with ice that he filled with cola, he strolled inside the store for a few minutes scanning the various products shelved on each aisle.

He really was not that hungry, but wanted it to appear to the clerk that he was in the store for more than to just get information. The floor had uneven features from years of wear, but it was obvious that it was well-constructed of solid wooden planks. Thin layers of fine white beach sand scattered on the floor indicated a steady business by the locals and tourists. The wooden floor creaked as he paced around the aisles looking for a pack of sugar-free breath mints. Jennings found the mints then opened a cooler, grabbed two beers, and approached the cashier.

A middle-aged redheaded woman smacked her gum from her perch on a black vinyl-covered barstool as she surveyed the gas pumps through dingy plate-glass windows. More customers drifted in as she kept an eye on the store's security monitors.

"Howdy, mister, will that be all for ya tonight?" the cashier said, in her *low-country brogue*.

"Give me a pack of Marlboro Lights, please. I think that will do it," said Jennings.

"Here you go, mister," she said, handing him the pack of cigarettes. "You ain't from around these parts are ya?"

"I don't live on the island, but I am from Charleston."

"I thought you wuz too well-dressed to be born and raised on Johns Island. Besides, we know everyone who lives here, except some of the rich people who built in the new subdivisions."

"Yeah, I guess you would know most everyone if you are raised here. Say, you didn't happen to see a dark brown Olds Eighty-Eight come through recently did you?"

"Hmm, well, the only one I can think of is one that belongs to one of our shrimpers, who lives here on the island. It's a dark color, but I don't think it's brown. What do ya need with him? You ain't from the IRS, are ya, 'cause I've known these boys since they were in grade school? We're a pretty tight-knit bunch 'round here."

"No, nothing like that, he told me I could look him up to buy some shrimp some time ago. I lost the piece of paper he gave me with his number on it. I am in the area and thought I would give him a call. My wife asked me to pick up several pounds if I came this way. We have a large freezer in the garage where we stock up on good deals."

The store clerk studied Jennings, puzzled for a moment, and then replied, "I didn't get your name, mister."

"It's Jennings, Mark Jennings."

"Okay, Mr. Jennings, that sounds like a reasonable request. My name is Mabel. It's nice to meet you. If it's who I'm thinking it is, then that's Bobby Spires. He lives about four miles from here out on the marsh. His family's been living on the island for at least three or four generations. I went to school with his mama."

"Yeah, that's his name, Bobby Spires. How could I forget?" Jennings said.

"I didn't know he was retailing shrimp now. He's usually a wholesaler. I buy my shrimp from him for the store. Let's see... I don't have his business card handy. I guess my shoppers picked 'em all up, but he lives out on Lost Creek Road.

"Do you mind telling me how to get there, Miss Mabel?"

"No, not at all. You seem nice enough. You go two miles from here straight down Island Road where you will see a blinking caution light, and then you turn left on Jakes Landing Road, and go about a mile and a half.

You'll turn right on the first paved road you come to. It's the third house on the left. You should see an old broke-down pick-up truck in the yard, red, I believe. If the Oldsmobile is in the yard, then he's probably at home."

"Mabel, I appreciate it. I'm planning on buying about ten to fifteen pounds of shrimp, so it won't be a waste of his time," Jennings said. As soon as he received the information, he turned on his heel and bolted for the door.

"Sounds good then, Mr. Jennings, and tell ole Bobby that Mabel says hi."

"Sure will, Mabel. Take care and thanks again," he said, glancing back over his shoulder.

Jennings followed the directions that Mabel gave him. He slowly drove by the residence surrounded by pine and palmetto trees, seeing only the red pick-up truck. Discouraged, he checked into a very modest motel made of cinderblock about two miles away from the Spires house, owned by a local Johns Islander, who lived on the back of the property. It looked as if it had been built in the sixties, but the rooms had been upgraded with new paneling, carpet, and paint. Jennings correctly guessed that anglers or low-budget couples on secret rendezvous frequented the inexpensive motel. Exhausted from the stress of it all, he figured he would drink his two beers, and wait for his call. Little did he know that he missed Spires' arrival to his home by only an hour.

Dropping his keys and cigarettes on the side table, he flipped on the TV and decided to call his wife. He wanted her to cooperate with him to pay the kidnappers.

He had enough in the bank to come up with it, but his wife had the bulk of the savings between them. Her grandfather left her two-hundred thousand dollars when he died, which she kept it in a Certificate of Deposit at his bank. Dialing Anna Leigh, he hoped she would cover half of the ransom money. She usually did chip in when it came to their children, but never before had they dealt with a large sum of money involving a kidnapping. And, never before had their relationship been so fractured and tenuous.

"Hello, Mark, I was wondering when I would hear from you."

"Anna Leigh, hi, listen, I'll get right to the point because I know how you feel about me being out here trying to find our son. You know already that I'm working with Russ and Paula to get Nathan back, and that I need to come up with fifty-thousand dollars in cash to meet these guys. Would you be willing to put up twenty-five of it? I'll put in the other half."

"Are you saying you don't have enough money, Mark?"

"I didn't say that, I was just wondering if you would split it with me."

"Mark, you need to be the one to come up with the money, not me. I'm willing to help my children in any way possible, but I did nothing to cause Nathan to be kidnapped, so I don't think I should be the one to put up money when you have it," she said.

"Okay, Anna, fine, if you want to play it that way."

"Sorry, Mark, but it's called accountability."

"Alright, I was just asking, never mind. Good night."
"Good night," said Anna Leigh.

Upset at her reaction, Jennings lit a cigarette and finished the second beer before turning down the covers and crawling in bed. He picked up the remote from the side and flipped on the TV, channel surfing until he fell asleep, hoping that tomorrow would be the day he would get his son back alive and safe from harm.

Eighteen

Paula's night at home was nothing out of the ordinary, which was just fine with her. Dinner and her daughters' homework were out of the way. Privately, she apprised Jim of the turn of events so that if she had to leave in the middle of the night, he would not be alarmed. Rachel and Christine were up to their usual silly selves, which set Paula's mind at ease after the rigors of her dramatic workday, which continued to unfold by the minute.

"I'm heading to bed early tonight, honey. We have a doozy of a case in progress," Paula said.

"I'm with you, dear. It has been a long day at work for me also. We got a new shipment of rugs in, and I've been fighting with those things all day getting them stacked and tagged. We hung a few, but not as many as I wanted. Very nice rugs, if I must say so myself."

"I'll bet they're gorgeous, Jim."

"They really are. All of these rugs came from Pakistan, Iran, and India, hand woven wool. Most of them are rather large, ten by fourteen…in that range."

"Wow, honey, when do I get to see them?"

"Anytime you want to shoot by the store, darling," Jim said, as he kissed his wife on the cheek, his arm wrapped around her, as they walked side by side up the deep red, carpeted staircase. "What about the girls? Are they still in the den?"

"Girls, time to hit the hay," said Paula, touching the button on the intercom when she entered the master bedroom.

"Okay mom, may we finish this one program? It's almost over," said Rachel.

"Alright, don't make me call you two again. Finish that one show and lights out."

"Thank you, Mom. We love you," said Christine.

"Love you too, good night," said Paula.

"Night night," they both replied, in unison.

"Jim, would you nudge me when you roll out in the morning? I'm going for a jog to get a couple of miles in before work."

"Sure, hon, but if it's running exercise you want, you can always come to the store and run the floor to help my customers," he said, trying to be funny.

"That's okay, dear. You're more of the professional at that."

Paula kissed her husband on the lips briefly then headed to the bathroom to prepare for bed. By the time she came out of the bathroom in her negligee, Jim was sitting up in bed reading a book, or pretending to. He slept in his boxers and T-shirt, his chest hair showing over the top. Paula liked what she saw and Jim was no different, although he played it cool, wanting her to know he respected her desire to get her sleep for the early morning jog that she alluded to earlier. She loved this about him, always being considerate, but she knew he was always ready for her, as well.

"What are you reading?" she asked.

"It's a book about a Caribbean sailor, who found a sunken treasure, and how it changed his humble life, his ups and downs, that sort of thing. He had friends he didn't know existed, until he hit it rich."

"I'll bet he did," she said, sliding into her side of the bed.

Jim glanced at her, but put his focus back at the page in front of him. Paula lay quietly on her side facing him. The sight of her husband being there with her faithfully each night caused her to become amorous. With one hand under the covers, she reached out and tickled his ribs. Jim jerked, almost losing his place in his book.

"Are you trying to start something, Mrs. Roberts?" he said. He put his book flat on his thighs, and gave her a mischievous look.

"What does it look like to you, Mr. Roberts?" Paula kissed his arm and gave another quick tickle on his side.

Jim jerked away playfully. "Oh, so you want to wrestle, do you?"

"Something akin to that, that is, if you want to call it wrestling. I prefer to call it other things," she said.

"And what other things do you call it, honeybunch?"

Paula did not answer. She snuggled closer to him holding on to his arm and wrapping her legs around his. Jim put his book on the side table, and the lovebirds caressed, kissed, and held each other. They listened as Rachel and Christine closed the doors to their bedrooms at the end of the hall. Paula switched the bedside clock radio to a soft rock station for a little cover music. Slowly, they loved each other in ways words cannot describe.

Relaxing afterwards, they drifted off to sleep. Both Jim and Paula slept well, and were up early by 6 AM. After toast, coffee, and seeing Jim off, Paula slipped out of her robe and into her exercise clothes, and running shoes. She bounded down the stairs, stretching on the front porch, then set out jogging at a slow pace, picking it up as she felt her energy level rising.

The recent events of the Jennings case rolled through her mind. She was determined to do all she could to return Nathan to his parents unharmed. She jogged past historic homes, careful to watch where she stepped because of the uneven sidewalks and brick roads. Rounding the last corner on her block, she completed her two-mile route. As she slowed her gait to a walk and to cool down, her cell rang. She liked the timing. Winded, but not out of breath, she retrieved the phone from her zipped jacket pocket.

"Paula, have you heard from Mark Jennings yet?" asked Baxter.

"Not yet, Russ, I'm a little surprised that he hasn't called me by now."

"Keep me posted, will ya?"

"You know I will. Listen, I might run by Shooter's Range and get some practice in. It has been a few weeks since I've taken the time to target practice. So, I could be out of pocket for about an hour. If you call and it goes to my voice mail, text me, and I'll see it."

"Sounds good, let's make texting, if no answer, standard operating procedure when something important comes up, Paula. Glad you brought it up."

"Ten-four, works for me. I'll talk to you later, Russ."

Mark Jennings woke up and drove off the island and up I-26 West to Summerville where he kept deposits from the drug proceeds. After withdrawing a total of fifty-thousand dollars from three different accounts, he drove back to his condo at Folly Beach to shower and shave. He did not care for the facilities at the little motel on Johns Island and needed a change of clothes. As he prepared himself for the day, he noticed a strange feeling had come over him ever since he had prayed. He no longer had a desire to get high. He wondered about the change he felt within, and remembered hearing stories of others who were "born again". *Could this have happened to me,* he wondered. He was not sure, but he knew something was different, and he knew he did not want cocaine, or any other kind of high. He just wanted Nathan and his family back.

With his condominium rented by the month, he considered his options whether to stay in the Charleston area, or to move elsewhere. He settled on this new place since Anna Leigh was divorcing him, and the investigation was still in progress. Thinking about other options in his life helped him to pass the time, which seemed to creep by, as if the world had gone into slow motion, waiting for the call from the kidnappers.

Nineteen

At the secluded hideaway, against his partner's advice, Arnie Jones continued to drink one beer after another. Standing up from the sagging sofa, he stumbled outside to relieve himself after consuming his ninth beer of a twelve-pack within a two-hour period. Staggering fifteen yards into the backyard, not far from the little dock, he looked up at the stars in the blackened sky, his face tingling with numbness from his beer buzz. Losing his balance, he pissed on his boots and jeans nearly falling on the grassy backyard that sloped downward to the waterway.

"Damn it, I wet myself," muttered Jones.

Knowing Jones was outside in the yard, Nathan hurriedly worked at the knotted ropes that bound him. Pulling and tugging at the hemp, he managed to get it loose from his wrists. Bending down, he slipped out of the rope, which held his legs and ankles, by pulling his tennis shoes off first. Sliding his feet back into his tennis shoes,

Nathan crept to the kitchen window in the back of the house where he could get a view of Arnie Jones shaking himself, as he began to zip up. Nathan's heart pounded within him from an adrenaline rush, which energized him into a state of readiness. He turned to look over his shoulder viewing the front room then eyed the front door, which was ajar. The screen door periodically bounced against the doorjamb at the behest of the waterway breeze blowing through the porous shanty.

    With Jones in the backyard, Nathan figured he could run out the front door and around the house as his captor walked up the slope to the backdoor. With another quick glance through a window, Nathan saw the ruffian light a cigarette, still standing outside, looking around and enjoying the night air. Seeing the opening to escape, Nathan crept stealthily to the front door on the balls of his feet. Opening the front door just enough to let himself get out, he did so with the least amount of noise possible.

    Nimble and light of foot, he darted as fast as his feet would carry him across the small front yard rounding the corner of the house then raced down the side to a corner by the backyard. Winded, Nathan squatted while he caught his breath, positioning himself on one knee. Leaning forward, he peeked around the edge of the house to see where Arnie Jones was located. Waiting for the crusty ole redneck to go inside, he wondered what he would do if the Jon boat motor would not crank. He reasoned that it was his best chance to get away, and dismissed his worries of a motor malfunction.

Nathan evaluated a stand of trees, mostly pine with undergrowth, twelve feet from the house. He figured that he could run through the woods and hide, if he had to, and eventually make his way to the road to hitch a ride. Playing "hide and seek" with his friends at the park, in his neighborhood, and at his uncle's farm, gave him the experience to be confident with this back-up strategy. Still, he liked his chances on the Jon boat in the waterway better than possibly being caught on ground and to be held again by these local desperados.

Jones took a long drag on his cigarette then flicked it down to the water's edge letting it sizzle then die out, as it floated, adding to the garbage already deposited in the waterway by those who did not care. Realizing he had been outside too long please his boss, he walked up the grassy incline to the back door. Nathan saw him disappear as he entered the back side of the house. He took a deep breath and made a run for it following the tree line, which led twenty-five yards to the water's edge.

Walking through the doorway to check on his captive, just after the short screened-in porch, which led to the living area, Jones saw the rope on the floor by the chair where Nathan previously sat for the bulk of two days. Shocked into a half-sober state, he was terrified of what Bobby Spires would do to him. He ran out the front door looking for the boy, and not seeing anyone in the front yard, he turned down the side of the house that Nathan utilized for a getaway. Loping down the side of the house to the corner, he got a view of the backyard. Darkness had set in and visibility was poor. He looked across the yard, his eyes attempting to adjust for a better view through the mist rising up from the waterway and floating over the yard creating an eerie fog.

"Alright boy, where are you? You better get back here right now, if you know what's good for ya," Jones shouted.

He knew his partner in crime would be furious with him, if he was to allow Nathan to escape. He remembered growing up with Spires and how that he had always dominated him. He thought about the time that his bully of a friend beat him, giving him a black eye, and putting bruises on other places of his body. He recalled the many times that Spires slapped him on the head and figured it would be much worse this time, if he did not find Nathan.

Nathan ignored Jones' beckoning voice and hopped into the small Jon boat. Quickly, he moved to the back by the motor housing. He had done it dozens of time before in the small lake behind his house. His dad had trained him, and more recently, his uncle had taken him out in a channel near Charleston. Nathan grabbed the orange rubber bulb on the black, rubber gas line of the deep red metal gas tank, pumping it five times. Then with one hand on the T-shaped handle of the crank-rope, and the other on the top of the motor for support, he pulled with all of his might. The motor sputtered. He gave another quick pull of the rope, another sputter. Grabbing the handle on the red five-gallon gas tank, he lifted upwards. It was almost full of fuel, which led Nathan to believe the boat had seen recent use. Encouraged, the young man pulled the cord again. Another sputter, but the sound lingered longer than before.

Jones trotted down the sloped backyard in the direction of the water where he heard the motor sputtering. Looking at the dock, and nearly slipping on the grassy slope wet with mist, he could barely make out the small shadowy figure of the boy in the boat hunched over the motor.

"You git outta that boat right now," he shouted, at the top of his lungs.

Nathan flinched in fear at the sound of Arnie Jones yelling at him. He continued to pull the rope cord in rapid succession. The motor sputtered again, almost cranking, but Jones was almost on top of him now. Twelve more strides and his captor would be on the dock. In desperation, Nathan yanked the rope again with every ounce of strength he could muster. The motor started with a muffled sound, and then burst into a loud rumble like that of a motorcycle racing its engine. Quickly, Nathan turned the handle to engage forward position. Turning the throttle as far as it would go, he revved the motor to full bore, and pulled away from the dock. The front end of the little Jon boat rose up high, as it shot out of the water facing the wide channel.

Jones landed one foot on the dock, and then the other, his feet pounding the wooden pier in the direction of the Jon boat. Nathan looked back over his shoulder seeing the awkward buffoon reach the end of the dock as he sped out into the dark waterway. Jones ran so hard that he lost his balance, and trying to stop, fell over in the cold murky water with a huge splash, his arms flailing about. Nathan, now fifteen to twenty feet away from the end of the pier, turned around laughing at the half-drunk knit-wit.

"Stop, and come back here boy!" shouted Jones, brackish water dribbling from his mouth.

"You stupid idiot, I just outsmarted you, and you can't do a thing about it, ha-ha." Nathan slapped his knee in glee and threw his head back laughing harder. Relieved that he was free, the sound of the purring motor was sweet to his ears. He felt amazingly comfortable on the water, the vibration of the Jon boat under him leading him to an uncertain, but for the moment, safe escape.

"Boy, I'm gonna git ya for this. You won't git away. I know every inch of this island. I'll find you!"

"You won't find me, you ole redneck!"

Nathan kept the throttle wide open as he veered right, heading to the middle of the channel. He looked back again, seeing the ripples in the water that the wake created. Arnie flailed about, wading in chest deep water to the ladder on the side of the dock. Nathan leveled out the boat, slowing the motor to three-quarters throttle. He looked around the channel for other places that he could dock. The area where he navigated was almost pitch-black and secluded. The only light that guided him was the full moon. The boat slapped the water as it bounced rhythmically up and down. Nathan settled into cruising mode on half-throttle in the middle of the waterway. He followed a moonlit path of soft bluish light shimmering in the water, as the *man in the moon*, who seemed to be his friend looked down upon him and smiled approvingly at his gallantry.

Twenty

❦

Bobby Spires arrived at Jakes Landing at dusk. A group of cars and trucks, mostly older models, was parked by the marina. Local men hung out there after work, drinking beer and shooting pool in a back room where sat two non-regulation, green, velvet-top pool tables. Patrons fed the tables four quarters to play. They talked about which fish were biting, as they slid their pool cues up and down in their hands preparing for their shots. Spires turned in a parking space at one end of the building, lit a cigarette, and then pulled out a little sheet of paper on which he had scribbled the phone number. He dialed his cell phone very deliberately, keypad beeping each time he hit a number. The phone rang as he put the handset to his ear and waited for Jennings to answer.

"Hello, this is Mark Jennings."

"Hey, Mr. Jennings, this is the man that's got your boy, Nathan. Did you come up with the money?"

"Yeah, I've got the money. I want to talk to my son now."

"Sorry, but I didn't bring him with me. You can talk to him when you bring me the money."

Jennings' jaw clinched in anger. "Listen, whoever you are. I need proof of life before I drive to some unknown destination."

I'll give you directions where we will meet, and then you can follow me to where you will exchange the money for your son."

"How do I know that you won't double-cross me... take the money and run? And how do I know that you have not harmed Nathan?"

"No, I don't guess you do. We have not harmed your boy at all. He's perfectly safe, although he has been a handful at times," Spires said. "We're just doing a job; it ain't nothing personal, you understand."

"He had better be unharmed," said Jennings.

"You are talking mighty tough for someone who ripped off the captain. I've got your son, and don't forget that."

"Look, whoever you are, I didn't rip off anybody. The captain delivered the goods and I paid him. It's not my fault that he got caught. That's the chance he took."

"We don't need to get into all that again, Mr. Jennings," said Spires. "Are you willing to come or not?"

"Yes, of course I'll come. You have my son. Where do I meet you?"

"Come on to Johns Island, go straight for three miles, then turn left at the road where you see the Jakes

Landing sign. Go down about one-half mile, and there's a place to pull over on your right. You will see a gravel parking area with two large, green, metal trashcans near the shoulder. I'll have my parking lights on, facing out to the road."

"Okay, I got it. From where I am, it should take about thirty minutes to get there, or do you have a time you want to meet?"

"You're going to have time. It's eight o'clock now; meet me at nine," said Spires. Follow my directions and you will see my brown Oldsmobile. Pull over at the parkway and flash your bright lights twice for a signal, but do not get out. I'll pull out, and then you follow me."

"Alright, I will be there. You know my car, don't you? It's the …."

Spires hung up before he heard all of what Jennings told him.

Dialing Paula's number, Jennings quaked inside from a combination of emotions. He feared for his son's well-being, and he was beside himself with anger. He hoped that the men who kidnapped his son would be punished. Still, he had to believe that he would get through this and get his son back safely. He thought it strange that he felt such a contradiction of intense emotions at the same time. The phone continued to ring. *Why isn't she picking up?* he thought. He thought of hanging up as Paula answered on the fourth ring.

"Hello, this is Paula Roberts."

"Paula, this is Mark Jennings. I got a call from the kidnapper. The man who has Nathan wants me to meet him at a roadside park, and then to follow him to the place where they are holding him."

"Where are you now, Mark?"

"I'm at Folly Beach, but I can meet you at a little grocery store on Johns Island. It's the first business on the right when you get on the island, the gas station there, just as you cross the bridge."

"I know the one," said Paula. "My husband and I stopped there when we took the kids clam digging on the island once. Park somewhere on the side of the store away from the door, okay? We can be there in about thirty minutes."

"I can do that, but listen, how are we going to stay together when I go to meet this guy?"

"We'll probably follow you, giving you enough distance ahead of us not to be conspicuous. We will cut our lights if we need to so this man won't suspect anything, but let's not get ahead of ourselves. Let me tell Russ what is happening, and we'll talk again when we meet in person. We should be there by eight-thirty."

"Perfect, the man who has Nathan wants me to meet him at nine."

"Alright, Mark. Let us know if you have a problem, or need to adjust the time, and please don't do anything until we get there?"

"No problem, Paula. I want you two helping, trust me. I'll see you in half an hour."

Jennings let out a sigh of relief that he did not have to change the time, and that the detectives were going to be there to help him. He could detect anxiousness in Spires' voice that indicated he was eager to make the deal. Making good time, Jennings crossed the connector bridge arriving at the convenience store ahead of Paula and Russ. He parked in a spot on the side of the store by the restrooms and switched off the engine. Flipping the key to accessory, he put the FM channel on a soft rock station. Rolling down his window halfway for air, he lit a cigarette and waited for Paula and Russ. Five minutes slowly trickled by. Glancing at his rear view and side mirrors, he kept looking for them to arrive. Ten minutes had elapsed when the detectives pulled in alongside him, and Paula rolled down her window. Jennings, noticing her window lowering, let down his driver-side window the rest of the way.

"Hey Paula, I see you two made it."

"Hi Mark, I remember this place. This is Russ Baxter, my partner," she said, motioning to Russ with her thumb, as if she was hitchhiking.

"It's nice to meet you, Mark. I'm sorry it's under these circumstances, though," said Russ, leaning over from the driver's seat so that he could make eye contact. "We will do all we can to get your son back to you safe and sound."

"It's nice to meet you also, Russ. Anna Leigh and I appreciate both of you helping us. What do we need to do from here?

"This is how we will play it, Mark," said Paula. "We'll be behind you seventy-five to a hundred feet. You maintain speed around thirty-five miles per hour when following the man who has your son. We will follow you to wherever he's taking you. We might have our lights off periodically, so don't worry about that, we will be there. When you meet with this man, you need to comply with what he requests. We will stay hidden and step in when the time is right."

"What if it doesn't happen like that?" Jennings asked.

"You mean if there's a double-cross?"

"Yeah, that's exactly what I mean!"

"We'll be watching and ready for that. If we have to come in suddenly, you grab Nathan and high tail it behind cover as fast as you can," she said.

Baxter sat amazed as he heard Paula explain the plan and give Mark instructions as if she had been doing this for years. She spoke with a confidence that added to his assurance that things would work out fine, if they just stuck to the game plan.

"Yeah, I can do that. What do we do when we get to where they are holding Nathan?" asked Jennings.

"It depends on how things unfold, Mark. As I said earlier, we will be nearby, so just know that we have your back. Don't do anything suddenly, unless you absolutely have to. Be very deliberate; even stall him if you can. That will give us time to get back through the woods to the location where they are holed up. We will prepare to come in from the best angle."

"Okay, sounds good to me. If he gives me Nathan in exchange for the money, and lets us go, that will be great. If he does not release Nathan, then thanks in advance, for what you two will do. I'll see you there," said Jennings, as he cranked his car.

Paula made eye contact with Jennings once more. "Don't thank us now, yet. Let's go see what we can do."

Jennings pulled out slowly and started down the small state road that led to a portion of Johns Island marshland that backed up to the waterway. Paula and Russ pulled out when they saw his taillights growing smaller, following at a safe distance.

Twenty-One

❦

Rachel and Christine smelled the aroma from the kitchen as they followed their noses to where Jim was preparing a meal that he threw together in short order. He decided on a quick nutritious meal consisting of a cheese-covered, tuna casserole with cheese, green beans, and buttered dinner rolls, a quick recipe he learned from his mom in upstate New York. He had tried it successfully on the girls a few weeks prior, and to his surprise, they requested it again. Adding butter and seasoning to the green beans, he jiggled the pot a little over the stove eye.

"Where's Mama tonight, Jim?" asked Rachel.

Christine tagged along behind her sister, looking over her shoulder, as she listened for his response.

"She called in a while ago, girls. There is no need to worry. Mom is working late tonight. You know her job requires that sometimes," he said.

"I bet she is out somewhere chasing a criminal like before," said Christine, attempting to be a wisecrack.

Rachel reacted with a laugh, and then frowned quickly at her little sister. "No, she's not Christine! Mom isn't doing that kind of work anymore. She said that she stopped all that after her last job."

"Girls, let's not fuss about what we don't know. Your mom is a hard-working woman and very smart. She will be fine no matter what she's doing."

"Yeah, Rachel, let's not fuss," said Christine, giggling.

Christine knew that she was responsible for the controversy, yet she got a kick out of seeing Jim play referee. She loved Jim, but liked to create a little mischief occasionally to get his reaction, more than a little like her mother. She had never experienced emotional bonding with a man before, except her grandfather, but after a year, a substantial amount of bonding between the two of them occurred.

Jim was not oblivious to Christine's tactics, but she still managed to take him off-guard when he was not on his toes. The fact of the matter was that he enjoyed it. He loved being part of the family and helping manage the domestic affairs. He and Paula had been married a little over a year, but most people never would have guessed it because of how they interacted as a family unit. Outsiders saw how the girls responded to him and thought that he was their biological dad. This was the one special thing about Jim that Paula and the girls loved so deeply that it could not be translated into words.

Jim had bought a book teaching him how to respond to his stepchildren. In this book, "The Blended Family", he read how not acting like a drill sergeant with Paula's children, but more like a wise mentor, would be much more beneficial. He tried his best to do as the book suggested, which stated that the *stepparent* should allow the *natural parent* to be the disciplinarian, when needed. Jim also read that it takes about three to five years to bond with someone else's children in a blended family. Their relationship was the rare case, in which the bonding to each other evolved in hyper-speed. Three years of bonding were accelerated into one. So many factors played into this phenomenon, yet everyone was hungry for the closeness they enjoyed.

"We're eating soon, girls. I need you two to set the table, ice the glasses, and pour the tea. I'm putting your favorite dish, from me anyway, on the table."

The girls did as Jim asked without question, their taste buds salivating like Pavlov's dog at the announcement of their favorite dish being served. After their meal, the girls chatted with Jim, asking him questions about his day at work. They had learned how to emulate their mom in this area. Jim thought it was cute and made the conversation fun and interesting, teaching them about antiques, as he told them stories of what customers had purchased, and the funny things they said and did. He asked Rachel and Christine about their day, to which the girls were never short for words.

"Okay girls, let's clear off the table and rinse the dishes, please. You two can load all the dishes and silverware into the dishwasher. Leave the two pots for me, and I'll take care of those."

"Yes sir," said Rachel. "Let's get it done, Christine."

"Do we have to?" pleaded Christine.

"Christine, you know we do. Mom would ask us to do the same thing, so don't try that on Jim," said the older sibling.

"Thank you girls, I appreciate it."

Jim watched them interact as they playfully completed their task, and smiled, without acknowledging the girls' antics. He remembered his teenage boys and thought about how similarly they behaved, though a different gender. *Teens are teens and there is no getting around that,* he thought.

Paula and Russ continued following Mark Jennings, as he made his way down the country road to the corner of Jakes Landing Road where he would turn to meet Bobby Spires. Paula thought about her family. It felt good, on one hand, to know that the girls were safe with her husband, yet on the other, she wished she were there. She knew her husband was the cream of the crop with a huge heart for kids. The catch she made when landing him went far beyond marrying for financial stability, or out of loneliness. He worked hard and made a decent living, but more than that, he loved her without measure, and cared for her daughters as if they were his own. She knew that she could never take this special man for granted, and she felt guilty that she was not at home in a mother's traditional role.

"Russ, I'm going to make a quick phone call to Jim to check on the girls. Do you mind?" asked Paula.

"Not at all, Paula, you should know that."

"Well, I'm still fairly new and I don't see you calling your wife."

"Hey, that's just it, you are new, Paula. My wife knows me by now, and vice versa. I do check in with her; mostly when no one is around, but I understand totally, so don't give it a second thought."

"Okay, thanks, I'll just be a minute," she said.

"No problem."

Paula pulled out her cell phone to give her husband a quick call.

"Jim, honey, it's me. Is everything going well at home?"

"Hey, love, yeah, it's going great. The girls are behaving, and they managed to live through my cooking. In fact, they enjoyed it and are cleaning up the kitchen right now. How are things at work?"

"They're fine, just another stake-out type of thing, I shouldn't be too late."

"Are you alone?"

"No, I am with Russ on this one, so it's a team effort. Well, honey, I just wanted to make a quick call to check on y'all. I'll call you when I start home."

"Sure, that would be great, I'll rest easier knowing you are on the way home," he said. Something in his soothing voice always bolstered her morale.

"I'll see you after awhile. Leave a light on for me, like the motel people say."

"I sure will, honey," said Jim, chuckling at his wife."

"Oh, and thanks for helping out with the girls. I love ya."

"Love you too. See ya soon, be safe, and come home in one piece."

"Alright Russ, I'm feeling better now. Let's get a strangle hold on these child snatchers and put them below the jail where they belong," Paula said.

Paula and Russ saw the red taillights of Jennings' car up ahead as he turned off on the side of the road. They saw the lights of the waiting Olds positioned at the far end of the parking area. The detectives pulled off the road fifty yards behind Jennings, quickly shutting their lights off.

"He's making a stop to meet his connection, like he said. Let's sit tight and see what happens," said Baxter.

"I'm sitting on ready, waiting to go," said Paula.

Jennings flashed his bright lights twice for the signal that he was ready to follow Spires. The Olds pulled away from the roadside with Jennings following. Paula and Russ allowed a few moments the first car a head start down the road, and then followed Jennings.

"This is it, Paula. Are you ready for some excitement?"

"Russ, I didn't bring "little stubby" along for nothing. I hope I don't have to use it, but she's ready if need be. I got in some practice recently when things were slow at the office."

"Say it ain't so, Annie Oakley." Russ chuckled at his gung-ho assistant.

"Well, I'm sorry, Russ, but kidnapping a child riles me up. I don't care what the reason is. I can imagine my girls, or Jim's boys, being in the same position. I would show no mercy, if it were them."

"I know how you feel, Paula, and I feel the same. You know that, but let's remember to keep a cool head out there. These guys may not be the sharpest tools in the woodshed, but they know how to fish, and to hunt. They know how to survive, and quite often, that makes for an unpredictable outcome."

"I hear ya, partner. That's good advice. Cool heads prevail, Uncle Charlie always said."

Up ahead, Jennings' car was slowing. Paula and Russ noticed the red brake lights shine brighter as he turned off the two lane paved road onto a dirt road, which led a hundred yards through a stand of trees to where the men were holed up. Jennings kept distance from Bobby Spires' vehicle, as instructed, a few car lengths behind. The thickly populated trees, whose branches intertwined overhead, covered the flat road leading to the hideaway. Sporadically, patches of moonlight broke through the dense foliage.

Baxter switched his headlights off again and turned in behind Jennings. The plan continued to evolve. Instead of pulling onto the side of the road, and trekking through the woods, they chose to follow on the same road because there did not seem to be another entrance.

"We'll find a place to pull over, if we see them stop. I don't know how far back he's going, but from the looks of the woods and marsh, we're be better off following by car, than traipsing through the woods," said Baxter.

"I totally agree," said Paula. "Besides, I'm not very fond of running through the woods at night, unless we have to. It looks like we're in some swampy, snake-infested terrain."

The moon beamed down, giving the light needed to travel the sandy road mixed with shells. Slowly, they made forward progress with the car in drive without pressing the gas pedal. Grass grew upwards in the middle of the road, brushing the undersides of the vehicle. A lone Great Horned Owl sat atop a tall oak tree, which stood majestically, out of place, among the thicket of pines. The great bird, with a wingspan of five feet, let out its familiar sounds..."whoo-whoo-whoowha", almost an octave lower than its cousin, the Barred Owl, then turned its head peering down on the activity below.

Ahead, Jennings' 300-Z bounced up and down, bottoming out here and there, as it crept behind the sedan that Spires commandeered. Jennings looked in his rear-view mirror, barely able to discern Russ's dark green Cherokee about twenty yards behind him. The owl suddenly jumped from its perch and swooped down in front of Russ's Jeep letting out an earsplitting cry, permeating the night like a siren. Paula and Russ heard the flapping wings of the largest among the four owls, which breed in South Carolina.

"Holy crap! What the heck was that?" asked Paula, startled by the enormous bird.

"Oh, that was just a large Great Horned Owl. They hang out in the woods around here."

"Yeah, well I knew they existed, but didn't know they got that big. Look, Russ, they're putting on the brakes."

"Quick, pull over on the shoulder of the road and park."

Baxter did as his partner requested. Quietly, the sleuths opened the doors and slipped out of the SUV. Russ led the way with Paula not more than six or seven feet behind. Stealthily, they trekked along the side of the road, hiding behind the trees as they sought cover behind one tree trunk then another. Russ drew his .45 caliber Glock from the holster, holding it down by his side. Paula held her .38 caliber Smith & Wesson, pointing to the ground, low just below her waist, with the safety on.

"I'm going to run across to the other side of the road," Russ whispered. "We need to spread out. Keep an eye on me, and I'll give you a signal when to make a move."

"Go, Russ. I gotcha covered. Whenever you signal, I'll be ready."

Daniel Easterling

Twenty-Two

❦

Nathan maneuvered the Jon boat, cutting through the waterway as he passed by other docks and residences that line its banks. The lit houses were barely visible because of the fog rising off the water that shrouded the banks. It was rather spooky for an eleven year old to think about approaching one of them so soon after his escape. Still wanting to put more distance between himself and his former captors, Nathan continued to cruise through the dark brackish water. The moonlight, faithfully beaming, served as his guiding companion. He spotted a cove to his left, which piqued his interest. It was wider than two he had passed already. He figured that if someone tried to come up from behind him that he could get in and out without extreme difficulty. He also surmised that he might be able to find other smaller coves where he could hide, if necessary. Although there was no other boat at the little dock where he heisted the Jon boat, Nathan wondered if the men could somehow be out on the water hunting for him.

So far, the trip through the waterway was uneventful. He felt very small out in the middle of the large waterway, yet the smell of fish permeating the air gave him a familiar marker. Up ahead about eighty yards, Nathan observed a large boat coming into view. It looked like a pontoon of some kind, with size enough to hold a large group of people. He could make out lights around the top and sides, and hear the faint noise of people laughing and music playing. Steering his boat directly toward the cruising party boat, Nathan hoped to get their attention to tell them what happened to him. His hopes of rescue leaped in his chest as he opened up the throttle of the ten horsepower motor and sped towards his newfound savior.

Bobby Spires pulled up close to the front porch of their hideaway, hopping out of his car. Arnie Jones came running from the back of the house waving his arms, as if he were fleeing from a swarm of bees, hot on his trail.

"Bobby! Bobby! The kid got away!"

"What do you mean he got away? I told you to watch that boy good, you idiot!"

"I was, Bobby, I was. One minute I went outside to take a leak, and he was tied to the chair. The next minute I walked back in and he was gone. I ran around the house looking for him and found him at the dock. He stole the

Jon boat before I could get to him, and took off out in the waterway. I didn't know that boat had any gas in it."

"Damn it, Arnie! I knew I shouldn't have trusted you to watch the boy. Now, what have we got? Nothing, you freaking numbskull! We're gonna be charged with kidnapping, if they find us, and we don't even have the boy now."

"I'm sorry, Bobby. I didn't mean for it to happen." Jones looked at his leader remorsefully for guidance.

"Shut up and listen to me, Arnie! Which way did he go? Can you tell me that?"

"Yeah, Bobby, he went out in the waterway heading toward the ocean."

"That little twerp! Let's go inside right quick. The Jennings man followed me here to get his son. You let me do all the talking," said Spires.

"Okay, Bobby," said Jones, sheepishly.

Jennings pulled in behind Spires' car and parked. He opened the door of his sports car and got out. Spires stood at the screen door watching him, and then stepped out with a gun in his hand lowered by his side.

"Where's the money, Mr. Jennings?" Spires barked.

"Where's my son?"

"Give me the money first, and I'll give you your boy."

"I'm not giving you anything until you turn over my son alive and well."

Spires walked toward Jennings, who was standing by his car door, his face grimaced in anger.

"Put your hands up in the air where I can see them, Jennings. I don't want to hurt you, so just give me the damn money, and you'll get your son back," demanded Spires. He pointed his forty-five caliber pistol at the midsection of Jennings.

Jones stood behind Spires watching and waiting to see what would occur. "Yeah, give us the money, if you want your son back," he said.

"Shut up, Arnie! I told you I would handle this!" said Spires. He clinched his jaw at the interruption.

Jennings glanced down at his nine millimeter Glock hidden in the pocket of his car door. He thought for a moment about ducking to grab the loaded gun. Basic training at Fort Jackson some twenty-four years earlier flashed through his mind. He had since fired the revolver a few times at a shooting range, but did not trust his accuracy. He recalled what Paula and Russ told him about not endangering himself, unless necessary, and did not want to take a chance on possibly never seeing his son again. Complying with Spires' command, he raised his hands in the air.

From her hidden position, Paula could see that things were not going well. She saw Spires walking slowly toward Jennings, gun pointed. Across the front yard in the tree line, Russ remained crouched and hidden, as well, watching for the precise moment to make a move. Russ and Paula made eye contact. He gave her a signal to wait, and then stood up from behind the tree trunk.

"Drop it now! It's over," said Baxter, his revolver pointing straight at Spires' from twenty feet away, as he continued to move closer.

Spires flinched, but did not budge. He glanced at Baxter, but kept his aim dead on Jennings as he moved a little closer – now twelve feet from his target.

"I'm not dropping anything. Stop right where you are!" growled Spires, hoping Russ Baxter would succumb to his bluff. "Now, drop the damn gun, or I'm gonna waste this man right here and now!"

"Okay, wait," said Baxter.

He put his left hand in the air, and with his right, he released his grip on his pistol allowing it to hang by an index finger. He figured Spires might be bluffing, but calculated that it was not worth the risk when dealing with someone unpredictable. Paula had a bead on Spires, so she kept her position in the bushes until the right moment to strike. Baxter stretched forth his arm, dropping his gun to the ground, then nodded his head to Paula indicating that she make her move. No sooner had he nodded than she bolted out from behind a large bush by the edge of the road with her pearl-handled Smith and Wesson drawn.

"Drop your gun! I won't hesitate to use mine if you don't," said Paula, from behind where Spires stood at an advantageous position.

Spires knew that he was at a huge disadvantage, but would have none of a woman telling him what to do. He spun around to fire his revolver at Paula. As a shot rang out, she dove to the ground, rolled over once, firing twice from her belly, two bullets, one to his torso, and one to his thigh dropping Spires, like a lumberjack felling a tree. He dropped his weapon, bleeding and writhing on the ground in pain, then lay motionless, as one dead, but eyed his gun not far away. After ten seconds of playing possum, he rolled over and stretched for his gun. Baxter, who had recovered his weapon, beat him to the gun, kicking it out of his reach. He stood on his back with his other boot pressing down hard, his revolver pointing at his target.

Spires should not have trusted his mentally slow friend with a gun, and it was painfully obvious now. Jones stood dumbfounded in amazement watching everything transpire, while forgetting about the gun tucked in his pants. With Spires under control, Paula had time to get a better look at Jones, who had the tip of the gun handle protruding from his pants.

"You, over there, drop that gun to the ground," said Paula. Lift your hands where I can see them."

She glared at Jones with her aim on the buffoon sidekick. He lifted his gun from his pants and dropped it, then raised his hands to the sky. Russ put Spires in cuffs, while Paula did the same to Jones.

Mark Jennings ran to the injured Spires and bent down to face him. "Where's my son?" shouted Jennings.

"We don't have him," he said, wincing in pain. "He got away just before I drove up."

"You're a liar! Where is my son?"

"I'm telling you the truth. He escaped before we got here."

"And how did he do that?"

"In a Jon boat from the dock out back," said Jones, speaking up for his partner who could not speak again due to immense pain.

"Which way did he go?" asked Jennings. He walked up to Jones, who was standing by the porch next to Paula.

"I saw him going up the waterway toward the ocean."

"No funny business, man. You are already in serious trouble." shouted Jennings.

"That's the truth, man. I saw him leave in the Jon boat that was docked behind the house."

Jennings ran inside the old house, giving it a quick examination. "Nathan, are you here? Nathan!" he called frantically, as he ran to each room looking. Not finding him, he ran out the back door, then down the lawn to the dock to inspect for evidence to support their story. He saw the wet rope stretched across the dock that Nathan had tossed when he untied the boat. Satisfied that the story was legitimate, Jennings ran back to where Paula and Russ stood with the captured men. He listened in as the sleuths strategized.

"What did you find, Mark?" asked Russ.

"A tie-rope missing its boat was lying on the dock. Seems like he is telling the truth," said Jennings.

Baxter turned to his partner. "Paula, I'll call the police, and have these two men picked up and booked. This one needs medical treatment and an ambulance, as soon as possible. Why don't you go with Mark and look for Nathan."

"I'm on it, Russ. Mark, are you ready to go?" asked Paula. She shoved Jones closer to Baxter. "Sit down on the ground, next to your buddy," she said to Jones, who complied, wincing at the sight of his bloody friend on the ground.

"I couldn't be more ready," Jennings said. He pulled his car keys from his pants pocket. "It's open, Paula. Hop in."

Paula jumped in the Nissan 300-Z. Jennings cranked the sports car, and spun his wheels on the sandy parking area as he turned around, flinging debris in the air. The rear end of his vehicle fishtailed and straightened on the dirt road leading out of the marsh.

"Where do you think Nathan might be headed, Mark?"

"I don't know for sure, but if I know my son, he will try to find the first group of adults he thinks he can trust."

"How well does he know the waterway?" she asked.

"I've taken Nathan fishing out here one time. We went out from Jakes Landing in our own boat, as a matter of fact, so we both know it to a certain extent, but we fished during the day, not at night like this," he said.

"That does make a difference. Why don't we go to the landing, since it's close by, and see what we can find out," said Paula.

"Exactly my thoughts. Let's do it," he said.

Reaching the end of the dirt road, Jennings turned onto the paved road that led to Jakes Landing. He shifted into second gear and hit the accelerator, tires screeching, as they bit into the asphalt. He slammed the shifter into third gear accelerating more, and then into fourth. The sports car reached ninety miles per hour in seconds flat, pressing Paula back against her bucket seat. She flinched, but shook it off, leaning forward to watch the roadway for any sign of Nathan. Two miles down the road, they saw a big white sign painted on plywood and supported by a couple of tall telephone poles. "JAKES LANDING", it read in black and white, with a red arrow pointing to the left. Jennings downshifted, grinding the gears, as he slowed the sports car to an acceptable speed to make the turn. The marina did not close until 11 PM, about an hour after their featured party boat was scheduled to dock from its dinner cruise of the surrounding islands in the Charleston harbor.

Twenty-Three

✦

The night air chilled his body as the sea breeze picked up. Nathan did not know if he would be safe or not, but he figured nearly anything beat being out in a small boat at night on a dark, treacherous waterway. He continued to guide the Jon boat in the direction of the party boat when suddenly, and inexplicably, the motor, which had purred like a Singer sewing machine thus far, sputtered and skipped to a stall. A good fifty yards away from the pontoon boat, he crouched over the back of the boat, and grabbed the handle to crank it. He gave the rope a couple of jerks, but the motor only sputtered. The strong stench of gasoline invaded Nathan's nostrils, burning his mucus membranes and his eyes.

He figured from what his father taught him that the motor was flooded, and that he had to let it air out before attempting to start it again. He remembered when Uncle Frank allowed him to drive his boat, and wished it would crank as easily as his boat did. Uncle Frank, Anna Leigh's brother, had taken up with his nephew about a year and a half earlier when Mark Jennings began to behave erratically, not spending the time with his kids as he once did. It was the beginning of the period when Mark sunk into his downward spiral of cocaine use, hanging out at all hours of the night.

    The Jon boat began drifting with the current away from the party boat. The hope of being safely rescued began slipping from him. He realized that all the music and commotion on the boat made it unlikely that anyone would hear him, but nonetheless, in desperation he stood up, cupped his hands to his mouth, and shouted, "Hello out there! Can anybody hear me? I was kidnapped. Help me!"

    Nathan lost his balance and fell over forward, catching himself with two hands on both sides of the aluminum boat as it shifted with the current and small waves. Discouraged, Nathan sat on the backseat to catch his breath. Propping up his head by his cold hands, elbows resting on his knees, he gathered his wits. He raised his face up once again, trying to catch the movement of the people on the deck of the pontoon boat. They were just shadows from where his boat had drifted to now, sixty-five yards away.

    Collecting his thoughts, Nathan decided that his chances of being found improved markedly, if he were to wear all white on the upper half of his body. Despite the chill in the air, he stripped off his burgundy polo shirt leaving only his white T-shirt on his upper body. Careful to keep his balance, he held to the sides of the Jon boat until he overcame the wobble that threatened to toss him overboard. Erect now, as a crowing rooster balanced on the apex of a roof, Nathan took a deep breath and shouted at the top of his lungs in the boat's direction. With no response from the distant boat, he thought of how he might employ a more effective method of gaining their attention.

The Jon boat continued to drift farther away from the party boat, the noise and music getting fainter. Knowing his chances were dimming by the minute, Nathan reached down to the hem in the bottom of his T-shirt and yanked it off in one quick movement, like he would on a hot summer's day after being saturated by sweat when playing with his friends. He slipped his polo shirt back on for warmth, and then lifted the white T-shirt overhead swinging it back and forth, and shouting again, as loudly as his youthful lungs could muster.

"Hello! Hello! Hey, anybody, help me!"

Nathan felt his voice growing hoarse, as he looked down around him. He heard the murky waters lapping against the sides of his boat, and wondered what creatures might be beneath him. He remembered his dad telling him that sharks inhabited the brackish water where fate had placed him on this foreboding night. He hoped that none of these creatures were near him. As this very thought haunted his brain, he looked out fifteen yards away to see an ominous-looking, triangular object raised out of the water smoothly gliding in his direction.

A young couple strolled arm in arm to the end of the party boat to get a reprieve from the loud music. Reaching the stern, they leaned against the safety rails for privacy to talk while enjoying the night air. The man pulled his companion close to him as he leaned against the back rail of the boat. Looking in her eyes for a moment, he closed in for a kiss, but was distracted by what he saw over her shoulder out on the water.

"Look Megan!" Randy said. "There's something white out there moving back and forth. It looks like a flag, and I think I hear something, as well."

Randy turned her around so that they could see better in the direction where Nathan was located, his hands resting on her shoulders.

"Where, honey?" Megan replied.

"Look straight out across the water as far as you can see in line with that lighted house in the background."

"I see it. Good grief, Randy, it looks like someone in distress."

"Let's watch for a minute," he said.

Nathan again shouted for help, waving his white T-shirt. "Help, anyone! Help me!"

"I hear it," Megan. Let's go tell the captain. What's his name? Do you remember?"

"I think he said his name is Captain Bill. Yeah, that's it. Let's go find him. There's definitely someone out there waving something white and crying out for help."

Beneath the water's surface, an eight-foot Bull shark in search of an evening meal swirled and zigzagged in its hunting pattern. The shark sensed movement and noise ahead, and continued to move closer to the Jon boat. Nathan was sure it was a shark now. He could see the sizable predator heading in his direction. Judging from the size of the fin, he knew that he should sit down and brace himself, in case the monstrous fish was to ram the boat. The little boat was heavier than it would have been with an electric motor, but it was questionable as to whether it would survive the impact of a charging shark of this size. Nathan positioned himself squarely in the middle of the Jon boat. He sat hunched forward, his hands tightly clutching the cold aluminum sides. Not knowing if anyone heard his panicked plea for help, he knew that this was not the time to worry about being rescued. Instead, he went into survival mode, as he watched the shark's fin picking up speed. The vicious shark made a beeline directly at him.

The couple located the captain of the party boat. "Captain Bill," said Randy. "We're sorry to interrupt you, but there's a person out on the water on a small boat who is swinging a white towel, or something, over his head, and shouting for help."

The captain, alarmed by the news, quickly retrieved his binoculars then lifted them to his eyes, looking in the direction where the helpful passengers pointed. "I can't see very well with these at night. Let me put a light out there. Are you sure you saw a distress signal?"

"Yes, Captain, we both saw it," Randy replied. He looked at his girlfriend who stood with him, nodding her head in agreement.

"Shine a fog light starboard!" Captain Bill shouted to one of his crew. With the crew moving the light back and forth slowly, the captain spotted the small Jon boat drifting listlessly on the waterway. "It looks like a kid on a boat just sitting there. I can't tell for sure, but it's worth checking out. Thanks, you two," said the captain. "Hey listen, keep this between us for now. I don't want to make a commotion among the party-goers. The people are having too much fun, if it turns out to be a wild goose chase. I'll make an announcement, if we need to inform everyone."

"Yes sir," replied Randy. "We totally understand. We won't say anything,"

The shark, weighing around five-hundred pounds, dipped beneath the surface twelve feet from the little boat, swiftly swimming and rising just before impact with enough force to jolt Nathan temporarily from his grip. The last time he was rocked with such force was on a bumper car ride at the Pavilion in Myrtle Beach. He quickly regained his composure and squeezed the metal seams of the boat, which rocked back and forth taking on water from each side. Looking at the bottom of the dark Jon boat, Nathan noticed a wooden paddle lying in a puddle of water. He grabbed it and placed it across his knees, then watched the water for the fin to appear again thinking that a good sharp whack of the paddle might scare the vicious Bull shark away.

His knees quivered as he thought about the possibility of being knocked overboard and eaten alive by a shark. He had heard stories on CNN of surfers in Florida who claimed they did not feel much pain at first when a shark had severed a limb. Experts say it is because their teeth are incredibly sharp and their jaws are extremely powerful. The fin surfaced as Nathan expected. He stood quickly, turning his paddle sideways so that the edge would strike forcefully on the shark's dorsal fin. Raising the paddle overhead, knees still trembling, and stretching his rib cage so that his intercostal muscles screamed in pain, he swung with all of his might, smacking the beast on its spine. The old cypress paddle splintered from the force of the collision with the back of the massive creature.

Nathan sat down quickly grabbing the sides of the boat again, hoping his offensive move had some effect. The Bull shark shook violently from the paddle's impact, hitting the side of the boat with its tail. The fish swam beneath the surface of the water out of sight. Nathan, frightened out of his mind, but doing all he could to survive, looked up to see the large pontoon boat moving towards him. The captain shined fog lights in his direction, blinking them off and on a few times in rapid succession. Nathan picked up his wet white T-shirt from the bottom of the boat waving it again.

"Hurry up!" screamed Nathan. "There's a shark ramming my boat!"

This time Captain Bill heard the boy's distress call. "Hold on son, we're on the way. We'll get you out of there," the captain announced through a megaphone.

Nathan looked around his boat again, and to his surprise, the dorsal fin surfaced for a third time ten feet from the boat. He had hoped that smashing the animal with his paddle had scared it away, but the Bull shark, an extremely aggressive species, continued to hunt its prey. The shark moved swiftly in his direction again, the Jon boat already taking on several gallons of water, sat lower in the water. Nathan tensed every muscle in his body hoping to survive a direct hit. The shark cut through the water like a WWII torpedo. Nathan braced himself for the force of another ramming. A loud crash occurred, but no one seemed to hear, or know, but Nathan.

Twenty-Four

❦

Two vehicles dispatched from the South Carolina Law Enforcement Division (SCLED) and two from Charleston County Sheriff's Department. Blue lights flashing and sirens blaring, they sped their way down to the marsh where Spires' old homeplace was located. An ambulance tucked in the middle of the sheriff vehicles was escorted for the injured kidnapper who lay prostrate, cuffed, and bleeding into the very ground on which he was raised. Russ Baxter pressed a blood soaked hand towel that he retrieved from his vehicle against Bobby Spires' torso, but wondered if it would slow the bleeding enough until the medical personnel arrived. Arnie Jones sat on the grass ten feet away from his partner with his hands secured behind his back.

"I feel like I'm sinking in a deep hole. I don't know if I can hang on any longer," Spires said. His eyes fluttered and sank back in his head, as he rocked side to side in pain.

"Hang in there, man, I hear the ambulance coming now." Baxter looked down the dirt road and saw the box-shaped emergency vehicle come into view, and jostling its way on the uneven drive-way, branches scraping the top and sides.

Suddenly, Spires let out a loud cry. "Damn it, Arnie! This is your fault for letting that kid get away."

"Oh, sh...shut up, Bah...Bobby, this whole thing was your idea," Jones stuttered.

"Both of you keep quiet," Baxter demanded, taking control of the situation. "You'll have your chances to talk all you want pretty soon."

Charleston County deputies arrived with pistols drawn were first to assist Baxter with the captured kidnappers. SCLED officers were right behind.

"Drop your weapons," the first arriving officer shouted to Baxter. Evidently, the officer did not completely understand the situation, nor did he want to take a chance.

"Officer, I'm Russ Baxter, a private detective from Charleston," he said. "Could I show you my ID?" Baxter pointed to his back pocket.

"Yeah, but do it slowly," the officer said.

Baxter held up his wallet with one hand, his constable's badge shining in the bright lights of their vehicles, still holding his gun in the ready position. The officers relaxed seeing that the situation was under control.

"Put your guns away, men. What have we got here, Baxter?" bellowed a senior officer, who made his way to the front of his men. The officer recognized him from past activities when their cases coincided.

"Captain Elliott, nice to see you again," said Baxter, recognizing the SCLED officer. "My partner, Paula Roberts, and I, nabbed these two men who kidnapped a young boy, holding him for ransom. The boy, Nathan Jennings, apparently escaped in a boat."

"Where's your partner, now, Russ?"

"She left with the boy's father to search for the missing boy. He got away from the men and was able to commandeer a Jon boat from a small dock behind this old house. He's only eleven, but sure as hell took out on the waterway by himself."

"You don't say, Baxter," said the captain. "That's one brave eleven year old."

"That he is, Captain. That he is."

The driver of the ambulance positioned the emergency vehicle on the small patchy front yard. One EMT relieved Baxter from applying pressure to the wound. Another quickly cut away the clothing necessary to apply pressure with fresh gauze directly to the bullet wound. Working in tandem, an EMT attached a BP cuff around Spires' upper arm, checking his pressure. He reached to his wrist for a pulse check.

"How are his vitals?" the senior EMT asked.

"Not good," his partner replied. "His BP is very low, 75/48, pulse is rapid... 165, but weak."

"Insert an IV immediately," said the lead EMT.

"What's your blood type, sir?" asked the other EMT. Spires was unresponsive. He tapped him on the shoulder, and then gently slapped his face a few times. Spires' eyes fluttered.

"Does anyone know his name?" the other EMT requested of the officers standing nearby.

"Yes, it's Bobby Spires," said Jones, watching like a dumbfounded teenager.

"Bobby," said the EMT, "what's your blood type? You've lost a lot of blood. We need to get two units of blood in you as fast as possible."

Barely able to respond, Spires saw the EMT through a haze, as if in a dream. Hallucinating, he thought he saw the eyes of Jesus in the medical worker's face.

"My blood type is...my blood type is...," Spires murmured, then relinquished into unconsciousness, closing his eyes.

"We have a code blue," said the EMT into the microphone on the radio attached to his shoulder. "I need his identification immediately. I need his blood type."

"Let's turn him over on his side so I can get to his wallet," said his co-worker.

"I know what it is," said Jones. "We been friends ever since we were kids. He cut himself with a fishing knife once, kinda bad. They gave him O positive."

"Are you sure?" asked the senior EMT.

"Yeah, he told me never to forget it in case he ever needed it again."

"He's a lucky man. We carry two types of blood with us. One of those is the most common of all, O positive," said the EMT.

The other EMT rushed to the ambulance, retrieving two pints of bagged blood, and paraphernalia to administer the life-saving liquid. After administering the blood, they secured their patient on a spinal board and loaded him into the back of the ambulance. With lights swirling and siren screaming, the ambulance spun its tires ripping up the dirt drive en route to the blacktop. Bouncing its way on the road, it sped back to the mainland, one officer riding in the back, as is the protocol for an arrested person suspected of a crime.

Two SCLED agents grabbed Arnie Jones by his elbows and escorted him in the direction of their vehicle.

"Officer, do you mind if I get my handcuffs off of him?" Baxter requested.

"Not at all," said the SCLED agent, as he jerked his cuffs off the backside of his belt. The two muscular officers, both ex-military, spun Jones around, holding him firmly in position for Baxter to unlock his cuffs. "Go ahead, Mr. Baxter and get your cuffs. I'll be all too glad to use mine," said one of the men.

"Thank you, officers," said Baxter, as he slipped his cuffs off and clipped them to the back of his belt.

"Thank you for all that you and your partner did in helping us get these two men," said Captain Elliott. "As you know, there's an APB, and an Amber Alert out on this case. I hope we can get the boy back safely to put a good ending on it."

"I've got a feeling we will," said Baxter. "And for the record, my partner, Paula Roberts, is the real hero in all this. The guys had me in a cross-fire until she stepped in and wounded the man who was carted away by the ambulance."

"That's great, Baxter, I'd hang on to her," said Captain Elliott. "Looks like she's a keeper."

"I can only hope for that, but that's another story. Okay, guys, thanks a lot for getting here so quickly. Maybe it will save the man's life, and more importantly the life of Nathan Jennings'," said Baxter.

"Yes sir, no problem. By the way, we need you to come by our office tomorrow and give a statement. One of the men just got word over the radio that there's another hot case we need to chase," said the captain, as he handed Baxter his card.

"You got it, Captain Elliott. I'll be there."

Baxter looked down at the card, and tucked it in his shirt pocket. The law enforcement vehicles turned around and sped out through the cloud of dust the ambulance created. Arnie Jones was transported to the mainland where he was booked and locked in a cell at the county jail. Baxter drove behind the vehicles, phoning his partner.

"Hello, Russ," she said.

"What's going on? Where are you now?"

"We're not far from Jakes Landing. We're gonna ask some questions around there and see what we can come up with."

"That sounds good. I'll join you guys as soon as I can."

"I saw the blue lights whizz by the road we turned down, Russ. Did you wrap things up there?"

"Signed, sealed, and delivered, Paula. I don't know if that one guy, Spires, will make it. He bled out pretty bad. I stopped the blood flow as best I could until the EMTs arrived. They did their thing, and took the injured Spires away, administering blood as they left."

"I'm more worried about Nathan right now, Russ. I'll talk to you when I see you, I gotta run for now."

"See you soon, Paula."

Twenty-Five

❦

The pontoon boat closed in within twenty-five yards of the Jon boat. Nathan could hear the sloshing of the water and rumbling motors of the larger vessel as it approached. Adrenaline coursed through his veins as his hopes began to rise again. The captain handed a bullhorn to his assistant.

"Get up front, Roger, and let him know we're moving in to get him."

"Yes sir, Captain. I'm on it." The first mate grabbed the bullhorn and scurried into position. "Hello out there, young man on the boat, what is your name?" said Roger.

"I'm Nathan Jennings," the boy shouted, standing up briefly.

"Nathan, please remain seated. We are coming to help you." The pontoon was twenty feet from Nathan.

The Bull shark swam away from the Jon boat then turned back to make another run at capsizing it. The vicious beast gathered speed from fifteen yards away, flexing its massive muscular body as it barreled full-speed ahead toward the Jon boat. Nathan fixed his gaze on the pontoon boat, en route to rescue him, because he could not bear looking directly at the Bull shark closing in at such a high rate of speed. Glancing down and bracing for impact, Nathan held tightly as the Bull shark crashed with violent force into the fourteen-foot aluminum boat once again. He had never felt such a jolt in all his life. Nathan's arms flew up in the air as he fell backwards into the cold, murky abyss.

    This time the shark was successful, and the boat bounced in the water like an angler's bobber at the tug of an over-sized fish. Instinctively, Nathan began to tread water as soon as he could right himself and get his bearings. Not knowing where the shark was, he knew his best chance at survival was to get on top of the capsized boat. He stretched himself out in the water and swam as fast as he could in the direction of the capsized boat, which had scooted away a good six, or eight feet.

    Night feeding was normal for the huge behemoth, and not much challenged it, except for Homo sapiens with a weapon. Aware of this fact, Nathan knew he had seconds to get completely out of the water. His goal was to position his body on the bottom side of the capsized boat before the shark would sense his flailing and chomp into his flesh. He kicked and flung his arms wildly as he pulled his head back and forth sucking air. Swimming as fast as his body would carry him, water splashed into his opened airway. Coughing the water droplets from his lungs, Nathan swam undaunted.

The first mate and the captain watched in disbelief, the hair standing up on their arms and neck. They weren't sure at first what happened, darkness rendering a partial view of what lay in the water near Nathan's boat.

"My God," said the captain. "The boy has fallen out of the boat! Move in quickly."

"Moving in, Captain, as fast as we can without running him over," the first mate replied.

The Bull shark turned as quickly as an Olympic swimmer executing a kick-turn, as it sensed the kicking of Nathan's tennis shoes in the water. From fifteen feet away, the predator made a move to attack its prey. Nathan reached up as high as he could with one arm, putting his hand on a bottom seam of the underbelly of the Jon boat, now floating upside down in the water. His first try was unsuccessful and his hand slipped off. The shark closed in, now only ten feet from the boy. Nathan looked over his shoulder to see the beast moving swiftly towards him. Closing in on the Jon boat from less than ten yards, the first mate got a good look at the situation.

"Captain, look, the boy is about to be devoured by a huge shark! I can see its fin moving in on him now."

The rushing water streamed off the sides of the powerful shark as it narrowed in on what would be his evening feeding. His jaws opened to maximum capacity, easily wide enough to sever a leg, or even bite the young boy into two pieces. The smell of fish permeated the salty air. A scene from Jaws raced through Nathan's brain. Sensing the awesome power of this untamed beast, his life shot through his mind like a fast-forwarding movie. A huge surge of adrenaline coursed through his veins and with one last lunge, Nathan catapulted three quarters of his body out of the water onto the bottom of the boat. With one hand, he gripped the cold aluminum seam, and he pulled with all his strength, allowing him to reach the other bottom seam with his free hand. The shark was only two feet away as Nathan yanked the rest of his body up, stretching out on the boat's bottom just in time to miss the huge, opened jaws with several rows and hundreds of teeth ready to sever his legs.

"Hold on!" shouted the crewmember. "We're right here."

"Hurry up," said Nathan, "there's a big shark right here by the boat!"

The captain, hearing what Nathan said, reached into a slender compartment near the wheel where he kept his rifle, and other emergency items. He quickly checked the rifle's chamber for bullets, and finding that it was loaded, he ran down to the front of the deck. While the first mate shined a light on the boat, the captain spotted the shark swimming around in an attempt to find any portion of the boy that it could bite. Suddenly, it dipped under the water.

Spellbound by the commotion, the passengers, and staff from the party boat watched in horror witnessing a live shark attack. Many of the people had seen programs on television where sharks were feeding in a staged environment, but never in this fashion. Clutching the guard railing on the pontoon boat, the partygoers anxiously awaited the outcome. The shark surfaced again between the pontoon and the Jon boat, still determined to find its prey. The DJ wondering where his dancers had gone, turned the music off and ran to the side of the boat to join the rest of the crowd. All they heard now were the eerie sounds of the water lapping against the boat, and people murmuring their frightful expressions as they watched.

"Hold very still young man," shouted Captain Bill. He fixed the rifle firmly against his shoulder.

"Go ahead, shoot," said Nathan said.

Captain Bill waited patiently for a good shot on the beast, as he narrowed his aim. Drawing a bead on the shark, the captain squeezed off two rounds at his target. Blood squirted up in the salt-filled air splashing Nathan across his back, as the hollow-point bullets tore into the flesh of the gnarly beast. The Bull shark shook violently for a moment as the water around it turned dark red. The captain fired a third shot striking the shark in the head, submerging it below the surface.

"Are you alright, son?" the captain shouted to Nathan.

"Yes sir, I am now, thank you."

"Hold on son, my crew is lowering a raft right now to get you out of there. It's going to be fine."

"I will, sir. I'm waiting right here. Is that shark gone?"

"Yes, I believe he is," said Captain Bill. The captain watched the shark sink listlessly, below the surface until it was out of sight.

Seeing that he was out of danger, Nathan relaxed from the rigid position that he had held for the last several minutes after capsizing. It seemed more like a couple of hours to the youth as he felt his heart pounding against the cold wet aluminum, his skin growing numb from the chill. Nathan loved a good thrill at the amusement parks, but this type of excitement, with his life in danger, was beyond his wildest dreams.

Captain Bill radioed the Charleston County Sheriff's Department. "Charleston County Dispatcher, state your emergency please."

"Yes, this is Captain Bill from the party boat out of Jakes Landing. We are in the process of rescuing a young man who looks to be about twelve years old, over."

"Captain Bill, could you find out the boy's full name. We have an Amber Alert out for a young man about that age," the dispatcher said.

"Yes ma'am. I can do that. Hold the line for a minute, please."

With the call in progress, the two crewmembers in the boat reached Nathan's capsized boat, loading and returning him safely to the pontoon. Once aboard, they took him to the waiting captain.

"What is your full name, son? Where you from, and what are your parents' names? I have the Sheriff's Department on the line."

"It's Nathan Jennings from Charleston. My dad is Mark Jennings, and my mom is Anna Leigh Jennings."

The captain switched the conversation to his radio. "Hello, Dispatcher?"

"Yes sir, this is the dispatcher. Go ahead."

"Yes ma'am, this is Captain Bill, again. The boy says his name is Nathan Jennings, son of Mark and Anna Leigh Jennings of Charleston."

"That young man is our missing youth, Captain. Congratulations on your rescue. Where can I dispatch deputies to pick him up, sir?"

"I'm returning to Jakes Landing in an hour by our schedule, ma'am."

"Can you cut your trip shorter, Captain? This boy needs to get back to his parents ASAP."

"Yes, that won't be a problem. We'll head back immediately. Let's see, it is twenty-one-hundred hours now. We'll arrive at Jakes Landing by twenty-one thirty, ma'am."

"I use military time, too, Captain Bill, but just to be sure we don't get our wires crossed, that's 9:30 PM when you estimate you will arrive at on Jakes Landing. Is that correct?"

"Affirmative, ma'am, I'll have the boy by my side at all times until I release him to your deputies."

"Hold the line just a moment, sir. Let me contact a deputy in the area now. This is an APB to Units 44 and 45 on Johns Island, come in, over."

"This is Unit 45, Deputy Moody speaking, come in, over."

"Yes, Deputy Moody, this is Corporal Delfino. I need you to pick up the missing Jennings boy at Jakes Landing. Captain Bill from the party boat, which launches from there, will have him by his side. The boy's name is Nathan Jennings. He's the one on the current Amber Alert. Can you be there by twenty-one hundred hours, over?"

"Roger that, Corporal Delfino. I'm on patrol at Nestlewood Subdivision about ten to fifteen minutes from the landing. I'll be there waiting for him, over."

"Ten-four, Deputy Moody, bring the boy directly to the Charleston Sheriff Department Complex, over."

"Roger that, Corporal Delfino, I'll radio back with a progress report, over and out."

"Ten-four, Deputy Moody, over and out."

"Captain Bill, come in, this is the dispatcher."

"Yes ma'am, go ahead, I can hear you?"

"Please continue as planned. Deputy Moody from the Charleston County Sheriff's Department will be waiting for you at Jakes Landing."

"Yes, ma'am, I'll have him there. May I get your name, ma'am?" asked the captain.

"Yes sir, sorry, this is Corporal Angela Delfino."

"Thank you, Corporal Delfino; we have a protocol, also."

"No problem, sir. I understand, and thank you for doing your duty."

"It's always an honor to rescue a child, ma'am. It doesn't happen often, but it does happen from time to time out here on the water."

"I'm sure it does, sir. Good night, Captain Bill."

"Good night, Corporal Delfino."

Twenty-Six

❦

Mark Jennings and Paula Roberts pulled into Jakes Landing about 9:30 PM hoping that Nathan would have been seen by someone, anyone. Upon arrival, they noticed a Charleston County deputy's vehicle with its blue light flashing, but no sign of the deputy. His car was abandoned and still running, against protocol, the driver door flung open.

"What's going on here? Looks like it could be serious," said Paula.

"I hope not," said Jennings. "We've got enough serious stuff going on. All I am concerned about is getting Nathan back."

Jennings parked his Nissan 300-Z behind the patrol car, the spinning lights casting a blue glare over his windshield. They walked around the marina's restaurant to the dock, which housed thirty-five boat slips, hoping to find Nathan.

"Let's go in the back door and look around inside," said Jennings.

"Wait, look down the dock...there! See the big pontoon boat all lit up, pulling in? Why don't we check out what is going on first, then we'll go inside."

"Yeah, I see it. I'm with you, Paula. Let's go."

Quickly, they scanned the slips where there were several speedboats, small fishing boats, pontoons, and a few houseboats, but all were considerably larger than a Jon boat. As they continued to walk farther out the pier, they passed two jet skis rocking gently in the water, tie lines on either side. Jennings remembered jet skiing with his children the previous summer. Seething with anger that a sorry, worthless piece of humanity would take his son, he plodded forward with purpose. It was the worst kind of violation he had ever felt. The determined dad and Paula Roberts walked toward the end of the pier where the big party boat eased into its reserved, over-sized slip. The crew finished tying off the ropes, and jumped back onboard to assist the existing passengers.

"Do you see the deputy talking to those men?" asked Paula.

"I don't see him," said Jennings.

"Let's go see what they are doing," said Paula.

Deputy Moody stood on the pier talking to Captain Bill. Passengers began unloading and filing off the boat single file past them as they made their way to the marina.

"Deputy, I'm Paula Roberts, a private detective from Crescent Moon Investigations in Charleston. This is the father of Nathan Jennings, the missing boy being broadcast on the Amber Alert. Sorry to interrupt, but we're looking for his son, and wondered if you have seen a Jon boat here in the last…"

"I'm Deputy Moody, ma'am, and this is Captain Bill Snelling, captain of Jakes Party Pontoon," said the deputy, cutting her off, and shaking hands with Paula and Jennings. "It appears, from what the good captain just told me that you have excellent timing. The captain and his crew rescued Nathan from his capsized boat just thirty minutes ago on the other side of the waterway. Isn't that right, Captain Bill?"

"Yes sir, the young man's a fighter," said Captain Bill. He stepped forward to shake their hands. "His boat capsized when he was attacked by a large Bull shark about six or seven feet long. From what he told me, he had to fight the shark off with a paddle before I was able to get close enough to sink it with my rifle."

"Where's my son now?" Mark Jennings blurted out. "Is he alright?"

"He's fine. He should be up any minute," said Captain Bill. "We sent him below to take a hot shower. We were concerned about hypothermia. My first mate, Roger, found some dry clothes that he might be able to fit in to. He's a fairly tall boy for his age, but one of our crew is a diminutive man, so he loaned him a set."

"Yeah, he's eleven, almost twelve, but like you said, a good size young man," said Jennings. "Thanks for looking after him like that, Captain Bill. I'll be sure and get those clothes back to you. Can I go on board to meet him when he comes out?"

"Sure, Mr. Jennings," said the captain, who stepped aside to make way for the jubilant dad to step onboard via the connecting ramp.

As his father began to board the boat, Nathan appeared from beneath the deck, hair mussed up, and wearing baggy jeans with a colorful, oversized, tie-dye T-shirt, but he looked none-the-worse for the wear.

"Nathan, is that you?" said Jennings. He walked down one side of the boat quickening his pace when he saw his son.

"Dad!" shouted Nathan, seeing his father moving towards him.

Hearing his son's voice, Mark Jennings' heart leaped into his throat, as any father's would. Adrenaline rushed through his body as he ran to the silhouette of his son, who also ran in his direction. Elated, Jennings took a few more steps and came to a stop as Nathan bounded up in the air, latching onto his dad like an NFL linebacker tackling a quarterback.

"Son, I'm so glad to see you!"

Jennings buried his face in his son's neck, embracing him in a bear hug, the likes of which he had not given him since he made the Little League All Star team. Clutching his son in his strong arms and hugging him so tight it pushed the breath out of Nathan's chest, Jennings' eyes filled with tears of joy.

Recovering his son without harm from his kidnappers was the best thing that could happen to him.

Paula, Deputy Moody, and Captain Bill looked on together with joy at the reunion. The trio went back to chatting among themselves to give the father and son time to enjoy their moment.

"I'm happy to see you too, Dad, but could you ease up on the hug a little, I can't breathe." Nathan coughed, and they both laughed at themselves for a moment.

Jennings, and his son, holding a plastic bag with wet clothes in it, exited the party boat via the ramp where Paula and Deputy Moody stood waiting. Captain Bill stood nearby, thanking each passenger as they disembarked.

"Mr. Jennings, I didn't get all the details, but like Captain Bill said Nathan was in a Jon boat which had capsized, and was holding on for dear life. A shark was circling around the boat trying to get to Nathan," said the deputy.

"Good grief!" said Jennings. He bent down to look his son in the eyes. "Did that really happen, son?"

"Yes, Dad, I smacked that ole Bull shark on the back as hard as I could with my paddle, and he came back at me and flipped the boat over. The pontoon boat wasn't far away. Captain Bill got really close and shot him when he came at me again. It was way cool, Dad. The blood from the shark squirted in the air and landed on my shirt. I saw that big ole shark sink in the water after the captain killed it."

"That's an amazing story, Nathan," said Paula, who was listening with keen interest.

As Nathan completed his thrilling story, Deputy Moody, aware of his orders to take the boy to headquarters, interrupted. "Mr. Jennings, I hate to spoil your reunion with your son, but I've been instructed to bring Nathan to the station ASAP. The dispatcher made that very clear."

Taken aback that the deputy wanted to take Nathan from him, Jennings countered. "I've got my ID with me. I would like to take my son home, Deputy."

"I wish I could do that, sir, but I have my orders. I hope you understand, but I have to do as instructed, especially when dealing with an Amber Alert case. You can follow us to headquarters, though, Mr. Jennings."

"Deputy Moody, do you really need to take him with you? I think you can see that he's in good hands," said Paula.

"I'm sure of that, Mrs. Roberts, but the boy must be interviewed. It's protocol."

"I will guarantee his arrival for debriefing. Would you call in and ask, Deputy Moody? They may not want to do it tonight anyway, now that he is safely returned to his father. It is getting late, as well," said Paula.

"That's correct, Deputy. That would be great if you can work that out. I'll commit to that, as well," said Jennings.

"I guess I can do that for you and Mrs. Roberts. Hold on please, while I radio in for permission. If they agree, you can bring your son by the station tomorrow to give a statement."

Paula waited with Jennings and Nathan while the deputy went to his vehicle to make his call.

"I'd say you two are very fortunate people tonight," said Paula. She smiled approving their reunion.

"Paula, thank you so much for your help. I'm sure this could not have happened if it were not for you and Russ. Do you think that the authorities will let me take Nathan home tonight?"

"I don't think they will mind, Mark. For starters, a psychologist on call would have to come in to interview Nathan. He, or she, whichever the case may be, will probably be glad to wait until tomorrow. Secondly, you, and especially Nathan, need your rest after the ordeal you two have been through."

"You're right, Paula, it's almost ten-thirty, and Nathan's still cold and shivering a little. You know I can't say too much to the deputy, though. I'm not the most popular man in this county right now."

Deputy Moody returned from his car to the backside of the marina where the trio waited on the dock. "Mr. Jennings, and Mrs. Roberts can you be at the Charleston County Complex tomorrow with Nathan at 10 AM? They want all three of you there for an interview."

"We sure can, Deputy," said Jennings.

"We'll be glad to," said Paula.

"Very good, then. Nathan will meet with a Dr. Avery Brooks, a psychologist. You two will meet with Captain McElheny to give a statement. I assume you know how to get there, Mr. Jennings."

"Yes sir, Deputy Moody, I do. We will be there on time and without fail."

"Very good, sir, I'll escort you off the island if y'all are ready to go," the deputy said.

"Thank you very much. We're ready when you are, right, Paula?" Jennings shook the deputy's hand briskly.

"That's right, Mark. Let's roll."

"I'm sure I'll see you around, Mrs. Roberts. Y'all go ahead, and I'll follow you off the island," said Deputy Moody, as he walked behind them to his patrol car.

"I am glad to get out of here, Mark?" said Paula. "I've got a family waiting for me."

"Absolutely! I'm one hundred-percent with you," said Jennings, in a jubilant tone. "Let's get out of here, Nathan."

"I'm ready, too, Dad." Nathan skipped up and down for a few steps, as they started down the pier.

"I know you are, son. I know you are."

The happy threesome hurried around the marina on the wooden walkway, which deposited them on sand for a few feet to the asphalt parking area. Nathan jumped in the small backseat, barely big enough for him. Paula climbed in the front, riding shotgun. Jennings fastened himself and cranked the car.

"Buckle up you two, I'm not going to waste any time getting home."

"Works for me", said Paula. But let's not get a ticket, if you are referring to speeding, Mark."

"I don't think we will with Deputy Moody behind us."

Nathan tried to relax in the back seat while his dad and Paula conversed, but his mind was spinning. He thought about his day and the last few hours since he escaped from his captors. The smell of the shark and the sight of blood from the shark when the bullets from the captain's rifle tore into its flesh was still exceedingly fresh in his tender mind. Strangely, he felt as if someone bigger than his dad, or Paula, had taken care of him, but he didn't know how to process the inexplicable feeling.

He could not wait to get home and into some fresh clothes that belonged to him. Nathan had never worn anyone else's clothes, and it just did not feel right. Still listening to his dad chatter with Paula, he wondered about the two men who took him from his front yard. He figured that they would receive fair treatment, but hoped that they would be punished severely for doing what they did to him. He realized that it could happen to any one of his friends, or even his sister. As a result, he could not feel sorry for them, no matter the outcome.

The next day, Mark and Paula gave their statements at the Sheriff's Department while the psychologist and a detective interviewed Nathan. Kidnapping and extortion charges were brought against Bobby Spires, and his sidekick, Arnie Jones. Later, the District Attorney was successful in putting away the two men for twenty years without parole.

Mark Jennings moved to Miami to start his life over and recover from the divorce that his wife requested, citing unfaithfulness, which he could not deny. Jennings would have traded an eye to not suffer a divorce from his wife, but he had it coming, and he knew it. He did manage to escape charges on cocaine distribution for lack of evidence. The other positive taken from this perilous kidnapping was that Jennings laid down his drug habit shortly after the day he pulled over to the side of the road and prayed.

Anna Leigh Jennings continued her life in Charleston, having to go back to work as a teacher. She began seeing a man that she was not in love with, but did provide companionship. She wondered if it was possible to fall in love again after having children with someone else, or if it was a matter of time until she met the right man. She struggled with her feelings for Mark, even though he was unfaithful because she had known him since childhood, and he was the father of their two children. The dream of growing old with the natural father of her children and her first love would not die easily.

Twenty-Seven

❧

Twelve Months Later, Miami, FL

"What the heck did you expect her to do, Mark? You were screwing around on her. I mean, I know it's tough, but she did what she had to do to maintain her self-respect", said Matt, his younger brother.

"I know she did, Matt. I'm just venting, man. I hate not being near my kids. This job you helped me get is leading me nowhere. The most I can see myself becoming there is a loan officer. I haven't moved up since I hired on, and I get the feeling that unless I'm Cuban-American, or of Hispanic descent, I don't stand much of a chance at advancement."

"Mark, you know that's not the case, man."

"No, I really believe I'm the subject of reverse discrimination in that bank. I'm the only one there who is not bilingual, or brown skinned," said Jennings.

"But that's a huge part of the culture here, Mark. It's a bilingual community, and those who can mix and communicate better with the clientele are able to get a leg up," said Matt.

"But you fit in great, and have advanced," said Jennings. He shifted his position on his brother's sofa, grabbing a sofa pillow and holding it across his chest.

"Well, brother, I'm glad I took Spanish in college and moved here soon after graduation so that I could become fluent. I don't know what you want me to say, Mark. I can't change any of this. It's just the way it is."

"I know that, damn it. If you would just listen and understand a little, it would be helpful. I miss my kids, and it hurts like hell. I know I blew it with a good woman, the mother of my children. Now, I hear that she's dating some guy and it may be getting serious. It seems like my life is passing me by because of one big screw up."

"You played your cards the wrong way. What can I say? If you don't like the cards that you're dealt, toss 'em in and get a new hand. There's nothing wrong with getting back in the game," said Matt.

"What are you talking about?"

"You could start dating, instead of sitting around here with the remote when you're off work."

"I can't get Anna Leigh out of my heart," said Jennings.

"You're pathetic. If you love her, go win her back. You two were always good together, and you belong there with your own kids."

"Finally! That's what I've been waiting to hear, something positive from you. In the midst of all this crap, you are giving me a little encouragement instead of just telling me where I've made a colossal dope of myself," said Jennings.

"So, are you going to start dating again, or what?"

"No, I can't stay here anymore, Matt. It's become obvious to me that I don't belong here anymore. I've tried and it was good for a while to get adjusted to being single, but it has run its course."

"Yeah, I've been seeing it for some time, but you had to figure that out for yourself. So, what do you plan to do now?"

"What you said triggered an epiphany in me. I am going to move back to Charleston."

Without saying another word, Mark Jennings rose up from the sofa, and tossed the down-stuffed pillow at his brother, who barely had time to catch it as it smacked him in the chest. Dumbfounded, Matt watch as his brother scooted off to his room to pack.

Jennings' heart ached for his children more than any other time in his life. He missed seeing them grow up, the sound of their voices, and their touch. The hole in his heart grew bigger with each passing day until it seemed as big as the Grand Canyon. He was a dad that had strayed from the simplistic values that held a family together, and was paying the price for it. He loved his family, unlike many dead-beat dads and wanted the best for them. He wanted desperately to outlive the shame of the stigma that attached to him like a barnacle to a pier after the divorce, and being tagged as a failure by many of his peers. He wanted his family back, and if there was any way possible, he was willing to do whatever he had to do to get a second chance. The old adage of "you don't know what you've got until it's gone", was applicable to his situation, and how well Jennings knew it.

In less than an hour and a half, he had gathered his belongings, and packed his SUV. He had loved his 300-Z and hated parting with it, but it was no longer practical for him for trips with luggage from Miami to Charleston. He still thought fondly of the Z from time to time, referring to it as his baby. When he traded the sports car in, he managed to get low miles on a one-year old Infinity QX-56, with leather, plus all the bells and whistles. After he had made several trips to his vehicle, packing every square foot of space, he started the SUV, letting it idle for a moment.

"I'm done, little brother. I can't believe how much crap I've collected in the short time I've been in south Florida. Listen, thanks, I can't tell you how much I appreciate your help over the past year. You've gone over and above the call of duty."

"Don't give me all that mushy crap, Mark. I may need the help myself one day… you never know. Besides, you are my flesh and blood. Now, get out of here. Go, before you make me choke up."

Mark laughed and gave his little brother a bear hug and a couple of slaps on the back, as he stepped out on the porch toward the driveway.

"You do have a soft side," said Matt. "Having children has done something good for you. Maybe I should try it one day."

"Yeah, you ought to try it. Having children changes most everyone, Matt. I feel certain you would like it. Alright, I have to go, but you know where I am, if you ever need me. Or if you just want to stop in for a visit, I owe you one."

"You don't have a place to live anymore. How am I going to do that?" Matt said, laughing.

"I'll be in Charleston, you knucklehead! I am only a phone call away, you known that. After I find a job, I'll work on buying something again, but my most immediate concern is getting my family back."

"Alright bro, take care and give me a shout once you arrive safely."

"I'll do that. Goodbye, Matt."

Jennings pulled out of the drive and wound his way out of the neighborhood. Once on the expressway, he made a beeline to the interstate. Driving up I-95 North, he adjusted the rearview mirror, and then focused on the busy route ahead. He thought long and hard about his life from his childhood forward. If there was any way to make amends for his past mistakes, he would, not only for his children's sake, but also for Anna Leigh. He remembered their wedding, their honeymoon, the first several years of their marriage, and the good times they had. He thought about the time when he went astray, and the fact that it was totally his fault. The times for rationalization and making excuses were over. The time to own up to his mistakes, make amends, and be the father that his kids needed was paramount in his mind.

Could Anna Leigh possibly still have feelings for me? He wondered. *Furthermore, if she does have feelings for me, would she allow me back into her life again?* He still considered her as his one and only soul mate, his true love. No one he met after her measured up. The few times he met anyone in Miami to consider dating, he always compared her to Anna, and he could not go forward with more than one outing. It was a charade, and he knew it.

From their childhood days, he remembered pulling her pigtails in fifth grade, and chasing her around the playground equipment on the schoolyard. She had an incredibly cute giggle, bouncy hair, and sparkling eyes that caused him to love her from the beginning. He always dreamed of being with her when they grew up, and he was fortunate to have had his chance. Life seemed without purpose apart from her. He painfully relived his memories to the time when he went astray with drugs at his friend's house. He knew that was the door, which led to his infidelity. Thankfully, he was over that now, and he prayed for the chance to redeem himself, and he hoped he could find a little mercy from his own family upon returning to Charleston.

Jennings' heritage was not too shabby. His father, now deceased, was a prominent banker, and he had followed in his footsteps. His mother was still living and active in her life as a grandmother to all her grandchildren. A senator for an uncle, and other prominent businesspersons in the area, gave him roots there, and connections that he may need to launch a new career. Now that sufficient time had passed for memories to fade a little, he felt that finding work would be easier.

Reconciliation with his former wife, even if it was a pipe dream, and being near his children, meant everything to him, and nothing else mattered. It was the very heartbeat of his existence. He locked the cruise control on 75 MPH for the long drive up I-95 North where he would connect with I-26 East, then eventually turn east on Meeting Street to arrive at the holy city, Charleston, his birthplace on the Atlantic coast where he always felt at home in the salty air and fresh ocean breezes.

Paula Roberts P.I. - Johns Island

Twenty-Eight

❦

Paula progressed in her employment in her relatively short tenure at Crescent Moon Investigations, and was offered a full partnership. She already had autonomy and partnership to a great degree, so it was pretty much a formality when she accepted. She was becoming well-known in the community for her prowess as a cunning private detective, and especially good in divorce cases when the women involved preferred dealing with a female. She knew how to be both compassionate with her clients, and crafty with opponents in an investigation.

Meanwhile, Jim's antique business had taken off, as well. He was great at what he did, importing valuable hand-woven rugs from overseas. He had a knack for finding antiques in good shape and restoring them to pristine condition to get the best possible price. Upon moving to Charleston, he found an incredible restoration specialist and hired him on the spot. Customers brought their antiques to him for restoration and sprucing up. The restoration man, Danny Waddell, did a good job of keeping the floor looking good. Jim also allowed him to bring in his own projects, and paid him a percentage of what he restored, on top of his hourly rate. Danny appreciated the chance to earn extra money and the benefit was mutual to Unique Antiques of Charleston.

It was common knowledge that Jim was not in love with the fact that his wife was a private investigator, but he never complained, or harangued her about it. He had told her how he felt and let it go at that. She knew that, and she wished that her hours were different, but over the past year, she had worked out flexible hours with Baxter. It allowed her time to pick up her daughters from school, get them started on their homework, and at least start dinner most days. On days that neither one of them decided to cook they brought in pizza, Chinese, or some other type of fast food.

This Tuesday was no different from any other. Paula was at work at her desk making calls to clients, and creating reports, which were essentially progress updates on their cases. Occasionally, a super jealous spouse would hire Crescent Moon Investigations on suspicions only. Russ and Paula went about their jobs the same way they would for a legit case. Some of these cases were humorous to both detectives, but they only laughed about them among themselves, and strangely enough, some of the cases, to their surprise turned into something significant.

Cases came from a variety of sources. Some from attorneys, others were given by a psychologist friend, who was a former client of Russ Baxter. When the psychologist thought a case might have some merit, she referred the client to Crescent Moon Investigations so that an independent scientific approach could determine the truth regarding alleged infidelity.

Paula and Russ had just closed an embezzlement case for Charleston County in which a clerk was shifting funds to buy her family a boat and other recreational equipment for the summer. Paula would never forget the sight when she and Russ drove to a nearby lake, only to see Sheriff's Deputies arresting the clerk and her husband. The authorities impounded the boat, and two Jet Skis, while the bewildered teenagers looked on in disbelief. They both felt badly for the kids who were unaware of how their parents got the money to buy the water toys, but not for the couple who stole child support money from the county for their own selfish pleasures.

"Did you see the look on the lady's face when she was arrested, Paula?"

"I did, and did you hear her whimpering like a child when they took her into custody? She was like…"Ouch, Officer, the handcuffs are too tight…." I thought I was gonna lose it right there."

"Yeah, I heard the man mumbling to his wife something to the effect of," "I told you they would find out. Now, look at us," said Russ.

Mark Jennings continued his drive back to Charleston. He passed Savannah, Georgia on I-95, making good time, when he noticed a Chevy Silverado that he had passed earlier and was now following at a steady pace behind him. It was the same truck for the last fifty miles, but did not think much of it until it passed a car, which was between them, to get within a few car lengths of his vehicle. Both men in the truck wore sunglasses and baseball caps. The pickup settled in its position and backed off about twenty-five yards behind him. More than a little concerned about this vehicle, Jennings decided it was a good time to shake them from his tail, so he pulled over at the first rest stop that he came to just inside the South Carolina line and drove around to the back of the state-run facility. He got out of his vehicle to visit the restroom, and glanced to his left to the entrance of the rest stop. The Silverado following him turned in, as well.

Quickly, Jennings walked into the simply constructed concrete block building, erected in the sixties, which housed the men and women's restrooms. It had a covered outdoor lobby area with self-service snack machines from which travelers chose their refreshments. He dispelled the thoughts telling him that imminent danger was possible, and walked through the lobby area and turned into the restroom. The dank scent of worn, cold concrete and the heavy smell of the fresh paint from the block walls permeated the evening air. Jennings stood at the urinal relieving himself. Usually he thought about how good it felt to be in his home state again, but not this time. Before he could finish what nature demanded of him, he heard the shuffling of feet walking outside the restroom by the snack machines, which stood perched in the lobby like silent, impotent guards.

"Wait," one voice said. "We'll get him when he comes out."

"Shh," the other voice responded, "he'll hear us."

Jennings' heart pounded the walls of his chest like a drummer on a bass drum. He flushed the urinal, and quickly entered a stall, sliding the metal clip lock in place. *I was stupid to have stopped at this disgusting rest stop,* he thought. He decided to wait them out to see what they would do. Jennings' handgun, which was locked in the glove box of his vehicle, and buried beneath a car manual, maps, and maintenance records, did him no good there. He rarely touched the gun but sorely wished he had it on him now. There was only one-way out of the restroom, and he found himself trapped within. He heard the men talking, but could not make out what they were saying. As he waited, the voices grew louder.

"He must have heard us....he's not coming out. I'm going in to get him," said one man.

The other man responded, "Go for it, man. I've got you covered out here. I'll whistle if anyone else stops."

The first man drew his pistol out of his jacket pocket, as he walked into the bathroom looking for his potential victim. The weapon was an old .035 caliber revolver that his dad had passed on to him, but most people did not know the difference between it and a more powerful weapon. He looked to his left at the sinks and mirrors then to the right at the urinals. Carefully, he surveyed the three stalls. Two of the stall doors were partially open, the third one was locked. The man, dressed in jeans, gray pullover sweatshirt, and worn, faded sneakers with holes, walked quietly to the first stall and pushed it open. Discovering it empty, he repeated the same process at the next stall. He stepped back a few steps and bent down on one knee, peering down and under the third, locked stall. He saw two shoes, Mark Jennings' feet pointing outward from where he sat on the toilet ready to make some sort of defensive maneuver, if the man broke into the locked stall.

Twenty-Nine

❦

Anna Leigh Jennings spent most of the night helping Nathan and Samantha with homework. Both kids competed on sports teams and took music lessons on top of their normal curriculum. As a result, they were exhausted by the time they got home on most days. Nathan had fallen asleep on the sofa, watching his favorite TV program. Anna Leigh looked at him stretched out in his jeans and colored T-shirt, thinking that he had grown a few inches and had gained several pounds, seemingly overnight. She thought about how she almost lost her son a year and a half earlier. Samantha had gone to her bedroom when she got sleepy and had fallen fast asleep.

Over the past year, Anna Leigh kept her ex-husband apprised of their activities at school when they talked periodically. She discovered that she still had feelings for Mark, although she would not admit it to anyone, especially to him. She kept so many joyous childhood memories locked down inside because she felt that she could not allow herself to be vulnerable again. She had spoken to a psychologist about her pent up feelings, which relieved her somewhat, but still they haunted her because she could not let go of her dream of growing old with Mark. From childhood through college, he was the one and only male she loved. She became aware from her sessions with her therapist that dating the man she was seeing since her divorce, was a classic rebound. She needed adult time, and Robert was good to her and the kids, but the deep feelings required in order to commit a lifetime to someone had not returned to her, and she doubted that they ever would.

    She knew that her ex-husband was working because he paid child support on time. She also knew from her brother-in-law, Matt, that he was clean. Anna Leigh knew that her ex-husband had far more good qualities than bad, except for when he caved in with his high school friend, snorting cocaine, and taking the tailspin that he did. Since the divorce, she rarely interacted with him in person, but when she did, he showed genuine remorse, which was another reason why she could not totally shake her feelings for him. Having children tied them together in ways that were irrefutable, and he was showing her that he was truly sorry for the things he did which wrecked their marriage, and nearly put him in jail. Fortunately for them, the authorities were never able to piece together enough evidence to nail him. It did help scare him straight, and that was the best outcome of the whole, sorry mess.

Anna Leigh lifted her sleeping son by his arms to his feet. Nathan groaned, not knowing where he was until his eyes blinked a few times and opened to see his mother's face struggling to pull his thirteen-year-old body upright. She managed to get him started walking down the hall to his bedroom.

"You're too heavy, Nathan. Come on. Walk on your own, sweetheart."

He groaned again and moved in the same direction with his mother like a pair of lethargic dancers, yet in step. Leaning on his mother, as practically dead weight, she nearly dropped him.

"Nathan, stand up and walk," she said, frustrated.

"Okay, Mama."

Nathan moaned, as he struggled to stand, trying to satisfy his mom. Anna Leigh let go of him as he seemingly sleepwalked in the direction of his bedroom. He turned his head a little, hiding a tiny grin, as he gained full consciousness. Timing his surprise, he broke away from his mother, running down the hall to his bedroom, laughing as he went. Anna Leigh, quite alarmed initially by his unpredictable antic, smiled nonetheless. *He's such a ham, just like his dad,* she thought.

"Good night, sweetheart," she said.

"Good night, Mama."

After checking on Samantha, now fast asleep, Anna Leigh returned to the den to straighten the pillows on the sofa, and pick up snack remains left on the coffee table.

She looked at the pair of lamps on the end tables and thought about when she and Mark picked them out on a trip to Savannah. She smiled, remembering her husband's cute antics in the furniture store. He positioned himself behind a cardboard stand of a headless cowboy outfitted in western garb with holstered six guns at his side.

"What do you want me to do? Draw you a picture, little lady?" said her husband, mimicking John Wayne.

She always did love his imitation of *the Duke*. She sighed, thinking about her whole situation with a new boyfriend. It was all too confusing as to why she still had feelings for Mark. She knew of his adultery, yet deep down, she still loved him. She knew Mark had a hard time admitting that he had made a complete imbecile of himself, though he let her know by his demeanor. He was able, however, to open up verbalizing his mistakes to his younger brother who told her that Mark had not been involved with anyone since the divorce. She knew Mark, like a favorite book read repeatedly, and believed her brother-in-law's report.

Just as Anna Leigh reached the kitchen with drinking glasses and bread plates in her hands, the telephone rang. She placed the items down on the counter, and lifted the receiver of the yellow, wall-mounted telephone.

"Hello?"

"Anna, it's me, Mark."

"I can barely hear you Mark. Where are you?"

"You won't believe this, but I'm at a rest stop near Hardeeville on I-95. Call 911 for me and tell them to get here fast. Tell them there are two men here with a gun attempting to rob me, or worse. Hurry, I can't talk anymore." He hung up, worried that the men would hear his conversation.

"Mark! Mark! Wait...," she cried.

The phone call left Anna trembling. One minute she was in a dreamy state enjoying her children, and reminiscing about old times with her ex-husband. The next minute her heart rate shot through the roof, and Mark's call put her on the verge of going into a panic attack. She dialed 911, her hands shaking like an alcoholic with tremors. The dispatcher put her through to the South Carolina Highway Patrol dispatch, which sent a trio of patrol cars on their way to the rest stop. The dispatcher also alerted the county sheriff's department, who sent two, additional back-up vehicles.

The man with the gun stepped back to the doorway of the restroom speaking with his accomplice.

"He's in the last stall," said the man to his friend.

"So, kick the door in. We need the cash. We might not have enough gas to get home."

"Is anyone pulling into the rest stop?

"No, man, the coast is clear. Ain't nobody pulling in."

"Give me a shout if anyone pulls in. I don't want to use my pistol unless I have to. The cops will be on us like bees on honey."

"You can be sure of it. Now go get that dude."

The armed man crept softly back into the interior of the restroom, Jennings' shoes still motionless in his stall. "Listen to me, whoever you are, we don't want to hurt you, but you need to come out with your hands up. Hand over your wallet, and I won't have to use this gun."

No response came from behind the pale green metal door. An eerie silence blanketed the atmosphere within the concrete structure for a moment. Jennings remained still waiting for the man to make the first move.

"I said ...come out of that stall now, or I'm gonna kick the damn door in!" said the man.

Again, there was no response. Everything remained quiet except for the man's labored breathing. The husky man backed up a few steps, raised one leg up, and like a martial arts expert, and with his work boot, gave the metal door a fierce mule kick. The door bent, but did not cave in. He kicked it again, this time with more force, and the door swung open banging against the inside of the stall. The robber braced himself with his arms stretched forward, his gun pointing straight ahead. To his dismay, the stall was vacant. The pair of shoes was empty on the floor pointing outwards in perfect position, as if Jennings was seated on the toilet.

"That son of a bitch!" shouted the man. His face flushed red with anger. "Hey Willie, get in here. I want you to see what this jackass did."

"What the hell are you talking about, Paul?" inquired the accomplice, as he scurried into the restroom. Willie looked in the stall and saw the empty shoes. "Where did he go?"

"Look up at the ceiling tile out of place. He's gone up through the attic. He's a smart bastard, Willie. The way I see it, we've got two choices. We can try and find him, and take a chance on getting caught, or we can drive down to the next rest stop."

Jennings continued duck walking through the ceiling across the rafters. After moving more than twelve feet away from an outside wall of the restroom, he raised one leg a little higher to step over a cluster of wiring and missed the next foothold. Slipping off the joist, his foot pressed hard on the pink fiberglass insulation. He felt the sheetrock bend beneath him, and jerked his foot back quickly, balancing himself as he held on to the rafters above him.

"Hear that Willie? It's coming from outside, in the ceiling. He's moving around up there."

The two men ran out to the vending machines area, and looked up at the ceiling. They observed a few particles of ceiling tile, which fell from above the beverage machines. Jennings moved past the machines to the center of the lobby area. He calmed himself so that his breathing was normal, and held tightly to a support rafter holding his position for the moment. Both of his feet were hurting from walking the two by sixes in his sock feet. The bottom of his left foot stung like fire. Glancing down, he caught a glimpse of bright red on his sock. Jennings realized where the fire in his foot came from now. He had picked up a splinter on the wooden rafters.

While the shady characters attempted to locate his precise location in the ceiling, flashing lights and sirens of patrol cars approached the rest stop. Jennings, feeling much like a trapped squirrel, remained motionless, hoping the men would leave at the sound of sirens. The two highway patrol cars parked simultaneously at the front entrance. Bright blue, pulsating lights circled, casting their glare from the parking lot and covering half of the sprawling lawn leading to the concrete building.

"Let's get out of here, Willie. Someone has called the cops."

"I'm with ya, let's go."

The men walked briskly, but calmly, to their truck parked behind. Arrested before, these country boys knew how to appear innocent while making their getaway. The patrolmen reached the front of the building, pistols drawn, while the two men climbed in the Silverado. Paul took his small handgun out of his pants and shoved it under his seat. He cranked the truck and pulled out at a normal speed without lights until they reached the entrance ramp.

The officers announced themselves loudly to anyone using the restrooms. Seeing nothing out of the ordinary, one of the officers walked out the back entrance and saw the truck entering the freeway entrance. He observed as it drove away at a normal pace, doing nothing that warranted suspicion, except the fact that the driver of the truck turned on the lights as he began to enter the freeway. Without more back up, their training taught them to allow it to go, for now. Rushing in the dark up to a vehicle with two men in the cab was extremely dangerous and had gotten several patrolmen injured, or killed.

Turning their attention again to the lobby of the seemingly empty building, one patrolman radioed the dispatcher as they walked back in. "This is Corporal Mangrum, please be advised, a late model Chevy truck with two men onboard just pulled out of the Hardeeville rest stop. Apprehend this truck with caution. The men inside may be armed. I repeat, the men inside may be armed."

"Ten-four, Corporal Mangrum, I'll get right on that, over." said the dispatcher. "I still have three more units en route."

Mark Jennings heard the voices of the patrolmen beneath. He heard the sound of the other patrolmen in the background on the radio advising the dispatcher of the truck's description and location. Deciding that things were under control and that the two thugs had left, he made himself known.

"Officers, I'm in the attic hiding from two men who were trying to rob me. Can you men hear me?"

"Yes, we hear you. What is your name, sir?" responded one officer.

"I'm Mark Jennings from Charleston. I just left Miami early this morning to return to my hometown. I've been working down there for about a year."

"What are you driving, Mr. Jennings?"

"I'm driving the SUV parked out back, the burgundy vehicle. I had someone call 911 for me."

The explanation fit the description the dispatcher gave to the officers.

"I'm Sergeant Banks, along with Corporal Mangrum, and two other officers. Mr. Jennings. We were dispatched here by a tip from your wife, the dispatcher said. The men who were attempting to rob you have left. You can come down now.

Encouraged by the news, Jennings duck walked his way to an opening where he removed a large, rectangle of ceiling tile. "Yes sir, she's my ex-wife, unfortunately, but thank God, she made the call."

"We understand, Mr. Jennings. Can you find your way out of there?"

"Yes sir, I'm coming down, probably right above where you are standing, judging from the sound of your voices."

"Take your time, Mr. Jennings. Don't hurt yourself," said one patrolman. He looked up to see Mark's sock feet coming out first then his legs protruding from the ceiling.

"I won't, officer," he said.

The patrolmen assisted Jennings in lowering himself to the ground. Finally, with his feet on the ground, Jennings dusted himself off. After he showed his ID, and gave a brief report, he retrieved his shoes from the stall.

"Thank you, officers. I am so grateful you arrived when you did."

"It's our job, Mr. Jennings. We will get more units pursuing those guys. One of our units will escort you up the interstate, if you like?" said Sergeant Banks.

"Yes, that would be greatly appreciated," said Jennings.

Thirty

❦

"Crescent Moon Investigations, Paula Roberts speaking, how can I help you?" She took a quick sip of her large caramel macchiato that she grabbed from a Starbucks on the way to work. It became a favorite stop of hers since moving to Charleston. Her former hometown, Georgetown, had not acquired one of the fastest growing phenomena in coffee shop chains in the world, yet.

"Paula, I'm glad it's you. This is Anna Leigh Jennings."

"Yes, I thought I recognized your voice. How are you, Anna Leigh?"

"Oh, I'm fine, all things considered, but it was a pretty rough night last night. I almost called you. It turned out okay anyway, though."

"What's going on Anna Leigh? You sound shaky."

"Mark called me from near Hardeeville at a rest stop on I-95 on his way back to South Carolina. It seems that two men were trying to rob him. He said one of them had a gun."

"Oh, my goodness, Anna! What happened? Is he alright?"

"Yes, he's fine now, but for a while there the situation got dicey, he said. He called me asking that I call 911 for him. When he was speaking to me, he was trapped in the ceiling of a rest stop facility, while two men below were searching for him. He had to climb up in the ceiling from a restroom stall to escape these thugs. I made the call and the South Carolina Highway Patrol were there, *Johnny on the spot*. Their arrival scared the bad guys away, and they got things under control, so that Mark could come down."

"Wow! That is a hair-raising experience. I'm glad that he's okay. Listen, Anna, I hope you don't mind me asking, but what's Mark doing back up this way? Last thing I heard was that he had a good job down in Miami, and was living with his brother."

"Well, that's right, Paula, but he says he's moving back because he misses the kids too much, and being so far away is not what he wants anymore...," Anna Leigh paused midstream in her sentence.

"Yes, Anna?" said Paula, lifting her cup for another sip.

"He's sober now, and has been clean for over a year. He attended counseling down in Miami, and said that it helped him in the rehabilitation process that he was already undergoing. I believe he's returned to being the man I married. Paula, Mark's making it clear that he wants us to try again, if I'm willing to give it a chance." Anna Leigh stood to her feet and began pacing the kitchen floor.

"What are you going to do, Anna?"

"I don't know. I told the kids about their daddy moving back home and they were super excited, especially Nathan. They've always been so close and things they like to do together, like hunting and fishing, playing ball, you know, boy things, they'll be able to do again." Anna waved one arm in the air then drew her hand to cover her mouth, as emotion overwhelmed her.

"I understand, Anna," said Paula calmly, to comfort her.

"I know you have other things to do, but do you have any words of wisdom for me? I'm in need of an independent, more objective voice than someone close to me. My mother is against it. My dad won't talk about it. My friends are divided, but it seems that most of them are advising me against it."

"Only thing that comes to me, Anna, is that you are the only one who can decide that. It's your life, and your family. Although everyone means well, no one but you knows your situation like you do with all that you've been through."

"That's exactly right, Paula."

"And no one knows Mark like you do. You are in the best position to make the right decision after you have time to be around him some and see how he behaves. That being said, I suggest prayer in very tough situations like this, then wait to see how things play out."

"I'm so glad to hear you say that. It's just that the kids love their dad, and I'm not sure about my feelings. I mean, I know there is closeness to him because he is their dad, but we were a couple since we were in middle school, as well."

"Being their dad should not be your only consideration, though, Anna."

"Oh, absolutely not, but what if he remains totally straight forever and I refused to forgive him. How will that affect our kids growing up, to be without their natural father? And how does that affect us, when deep down, we may both still love each other?"

"Anna, don't put yourself under a "guilt trip" over this. It wasn't your fault. You did what you had to do at the time. Yet, if you still love him and believe he's truly changed, then what business is it for anyone else to judge you? If you do chose to try again, the main thing is that you forgive and forget it as best you can in order to move forward with your lives. If he's changed, then the worst thing will be to continue to bringing up the past. That will likely revive old wounds, and cause him to question his decision to pursue you again."

"Where did you get all that, Paula? You sound like a psychologist. That's good stuff," said Anna Leigh, as she grinned.

"Anna, you and I have confided about each others' situation. I divorced and remarried as I told you. I went to counseling at my church, and read several books on the subject, which were of benefit to me. I'll be glad to share them with you, if you like?"

"Sure, whenever you get them together, let me know and I'll swing by the office and pick them up. Thanks, Paula."

"No problem. It's my pleasure...just let me know when."

"Well, Paula, I'm not sure what I'm going to do, but I'll take your advice about praying and sort of waiting to see what unfolds. I've been seeing a man and it had gotten kind of serious, but it took a turn for the worse last week when we got into a silly argument about how I raise my kids. He thinks he can just jump in and be instant dad, telling us all what to do."

"We both know it doesn't work that way, and I don't consider that a silly argument." said Paula.

"Yeah, that's true, and those who have never had children, generally don't have a clue. He's never been married, nor had children. He still lives with and takes care of his mother. Now, I'm re-accessing things and considering what I'm feeling for Mark, and the children. If I never try, then I'll never know. On the other hand, if I jeopardize what I have now, then I may miss out on a guy who really seems to love me despite everything. It's a two-edged sword, you know?"

"I do, Anna, but the question you'll have to answer is do you love the new man, or is he just someone you feel secure with? Also, what will you do with these unresolved feelings for Mark, unless you explore them?"

"That's saying it better than anyone I've talked to about the situation. I can't seem to work it through it to the place where I feel good about what to do, yet."

"You will know in time, Anna…hang in there. You'll make the right decision, and things will fall into place as you take one step at a time."

"Thank you so much, Paula. I'm sorry I took so much of your time, but I knew you would understand. I'll let you go and keep you posted, if that is okay?"

"You better. You call me anytime, hon."

"Thanks, Paula, you're the best. Good bye."

"Good bye, Anna."

Paula returned to the agency and was working through her messages. Baxter came in shortly afterward. She noticed his contorted face, as he walked to his office, not his normal demeanor. Usually, he kept an even keel regardless of what was happening, but he barely spoke to her, as he threw a hand up for a quick acknowledgement. Sitting down, Russ picked up the telephone to return the messages that Carla had left on his desk. He retrieved one message from the bottom of the stack, pulling it to the top, the one that requested him to call his friend at the FBI, Mike Atkins. Baxter hit the speed dial button letting it ring until he picked up.

"Special Agent Atkins, FBI, can I help you?"

"Mike, this is Russ. I got your message to return your call. Is this about the shipment?"

"Yeah Russ, the word from my friends is that there's a boat coming in to Johns Island about 3 AM tomorrow morning."

"Damn! Don't these people learn? I bet one of the players is the same guy that Mark Jennings worked with in the past, Jimmy Snyder, right?"

"That's one of the guys, Russ. Snyder appears to be a key distributor and has made a lot of dirty money, but he doesn't have enough money to land the large amounts of cocaine and marijuana that he's been getting. We suspect someone else is involved with financing the operation. Apparently, after Jennings was scared straight, someone stepped up and decided to become a main supplier of cocaine to Charleston. This man is moving sizable shipments, from what one source at the DEA told me, nearly every month," said Atkins.

"Mike, it's like I told you over a beer last week, I believe the financier for the operational end of it is my client's husband. He was already a user, but I believe he stepped in and offered Snyder to front the business, if he would keep moving product. I need to intervene, if possible, before we lose him to the justice system and it screws up his whole family. His wife is a personal friend of my family."

"Okay Russ, I hear you, but I don't hear you. You don't have much time, and I need to run, so be careful man."

"You too, Mike. Thanks a lot. I guess I owe you double now."

"You know you do. Beer on you next time at happy hour, and invite me and the wife over again soon for that Beaufort Stew y'all make."

"Done deal, I'll give you a call soon. Goodbye, my friend."

Just as Russ hung up the phone with Atkins, Paula stood by his door waiting. "Hi, Russ, I talked to Anna Leigh Jennings at length today. She's wondering what to do about Mark moving back to town. He's made overtures to her about them getting back together."

"I thought that she was engaged to another guy that she's been seeing," he replied.

"No Russ, she's been dating that guy, but he's acting like the Gestapo with her kids, and if I know her at all, she's not going to stand for that."

"Yeah, but does she want Mark's problems again?"

"He's made a big turnaround, according to Anna Leigh. He's clean now for over a year. She said he got a counselor while living down in Miami with his little brother. Anna Leigh believes he's the man that she married, once again."

"It sounds good, and I don't want to appear to be throwing a wet blanket on it, but I just have to wonder if his old friends will drag him down after he's here for a while," said Baxter.

"We'll have to see and wish them the best. It's all we can do. So, what is going on with you, Russ? I saw you on the phone and you didn't look good when you came in the office a few minutes ago."

"You read me too well, Paula. Well, you know the client we picked up last week, Tommy Lane's wife, Cindy?" he asked.

"Yeah, I remember. Her husband owns that big car dealership out on 526, right?"

"That's him, and by the way, he and Mark Jennings were tight at one time. It's rumored that they partied together. I have it from a reliable source that Lane is financing the drug runs from the Caribbean now. He's using the same supplier that Jennings used, and the same middle man."

"Good grief! Why am I feeling that there's much more to this story?"

"Your intuition is correct, partner. A shipment of cocaine is coming to Johns Island tonight, and Tommy Lane is likely meeting the boat for the shipment."

"What else do you know about him, Russ?"

"Cindy says her husband is a good man, but works too much, and is possibly using cocaine."

"Well, yeah, we've seen this before. Sorry to interrupt. Please, go ahead."

"She wants us to stop him, and help her get him into counseling. I don't know why I took the case, except that I've known the family a long time. They go to my church, and I know Cindy Lane's mother and daddy."

"I understand, Russ. You want to help the family, which is commendable. I'd do the same thing."

"That may be true, but it's a stupid business decision."

"We'll help them, Russ. I want to help slow that drug traffic to this area anyway. We'll help a family while earning a living. It's as simple as that. Look how the

Jennings case turned out. He didn't go to prison, and is supporting his family."

"I wish it was that simple," Paula.

"What are you getting at, boss?"

"I took the job for much less than our usual fees. Her husband keeps a tight rein on the finances. You might as well say it's a pro bono case," said Baxter. He studied Paula to gauge her reaction.

"Then we'll deal with it, Russ. I am sure you had your reasons. I believe when you do something good for someone, it always comes back to you eventually, in one form or another."

"I was hoping you felt that way. I just wanted to make sure you were on board before I asked you to help with the case."

"I'm all in all the time. We're partners for Pete's sake, aren't we, so stop worrying. I am down for whatever comes our way. I have learned to trust you over the past year. Besides, there may be a time when I call on you for a similar type situation."

Baxter relaxed after he broke the news, and leaned back in his swivel chair putting his arms behind his head. "Okay partner, I do appreciate you understanding, and tip my hat to you for your blind trust."

"Oh, it's not blind at all. You said you know the family pretty well, eh?"

"Yeah, I remember when Cindy was a little girl in Sunday school. She was the cutest thing you ever saw with those curly blonde locks bouncing up and down when she walked, and a bubbly personality to match."

"Aw, that's sweet Russ. So, tell me...when is this deal going down?"

"I know it's rather short notice, but are you able to work late tonight?"

"I'll touch base with, Jim, but I don't foresee a problem. Cool, we will be in action tonight then. What will it involve, any idea?"

"Okay here's where it gets complicated. There's a DEA bust planned tonight when the shipment comes in. We have to stop Tommy Lane, and his flunkies from arriving anywhere on Johns Island. If they do bust Lane, the DEA will have enough on him to put him away for a long time."

"I can't say that I don't wish we had more time, but I think we ought to be able to pull it off. Why don't we start tailing him now?" said Paula.

"What do you have in mind?" he asked.

"I'll go by his car dealership now acting as if I'm buying a car. I'll figure out a way to speak to the owner. Maybe I can plant a bug in his office. Do you know who his flunkies are?"

"Yeah, they work for him at the body shop from what Cindy says. He's got an old high school buddy running the shop, and there are one or two more in the mix I garnered from our conversation."

"It sounds like I may need to visit the body shop, too. It's in the back of the dealership, right?"

"Yeah, it is, but..."

"No buts, Russ, I got this," Paula said, winking.

Baxter laughed at his trusty partner. He had seen spunk like this before in a few men, but never witnessed it in a woman first-hand. It seemed that she feared nothing at all. He was sure that other women like her existed, maybe on a police squad, or in a Special Forces unit in a branch of the Armed Services, but he had never worked alongside such a special woman. She had quickly evolved into such a person, working with Russ, with Denby the lawyer, and with helping her private investigator uncle.

Paula's uncle solved extortion cases, child abduction, and numerous domestic cases of spouses uncovering their cheating partners. Back then, she mainly ran the office for him, but she did go with him on a few cases. She found it exhilarating, but never thought that she would work as a P.I. after completing paralegal training, and working for her former attorney boss.

"All right then. We will be rolling with your plan on this one. You get them bugged, and we will wait for them make their move tonight. I'll get the tire spikes loaded up. That ought to stop them before they hit the rendezvous point."

"Sounds awesome, I don't think we've done this together, yet, but I like it," said Paula, excited at the action her partner described.

"No, first time, Paula...listen, when you find out more information, just let me know. I'll be waiting in the shadows, ready to go."

"That works for me, Russ. I'll head over to the dealership now to feign buying a car, and get things set up."

"That sounds great. Later on, tonight, I'm thinking you can tail them, and I'll be near Johns Island waiting. If I can place the spikes at the right spot at a precise time, it will prevent them from getting onto the island. You can radio me ahead when you're close, so I don't spike anyone else unintentionally," he said.

"Or, we can be creative and run them off the road if we need to," she said. Paula laughed as she picked up her things, and walked by Baxter. Waving good-bye, she sashayed her way to the door. "Ole Tommy boy sounds like he needs a few slaps in the face anyway."

Russ chuckled, thinking that Paula was worth her weight in gold. He wondered how long he could keep her working with him. Her husband's antique shop had taken off like a skyrocket in its new location and she really did not need to work. Yet, she felt that she wanted to make a difference in people's lives. Working with Crescent Moon gave her the opportunity to help people on many of the cases, while they fulfilled an important niche in the community.

Paula Roberts P.I. - Johns Island

Thirty-One

⚜

Mark Jennings arrived in the Charleston area mid-afternoon. Thoughts of his wife possessed his mind, not letting him go. Her presence seemed as if it followed him. He detested the fact that she was going out with another man. He could not stomach the thought of a strange man hanging out around his children, telling them what to do. He had heard about this man attending his kids' events in place of him, and could not wait to make his presence known to let the intruder know he was not welcome to act as dad to Samantha and Nathan. The more he dwelled on it, the more it perturbed him. He was determined to regain his rightful place in his family by attending their events, instead of Anna Leigh's boyfriend. *Maybe she will stop inviting this guy to attend now that I'm in town,* he thought. He picked up the phone and dialed his ex-wife.

"Anna Leigh, how are you?"

"Hey, Mark, I'm good, and how are you?"

"I'm fine, thanks. Listen, I finally made it back to Charleston safely, and would like to see the children and you too, for that matter."

"Mark, I told you we could talk about it, but now is not the right time. I need time to clear my head. This is all happening so fast for me, but you can certainly see the kids. They miss you."

"Anna, I'm not asking you to decide anything. I just want to see Sam and Nathan for a little while. We don't have to talk about anything, and just seeing you while I pick up the kids will be good enough for me," he said.

"That's the nicest thing you've said to me in four years, but like I said, I need time. As for the children, I'll have them ready for you if I know about what time."

"I can't keep going like this, Anna. I miss you and the family so much, and if you open your heart to me again, I'll never disappoint you or the children again."

Ignoring his ingratiating attempts, Anna Leigh responded, "Can you come by and get them about three-thirty? You can keep them until dinnertime. I don't want them to eat while they're out with you though because I'm cooking, so you can take them to play somewhere, or to a mall."

Mark recognized her evasiveness and didn't push the issue. "Okay, sure, I'll take them to the Poinsettia Park ...maybe toss a Frisbee. We can even take the dog along. How is Mr. B anyway?"

"He's great, full of energy as always. He will be glad to see you, too. He mopes around more than he used to with you gone. You and Nathan raised him from a puppy. Dogs don't forget things like that," she said.

"Yeah, I guess not. I'll see you around three-thirty."

"We'll be here, talk to you then, Mark."

"Good-bye, Anna."

Jennings clicked the red button ending the call, and dropped the cell phone in his loose shirt pocket. Immediately his mind went back to a time when the children were very young. He reminisced about Christmas mornings watching the children with excitement in their eyes as they bounced out of their beds to see what good things ole Saint Nick had left them. Samantha and Nathan always left a cold glass of milk and cookies on the kitchen table with a note to refresh Santa as he made his rounds through their neighborhood.

Thirty minutes later, Mark Jennings pulled into the driveway of his former home. Putting the car in park, he shut off the vehicle, and opened the door. Standing up next to his SUV, he saw Anna Leigh come out from under the carport. His heart thumped a little stronger when he saw her beautiful, angular face, and naturally blonde hair bouncing around her shoulders. Her frame had changed a little since having kids, but in his mind, it only made her that much more attractive.

"Mark, the kids are on their way. Nathan is getting Mr. B on his leash and Samantha ran down the hall to grab the Frisbee when she saw you pull up."

"Okay, Anna, thank you. It's really good to see you," he said.

"You too, Mark. You're looking nice with your south Florida tan, and a bit slimmer, I think."

She did not mean to let that slip, but it was true. He had a wholesome look again. He smiled at her, but when she realized that she paid him a compliment, she tried not to smile back and avoid eye contact. She knew then that she had feelings for him, but really did not want to reveal it, not now. More time needed to pass between them before she could allow herself to trust again, even if he was a changed man.

Samantha and Nathan ran from under the garage racing each other to their dad's vehicle. Approaching their dad on each side, they embraced him fervently. Mr. B, a larger than normal Pomeranian, in tow, jumped up and down against Mark's body like a kangaroo anywhere he could fit in between the children, hoping to get his chance for attention, a pat on the head, or a rub of his back.

"Daddy, daddy," they both said. "We missed you. Mom said you are going to take us to the park."

"Yes, I am, kids. Hop in. I missed you both more than you know," their dad said.

To their display of affection he responded with warm hugs then reached down to pet Mr. B, whose pink tongue with a blue spot wagged with excitement. The whole scene tugged at Anna Leigh's heart strings considerably more than she expected. She was barely able to hold tears back and was glad when they pulled out of the driveway. As they backed out in the street, she hurried into the garage, so they would not see her crying from happiness to see them together again.

The thought of making love to anyone else was something that Anna Leigh had not fully dealt with since she and Mark has split. Rick, her boyfriend, had tried to be intimate with her, but she resisted, not sure of her feelings for him. She always put him off stating that she wanted to wait until she felt comfortable. Afterwards, Rick came to believe that she meant if they were married, so he proposed. Again, she avoided a commitment because she knew in her heart that she did not love him like he loved her, and deep down something did not click.

Anna Leigh had seen the way Rick and the kids interacted, and did not enjoy what she saw. For her children the relationship with Rick was stilted, at best, with contrived politeness for a man who wanted to fit in as part of her family. A few days before Mark called, the spat over her kids occurred, and it was then that she realized she did not want to marry him, no matter what happened with her ex-husband returning to town. Walking into the den, Anna Leigh sank into Mark's old leather chair and threw her feet up on the ottoman. She wiped the tears away with tissue, and folded her arms thinking. The phone rang and she saw from the number on the LED that it was Rick, the last person that she wanted to talk to at the moment. She let the call go to voice mail.

Daniel Easterling

Thirty-Two

❦

Paula arrived at Lane's Auto Superstore around four in the afternoon. As soon as she got out of her vehicle, she was greeted by an eager, smiling salesman, dressed neatly in Khaki slacks, blue buttoned-down shirt, and striped tie. Paula had slipped on a v-necked, pull-over cotton sweater, a skirt four inches above her knees, and silky-smooth panty hose. Her perfume intoxicated the salesman as she inquired about a car. He showed her a couple of vehicles in the class that she described, and she decided to test-drive one.

On the return from her test drive, the salesman made an inappropriate comment following what he thought was Paula's suggestive lead. As they arrived at the car lot, she flipped on him, stating that she was highly offended by his lewd remarks. The salesman was taken aback and didn't know what to think. When Paula asked to speak to his supervisor, the salesman reluctantly complied knowing he had done nothing wrong, except for believing and responding in kind to her coquettish behavior.

The manager, answering his page, walked out of his office where he was reviewing sales numbers, and down the hall to meet Paula.

"That's him coming down the hall, ma'am wearing the sweater vest," said the salesman, who walked over to one of the doors which led outside to the parking area, and waited until he was sure that his manager and this mysterious female were communicating. Paula waited as the manager approached her.

"So, you are the manager," said Paula.

"I am the sales manager, ma'am. The name is Charlie Sly. What can I do for you?" he said, extending his hand to shake hers. She did not reciprocate, but stood with her arms folded.

"Well, your salesman was hitting on me during our test drive, and I don't do business that way, Mr. Sly. I believe he said his name is Carl. I really don't appreciate being treated like that while I am here shopping for a car."

"Ma'am, I'm sure he didn't mean anything by it."

"Oh, I'm quite sure what he meant, Mr. Sly. I'm just not in the mood to shop any more after his behavior."

"He's been working here for four years, and I assure you that he's got a good record," said the sales manager.

"Well, that may be true, sir, but it's not good thing when a lady can't go out to shop for a car without being cornered by a salesman with a loose tongue making sexual innuendo. He asked me out, after I had already told him I was married. I'm offended, and very upset by all this," Paula said.

"What did he say, or do specifically?"

"I was driving the car that I liked around a few blocks with him and he leaned over toward me, and looked down, saying I had nice legs. I also caught him trying to peer down the top of my sweater when I leaned over to look at a dash feature that he pointed out. I had to sit up quickly to prevent him from seeing anything. Then he asked if he could have my phone number."

"We've never had such a complaint before on him. Are you sure you are not mistaken?" Mr. Sly asked.

Mr. Sly, taken off-guard by her outrageous allegations, knew that the men were not above cutting up with the women to have fun, but never considered any of his men doing what Carl was accused of. During training sessions, the salespeople had to sit through a day of video recordings, and do role-play skits addressing these types of scenarios. They knew their jobs were on the line for inappropriate behavior.

"Just take me to the owner's office. I think my complaint is falling on deaf ears."

Mr. Sly started to ignore her demand and continue his dialogue attempting to appease her.

"I'm thinking about writing an editorial in the paper. Or, maybe you would rather read about it instead?" Paula responded curtly.

"Uh, no ma'am, please wait here just a moment while I go get him. May I get your name please?"

"It's Brenda Nichols, and that will be fine, Mr. Sly." she said, using a pseudo-name.

"I'll be right back with the owner, Ms. Nichols."

The salesman who tried to sell Paula a car stepped outside to smoke. He lit up and walked over to his colleagues who clumped together, like birds sitting side by side on a wire, as they waited for their turn at greeting the next customer. Glancing over his shoulder back through the window as he exhaled a puff from his cigarette, he wondered why he had fallen victim to her outlandish accusation. He admitted to his fellow salespeople that he was flirtatious with her, but he knew it was a mutual thing. It was an uncommon occurrence, but he thought it was all in good fun, so when she flipped on him so quickly, it made his head spin. Was he losing his mind, or was this woman up to something? He wondered to no conclusion, as he justified himself to his co-workers.

Paula checked her purse for the listening device, grabbed her lip-gloss, unscrewed the cap, and quickly applied a little then touched her lips together. She turned to look down the hallway which led to the offices and saw the owner, Tommy Lane, coming down the hallway with Charlie Sly close beside him. Lane saw this striking woman from a distance, and instantly sucked in his gut, stood a little taller, and swept his tongue around his teeth, wiping away any possible food particles from the lunch he just consumed. Approaching her with a big smile and his friendliest greeting, he attempted to assuage the complaint of the potential buyer.

"Hi, how are you ma'am? I'm Tommy Lane, the owner. I understand you are not happy with one of our salesmen. What can I do to make things better?"

"Nice to meet you, Mr. Lane, can I talk to you in your office please? I don't like to air dirty laundry in a public forum," said Paula, in a more pleasant tone than she had spoken to the Mr. Sly.

Lane resisted the urge to put her off. "Sure you can ma'am. I didn't get your name?"

"It's Brenda Nichols."

"Let's go back to my office, Mrs. Nichols," he said politely.

Lane dismissed the sales manager and led her down the thinly carpeted hallway, the shade of faded grass in the fall. Seated comfortably in Lane's office, Paula told her story about the negative experience with the salesman while Lane listened intently. She observed his desk littered with car title documents, and a few pictures. Without warning, in the middle of her diatribe, Paula sneezed repeatedly. She looked in her purse to as if to find a tissue, but found none.

"Bless you, Mrs. Nichols," said Lane politely.

"Thank you, sir." she said. "I'm sorry. It must be my allergies acting up. You don't happen to have a tissue, do you?"

"I don't, ma'am, but I'll get you some. Hang tight for a minute please, and I'll be right back."

Lane scurried out from behind his desk down the hall to the break room where he pulled out a box of tissue from a cabinet. Paula quickly placed the bug on the underside of his desk where she found a space without it being conspicuous. She lifted his phone receiver and unscrewed the mouthpiece to plant a bug to tape his conversations. Just as she sat down, she heard the clopping of Lane's wooden heels from his penny loafers. She composed herself, sat uprightly, and looked in her purse, pulling out her compact mirror and a used tissue.

"No, don't use that, Mrs. Nichols. Here's an unopened box."

"Oh thank you, Mr. Lane. You are too kind. Here I am in your office complaining, and you are getting tissue for my allergies." She blew her nose, feigning her condition.

"Oh, that's quite alright. My wife suffers from the same thing. Now tell me, Mrs. Nichols, was there anything else that you want to tell me about your experience with our salesman?"

"Mr. Lane, I'm sorry to have made a scene. I guess I should have given the man the benefit of the doubt. I could have misunderstood him, who knows. We were kidding around and I thought he went too far with it. After thinking about it and calming down, let's just forget about it, okay?"

"Are you sure Mrs. Nichols?"

"Yes, I'm sure. I got carried away in the moment. My husband says I'm quick tempered. I'll come back when I'm having a better day. We've just moved to Charleston from Georgetown, and I've been stressed out over a number of things, getting the kids settled in a new school, decorating and furnishing the house, things like that."

"I understand, Mrs. Nichols. I'm sure things will calm down after a little while. Please come back and ask for our sales manager, Charlie Sly, so that he can make sure you are served properly."

"I will, Mr. Lane. You have earned my business by the way you handled a difficult situation. By the way, how do I get to your body shop? I have a dent I want them to look at while I'm here."

"It's directly behind the main building, Mrs. Nichols. Drive your vehicle around the building, and you will see the sign."

Paula stood to her feet to take her leave. "I'll do that, and thanks again for your time, Mr. Lane," she said.

Leaving the owner's office, quickly she cranked her vehicle, and drove it around back to the body shop. After using her charm once again, Paula found a way to plant a bug in their shop office. Driving off the lot, she grinned, and even laughed aloud at the unsuspecting men who made it easy for her to plant the electronics. With both missions accomplished in less than an hour, she dropped by the shooting range and got in thirty minutes of practice before calling her boss.

"Hey Russ, it's me, phoning in with an update. I've got the bugs planted in Lane's office and the body shop."

Baxter sat at the office intently monitoring the phone calls made by Tommy Lane to his body shop working out details of when they would leave to make their connection.

"Hey, partner. Yeah, I know because I can hear them now. The word I'm hearing is that they won't leave from the body shop until around midnight."

"Wow! That was a stroke of luck to hear about their plans that quickly," she said.

"Somebody's living right, I tell you. Awesome job, Paula, you're amazing."

"Yeah, I know, right," she said, laughing. "Listen, since we're situated here, and you are on top of surveillance, I'm heading home to eat with the family and will be back out later in the night before our targets push off, if that works for you."

"That'll work, Paula. I'm going to stay with the radio. If there are any changes, or details that might help us, I'll let you know. Go and enjoy your family."

"I wish these men had the sense to enjoy their families instead of this crap," she said.

"We'll help these guys by stopping them in their tracks, but they won't see it that way. You do know what we are doing could be construed as interfering with justice. We can't breathe a word of this to anyone. I don't have to tell you that," said Baxter.

"What are we doing again? I can't remember." Paula said, eyes glinting as she teased him a little. "Not to worry, Russ. This won't go any further than you and me. I only hope, for his sake, that Mr. Lane wises up after his wife gets a chance to talk to him. Without a doubt, she is going the extra mile for him. If it were me, I would kick his butt then kick him to the curb."

"I'm sure you would, Paula."

"I'm outta here, Russ. I'll give you a ring when I'm back on the road."

Thirty-Three

❦

Mark Jennings returned to his ex-wife's house with the kids at the time she had requested. Anna Leigh looked out the kitchen window to see them pulling in the driveway. It warmed her heart, and she wondered why she was feeling this way. She knew it was more than just seeing the kids and their dad together, but tried to push the feelings down beneath the surface of her consciousness. Samantha and Nathan bounced out of the car onto the lawn with joy, their foreheads glistening with perspiration from their vigorous playtime at the park. More importantly, they were exuberant from seeing their dad for the first time in six months.

Not feeling too confident, Mark walked gingerly to the carport to see the children in. He desperately wanted to turn back the hands of time. All was right in the world then. Reminiscing, he thought about how he served as his general contractor, in building the home he now had to leave. He saved a ton of money, and was intimately attached to the domicile because of the process over overseeing every detail from start to finish. It was the first home of size that they built after the starter home they owned when the kids were toddlers. He hoped it was just a matter of time, and that his misdeeds had not sentenced him to a life of being a stranger in the home that he built and where his children were growing up.

Anna Leigh saw Mark standing at the concrete driveway where the garage door was raised, and had a nostalgic flashback to when times were different. A half a dozen scenes from the past rolled through her mind before she could shut the haunting memories down. She remembered greeting him as he came in from work countless times right where he stood now. She hurt inside because the habit of smiling, and greeting him with a kiss had been taken from her. Refrains of life not being fair rolled through her mind, though she was taught to believe that life is what you make of it.

Samantha reached puberty earlier in the year, and Nathan's voice was changing, as well. The preteens and early teen periods were a breeze thus far, but Mark and Anna Leigh knew how they were, and could not imagine anything different for their children. Mark wished he could be there to experience their teenage years and be a dad, their rock of Gibraltar. He never believed it was right for one parent to raise children, unless absolutely necessary. And although his ex-wife may consider it necessary, he could not let it go, not yet anyway.

"I can smell the food cooking from here, Anna Leigh. What is that? Wait...please don't tell me. I think I know from the aroma."

"You should know what it is. I'm disappointed," she said, half-serious. "I only cooked it, like, hundreds of times when we were married."

"It's been a while. I'm sorry, I can't place it."

The kids, still mulling around, watched with interest as their mother and father interacted. To them, they were right together; they did not know the details of the past, nor did they care. They loved them both and knew them as their mom and dad, who were both supposed to be there for them. Sam and Nathan knew the simplistic stories of forgiveness they learned in Sunday school and did not understand why their parents did not apply these basic principles to their problems so that their lives could be normal again.

"Daddy, are you staying for dinner?" asked Samantha.

It didn't occur to ask her mom before she blurted it out. Such is the way of an eleven year old. Mark watched as Anna smiled graciously at her daughter, but eyed her with a look that sent a message of disapproval.

"Sam, what have I told you?"

"Be easy on her, Anna. She didn't mean any harm," said Mark, defending his daughter, not knowing she really was not in trouble.

Nathan jumped in on the tail end of the conversation, "Mama is Daddy staying for dinner?"

"I don't know, Nathan." She threw up her hands in resignation then glared at Mark, putting the ball in his court. "Your dad hasn't said anything one way or the other," said Anna Leigh. After seeing that he would not answer, she addressed him. "Mark, do you want to stay for meat loaf and a few things that I threw together? I have a Dutch apple pie in the oven with natural vanilla ice cream for dessert, if you are interested."

Anna felt extremely awkward and did not really know what the right thing to do was, but yielded to the desires of the children. Her usual philosophy was that if the kids were happy, she was happy. She bit the corner of her lip, as she waited. Mark picked up on her facial cue, tickled at her dilemma.

"I thought you would never ask," he replied.

The family reunited for a meal for the first time in over a year when they last had Christmas dinner together. After everyone gathered inside, Mark took his old place at the kitchen table. He thought about how fortunate he was to be the father of two wonderful children, and that he was once married to this remarkable woman that stood before him preparing a family meal.

"Mark, would you like a glass of sweet tea while you wait? I've still got to butter the dinner rolls and pop them in the oven."

"That would be awesome, Anna, I am thirsty. I bought the kids something to drink when we went to the park, but left myself out for some reason." Mark felt the cottonmouth dryness from the activity with his kids, and salivated at the sight of a glass of cold ice-tea.

"Here ya go," she said. Anna Leigh placed the glass of tea in front of him. Her silky blonde hair fell around her face from one side as she leaned over the table. The fragrance of her perfume ignited him, as she passed in and out of his personal space. He was tempted to make a flirtatious comment but refrained. She felt a little nervous at the awkwardness, as well. Moving away from the uncomfortable encounter, she stepped into the den to speak to the children who had gotten comfortable in front of the television.

"Kids, dinner is almost served. It's time to wash up."

"Okay, Mama," they responded.

They sprang up and ran to the bathroom to wash their hands then returned to the dining area. Anna and Samantha put the dishes of food on the table and the family interacted almost as if there had not been any time lost to the grand thievery of divorce, and Mark's self-imposed exile to Miami. Mark and Anna glanced at each other periodically, smiling as they enjoyed the children's comments and the family interaction. Everyone ate heartily and the Jennings excused the children from the table.

"Anna, that was truly remarkable. I haven't had a good home cooked meal like that since we were together, besides an occasional cafeteria, which isn't quite the same."

"Thanks for saying so, Mark. It's what I do," she responded, rather flatly.

Adding a slight smile as she turned, she began clearing the table, dirty dishes in hand. Her feelings were confusing inside, but she knew the butterflies were not from being nervous only. She sensed an aura about him that was not present in the last two years before their marriage ended. His face looked healthy again, without the bags under his eyes when he was strung out. He was not fidgety, or anxious to go somewhere that he concocted in order to get a fix. She took comfort in seeing the change that had happened to him. It was no longer hearsay. His demeanor projected that of a new man, one who appreciated the simplicity of family life, and a good home-cooked meal.

Jennings was content and peaceful with himself once again, more so than he had been in a long time. He thought about how and when he had lost it so quickly. In a flash, he remembered drinking too much with his friends and succumbing to temptation. The pain of that memory haunted him like a nightmare from a horror movie after eating too much pizza. He realized that some former friends were not worth hanging out with anymore, even if they were among his best friends growing up.

Times change and the paths down life's highway offer different destinations for its travelers. He wanted to stay on the path of enlightenment that he had found and possibly earn another chance with Anna Leigh, and his family, if she were to allow him into her good graces again. Regardless of the outcome though, he had determined a new and healthy lifestyle, a clean conscience, and caring for family. Though some consider it boring, Mark Jennings, now more than ever, recognized deep down that this is what living really meant.

Thirty-Four

❦

Tommy Lane left his office walking down the corridor to a door, which led to a covered walkway. Striding across the concrete walk, he entered a side entrance to Lane's Superstore Body Shop, which stayed open late many evenings to complete a vehicle by a deadline. Tonight, although a few employees were still inside, the work had ceased. After closing for business, one side of the body shop turned into a place to play poker. It was a select club for a few of the men and Mr. Lane. They drank a few beers, smoked their cigarettes and cigars, and played poker. They also made trips to the bathroom to snort cocaine, about which no one talked openly. America's white plague continued to wreak havoc on hundreds of thousands of people affecting all socio-economic levels from the wealthy to the poor. This business was no different, a microcosm of an unedited portion of American society.

A couple of men folded out a portable card table along with four chairs. Tommy Lane walked by the table just after it was set up. He paused for a moment lighting his cigar, and then tossed a pack of playing cards that bounced squarely in the middle of the flimsy tabletop and flipped up in the air, then coming to rest, awaiting the dealer's shuffle. The men used to play cards at lunch, but were not allowed to anymore after running over the time limit one too many times. One of the men was stabbed in the hand one time for cheating, and there were a few similar fights over accusations and arguments, so Mr. Lane had taken the cards away. The work improved markedly, along with the productivity. Now he rewarded them by allowing them to play, but only when he was present to ensure civility. The few men that played tonight were the ones who assisted him with the drug deals. One of the men brought a bucket of ice with six bottles of beer and all three men took their seats at the card table.

"Five card draw, deuces wild, okay with y'all?" Bill, the shop supervisor said.

"Yeah, that's good. Let's play," responded Lane.

Bill shuffled the deck a few times and dealt the first hand. The other man, Darren, did not say much, preferring to let his boss, and Bill, do the talking. The men picked up their cards and spread them out in their hands so that each card could be read. After a brief gander at their cards the men anteed up and selected up to three discards, dropping them in the middle of the table, before they requested the same number of cards from the dealer to replenish their hands. Bill meted out the requested cards and the bets were placed.

"What y'all got?" inquired Lane, tossing his cards face-up the table. "I got a full boat, kings, and eights."

"Beats my pair of nines," Darren said, as he tossed in his cards.

"And, it beats my ace high," Bill said. "Damn, boss man, you are starting out of the gate hot."

"I was just lucky boys... just got lucky. Listen men, changing the subject for a minute, we'll need to leave about 1 AM for Johns Island. The meeting is between 2:00 and 3:30 AM. We'll take our time getting there. We don't want to be seen in the area until we need to be there. Got any questions?"

"Yes sir, we got it. Did you tell me that you're going all the way in this time, Tommy, rather than wait at the restaurant until we come out?" asked Bill.

"Yeah, I want to go in to meet this guy once. I want him to understand what I need and when, and under what conditions. You will be my point man from here on out, Bill. In the future, you will take the money to the captain, the product to the distributor, collect all the proceeds, and get back to me. You will get your cut like we already agreed. You know what that is. In addition, I don't want to be contacted by the supplier directly anymore. The captain has to understand that if I give him this kind of business once every other month that there should be some other concessions, other than just supplying the stuff. I want him to understand that if he gets caught, it's on him, the same way as it would be on me, if I were to be caught."

"Yes sir, I completely agree with you," said Bill.

Darren sat listening to the other two. He took a chug of his beer then began to deal the cards, showing off his skills. He told everyone that he used to deal cards on the American Queen, which ran tours up and down the Mississippi River, prior to a ferocious hurricane, which demolished the pleasure boat. No one ever bothered to verify his claim because he dealt the cards with flare and speed. Darren admitted first trying cocaine while working on the boat. He claimed it helped him deal with the schedule he kept, and the raucous crowds who were most often drunk every night.

"Bill, do you remember the Jennings boy who was kidnapped about a year ago?" asked Lane.

"Yeah, I remember seeing that on the television, and reading it in the papers. The way I heard it, the detectives at Crescent Moon caught the kidnappers, and helped find the boy, but it was near disaster for the Jennings' family," said Bill.

"That's right, Bill. I remember that now. I heard the sheriff's department had their men in the area, but it was Russell Baxter, and his partner, Paula Roberts, who caught the kidnappers, then rescued the boy after he escaped and took off up the waterway at night in a Jon boat. It's really a pretty fantastic story."

Darren dropped the un-dealt portion of the deck on the flimsy card table, and then spread out his five cards close to his chest. He glanced down at his hand, and then waited for the men to place their bets. Tommy and Bill studied their cards for a moment. After all three men anteed up again, Bill began the betting with the required minimum.

Darren sat quietly, waiting his turn to bet. He watched the other men place their bets, and decided to offer up his opinion on what he had just heard them say for the first time. "I hear that Paula lady is a damned good shot and not afraid of anything. Also heard she could rumble like a man if she has to," said Darren. "I wonder where the hell she came from."

"You know what's even more interesting guys," said Lane. "I think my wife may have hired them to watch me. There has been a van following me off and on for the past ten days. Also, there was a woman in the store today who put up quite a fuss, then reversed her position suddenly after I stepped out to get some tissue for her sneezing attack. She resembled a picture in the paper that I saw of that lady detective when the Jennings case hit the papers, now that I think about it."

"Hmm, what did this lady look like, Tommy?" inquired Bill.

"She was 'bout five-six, very fit, attractive lady. You know...perfect features, long-haired brunette with green eyes, the kind of look you don't forget easily."

"That sounds like the same lady who came back to the body shop today, Tommy."

"Yeah, I told her how to get here. What kind of issue did she have anyway?"

"Not much, she had a question about a dent on the right rear quarter panel of her SUV. As soon as I gave her a rough estimate she was gone."

"Did she wait inside while you went out to check out the car, Bill?"

"Yep, come to think of it. She did."

"Hmm, well I think she's up to no good, but I can't put my finger on it, yet," Lane said, as he placed his bet.

Time flew by, and after several hands, it was nearly time to go. The men continued drinking, laughing it up, as they settled-up on their small bets. Tommy Lane looked down at his watch.

"Let's get moving guys. It's that time," said Lane.

The men slid their chairs back in unison, and crushed their smokes out on the concrete floor. Turning off the lights, they locked the doors to the shop.

Thirty-Five

❦

Paula Roberts arrived across the street from Lane's Super Store around midnight at a twenty-four hour coffee shop, from which she staked-out the dealership. She parked on the end of the lot, out of view of the workers, behind a large, metal light pole that stood between her and the dealership. Paula did not mind stakeouts because it gave her time to clear her head while she worked. Like most women, she had always been good at multi-tasking. Something about raising babies gave them instincts that a man did not possess.

She put her leather attaché on her lap and flipped it open to retrieve the tools of her trade. She placed a digital camera next to her on the seat, and extracted her revolver, which she placed on the floorboard in its holster. She easily hid the Smith & Wesson on a clip at the small of her back by wearing a loose fitting jacket. Scooting down in her seat, she peered through infrared binoculars across the street to the exit gate and parking area by the body shop.

There had been no vehicles leaving the body shop since the time that Paula arrived, but she had learned patience while on stakeouts. She took short breaks from pressing the binoculars against her orbital sockets by flipping through a magazine that she used to cover her face. Putting her binoculars up to her face once again, she focused on the area by the body shop. Concentrating on her view, she heard the speaker on her radio crackle, and then Russ's voice squawking through. She grabbed the radio from its cradle answering it, lowering the binoculars briefly.

"Yeah, Russ, go ahead."

"Paula, they should be leaving the body shop any moment, according to the communications I'm intercepting."

"I can't see very well. The body shop is too far back on the lot, but I am ready… wait, Russ, I got something."

Suddenly, Paula noticed movement, as she gazed into the shadowy night. She lifted the binoculars to her face as fast as a gunslinger from the Old West. Three men walked to a black Expedition and climbed in. They backed out of Lane's reserved parking space where he kept his spare vehicle with dealer tags. The year and make of the vehicle changed often, by design, so that he could not be easily traced. Lane was driving, Bill rode shotgun, and Darren sat in the backseat of the large SUV, which headed toward the exit. Approaching the perimeter fence the metal gate shuddered as it rolled open.

"We have movement, Russ. They're leaving the car lot," said Paula, one hand on binoculars, the other attached to the radio.

"Roger that, Paula. Good job! I have been listening to them yak about all kinds of things from car sales to body shop repairs. I even got an education on how they run the bills up at the body shop."

"Why am I not surprised, Russ?"

"As you said, partner, it looks like they are on their way now."

"Let's switch this chat to cell phones. It will be easier to handle while I'm driving."

"You're right, Paula, I'll call you."

Russ hung up his radio and flipped open his cell. He pressed the speed dial button, and she answered, positioning the cell phone beneath her hair.

"Paula's grill, how may I help you?" she said.

"I'll take a shark sandwich, medium well," Russ said, humoring her.

"You'll have your shark in a few minutes," she said.

"There you go, Paula. So, you're going to follow them, keeping your distance, of course, but staying on their tail all the way to the Johns Island Connector, right?"

"You got it, Russ. I'll be back in touch with anything significant." She snapped her cell phone shut and fixed her gaze on the SUV across the street.

"Ten-four, Paula."

The black Expedition rolled out of the body shop parking lot, the electric gate sliding back in place, automatically closing behind them. Once off the car lot the black behemoth carrying the three men turned left and navigated its way to the bypass, heading towards the connector road. Paula pulled out shortly after the target and followed. Knowing that Tommy Lane was a smart man, she kept back a good forty yards, and let a car in between.

Exhilaration came over Paula each time she tailed someone. She first noticed this enthusiasm working for her uncle, the P.I. from Savannah, and then later when working for Thomas Denby as a paralegal when he sent her on undercover missions. She reminisced about when she began to thrive on this sense of exhilaration and excitement. She traced it back to her childhood when raised in Georgetown. Whether fishing, clamming, or playing hide and seek, she sought to satisfy her adventurous spirit. She loved to laugh aloud when she outwitted her male counterparts, leaving them embarrassed that they could not outsmart her.

Paula continued driving behind the black Expedition without drawing the attention of its occupants. Tommy Lane glanced down at his gas gauge then pulled into a gas station to fill up. There was no need to take any chances in a gas guzzler with a load of drugs. Paula saw him turning in and pulled into an adjacent convenience store across the street. After gassing up, Lane pulled out again en route for his rendezvous. Paula watched her second hand on her wristwatch then pulled out exactly fifteen seconds behind him. Lane approached the final stretch of marshlands on either side of the road before the connector bridge. As they traveled, Lane's vehicle came upon a local seafood restaurant located a mile before the bridge and pulled in.

Quickly, Paula snatched her cell phone from the top of her bag and dialed.

"Hello, this is Russ."

"Russ, we're about a mile or so from the bridge and the subject is pulling into a roadside diner. My guess is they're too early for their rendezvous and decided to grab a bite to eat to kill some time. Are you in position?" she asked.

"Affirmative, I'm in position, partner. I'm waiting on word from you when to lay out the spikes."

"Okay, I'll call you as soon as they get up from their table."

"That works for me. I'm ready to go on your word."

Paula resumed her stakeout from across the highway at a pay phone by a closed convenience store. She had a view inside to the checkout counter of the cash register. Using her binoculars again, she saw the men place their order with the waitress. When the food arrived, the men gorged on their cheeseburgers, and fries, and gulped down their iced tea in ten minutes. Paula continued to watch meticulously. Although, she did not enjoy seeing men inhale food, chewing with their mouths open, and dribbling remains on their plates, she knew that timing was everything in order to subvert Lane from his goal of scoring drugs.

Glancing down at his wristwatch, Tommy Lane checked the time, 2 AM. "Men, it's time we start rolling again." "We'll be there by 2:30 AM if we leave now." The men rose up simultaneously on their boss's lead.

Paula had the threesome in her view when they slid out of the red, vinyl booth and head to checkout. Grabbing her cell, she called her partner.

"Okay, Russ, they are on the move again. They are paying for their meal, and will be on the road shortly."

"Ten-four, Paula. You'll need to close in and ride their tail as soon as possible with your bright lights on to distract the driver, so he is less likely to be watching the road and avoid the spikes."

"I was going to say the same thing. Like my dad used to say, "Great minds think alike".

"I'll make my move now," said Russ. "We'll talk again after our subject is stranded on the highway."

"Okay Russ, good luck. They are cranking up, and backing out now. You don't have much time."

"I'm on it. Goodbye."

Russ Baxter jumped out of his parked van on the dirt road beneath the highway above. He was glad that the road was close because he had to carry the two three-by-four sections of black rubber spiked mats up a hill to place on the highway. With the heavy Kevlar mats folded under his arms, he trudged up the steep, grassy knoll, which led to the guardrail on the outer edge of the highway. He raised one leg, then the other over the silver alloy railing, and trotted onto to the highway just before the bridge where traffic enters Johns Island.

Russ used mental techniques he learned in the service, comparing past events and experiences, to harden his resolve when performing the rigors of a tough task. In training, Russ learned from a Navy Seal instructor who taught a class for two weeks on the topic of Survival and Tactics of Subversive Warfare. It was always amazing to Russ how a trained mind could overcome adverse conditions. As a boy he remembered carrying one-hundred pound sacks of feed over his shoulder to customers' cars when working at a feed store with one arm wrapped securely around the bag. In the Marines, he carried ninety pounds of gear through the swamps of Paris Island during basic training. *These mats are a breeze compared to then*, he thought to himself as the weight began to wear on him as he climbed up the steep hill. Russ ignored the fact that he was considerably older now, pressing through the discomfort he felt in his body.

He bent over on the dark highway putting the mats in position, placing them on the right side of the road where he found the well-worn grooves made from countless tires rolling repeatedly to and from the island. With the mats in place, he quickly scurried back over the guardrail and slid down the damp, grassy slope. Getting back into his van, he started the engine and without turning on the headlights, pulled down to the water by a boat dock. Hiding the van beneath a sprawling willow tree whose branches and leaves draped to the ground like a curtain on a stage, Baxter waited with both windows down, listening for the sound of a vehicle approaching.

Paula sped up in her SUV, and closed in on the rear end of the Expedition, flipping on her bright lights. Lane detected bright lights glancing off the rear view mirror, nearly blinding his view of the road. He hated when a rudely ignorant tailgater got on his bumper. Flipping an adjustment on the mirror to night view, he looked to see who was following so closely.

"Who's this son of a bitch on my tail?" said Lane.

Bill, riding shotgun, turned over his shoulder to get a look behind him. The lights blinded him from seeing anything inside the vehicle, except the shadow of a person.

"I can't make out the driver, Tommy, but it looks like a female. I think I see long hair, but I can't be sure because of the bright lights," said Bill.

"I'm gonna speed up and try to lose the bitch," said Lane.

He floored the accelerator and the engine responded robustly, all eight cylinders kicking into high gear with the influx of gasoline from the fuel injectors. The Expedition began to pull away from Paula's vehicle toward the bridge ahead when the sound occurred, "boom, boom, boom," three tires blew out. The sudden unexpected noise startled the men. Instinctively, they ducked wondering if someone was shooting at them. Lane held the wheel tight, struggling to keep control of the vehicle as it swerved to the right bumping the guardrail about fifty yards before the bridge.

Paula hit the gas pedal of her vehicle as the Expedition's tires were going flat, and sped around in the passing lane. With her right hand acting as a shield, she held it up against her face to protect her identity. Lane tried to get a look at the driver passing him, but failed. Russ and Paula's plan worked to perfection as Lane's bulky vehicle slowed, skidding and swerving to a stop.

"What in the hell just happened here?" exclaimed Lane, in anger.

"We hit something in the road," said Bill.

"I know that, damn it all, but what was it? It feels like all four of the freaking tires blew out all at once."

Lane skidded to a stop, barely able to maintain control of the large vehicle. The men all jumped out together and walked around the vehicle to inspect the tires. Soon they came to the same conclusion.

"Damn! Look at this crap!" said Lane. Three of four of the tires are flat as hell!

"How are we going to make the connection now, Tommy?" inquired Bill.

"We aren't, you dufus. It's thirty minutes until time to meet them, and by foot it's an hour and half," said Lane. "We are not about to go traipsing across that bridge, and across the island, then down a dark road to a cove to do a drug deal. It will have to keep."

The men looked around for anything in sight that was still open, but there was nothing except a closed gas station about one-hundred and fifty yards behind them.

"Let's walk back to the place where we hit that debris in the road," said Lane.

"That's fifty yards back there, Tommy," said Darren.

"You think I don't know that? I'm in no mood for your lackadaisical attitude. Just shut up and follow me."

Lane took long strides down the highway, swinging his arms emphatically. His men, chastised for their laziness, followed close behind, keeping quiet as their boss had ordered. Reaching the place where their vehicle hit the spikes, they found no sign of debris in the road, except for a few tire fragments.

"It was right about here where we hit whatever it was, and I don't see a damned thing in the road that we could have hit. Something is fishy," said Lane.

"What are we going to do now, Tommy?" asked Bill.

"I guess we'll have to walk our butts back to where my cell phone has a signal then call someone to come get us. I think I saw a telephone booth next to that closed convenience store back down the road. We can make a call from there, or on my cell," said Lane. "Let's go."

Russ Baxter sat in his van leaning on the steering wheel, out of sight and thirty feet below the embankment. With his windows down, he could hear the men talking, and cursing at what had just happened to them. The spiked mats were stowed in the back of his van. He smiled with satisfaction at a job well done, and waited until he could safely leave the area.

Thirty-Six

※

With the men out of sight and enough distance from the road so that he wouldn't be heard, Russ made a call to his partner.

"Paula, what happened? Did you see it?"

"Oh yeah, I saw some major braking and swerving in my rear view mirror when I passed those guys. How did things go on your end?"

"Hey, if it had gone any better I wouldn't have believed it. It was amazing. They came to a stop about fifty yards after they hit the spikes. I was able to retrieve the spikes from the road while he was still stopping. The dimly lit road didn't hurt anything either. By the time, I got the mats I saw your red tail lights speeding ahead of them. Great job!"

"Thanks, Russ. Not so bad yourself. I hope that idiot, Lane, will wake up and realize that someone is trying to get his attention. He's a hard-headed, arrogant son of a gun."

"That's all we can hope for, Paula. I told his wife that this intervention is a one-time thing. We cannot keep interfering with potential drug busts like this. Cindy is going to have to convince him to change his ways from here on out."

"Did you give her any advice?"

"Yeah, I told her that she needs to lay it on the line, and just to level with him. I also told her that if she has any problems out of him….you know… domestic violence issues, to call me."

"Good idea, Russ, I kind of like the ultimatum thing. At this point, it can't hurt. That may be more than he deserves, but it is an attempt at preserving the family unit, and I certainly believe in that."

"That's it, Paula. The children didn't do anything to deserve this."

"I agree. Listen, partner, unless you need me any further, I'm heading home. I need to get some sleep so that I can be rested and in a normal disposition for my family tomorrow."

"No problem, Paula. Have a good one. You're the best!"

"Ditto, Russ. See you at work. I may be a little later than normal, if that's okay?" Paula said.

"No problem. I may be in a little late, as well.

Paula made a turn on the highway and headed back across another smaller bridge to the mainland. Oblivious to her surroundings, she drove, deep in thought about her family, wishing her job had normal hours, though she did like the work otherwise. She and Russ had already done many good things together, and she had earned a considerable amount of money for her family.

She never realized how much a good private investigator could make, and how rewarding some cases could be. In some cases couples decide not to divorce and to reconcile. In the Jennings' case, she witnessed a couple split up when there seemed to be no other way, and by a miracle, they reconciled. The sad part was when family units were destroyed through hard-headedness and infidelity. These were the bulk of domestic cases they handled, but to her, the most interesting. Business cases got interesting when they caught a partner embezzling. Missing persons had only come up once since she was working at Crescent Moon, and it was extremely rewarding to find the loved one.

Turning off the highway, Paula traversed through the residential areas until she came to her neighborhood street. Whenever she came home after midnight the family was sleeping. Choosing not to open the garage door because it made a huge racket, she parked in the driveway, and quietly closed her car door. Glancing at the luminous dial on her watch, she sighed.

"Three-thirty in the morning," she muttered.

Opening her car door, she stepped onto the flat, gray, slate walkway that lay flush with her green centipede lawn. One by one, she lightly stepped on the stones to her wooden porch then front door, and eased the key in the lock. As she turned the key to enter the door, a vehicle suddenly appeared rounding the corner of her block. She heard the sound of the engine roaring, and the vehicle's tires squealing as it straightened out on her street of red bricks.

Bright halogen lights lit up the yard as if someone had flipped a switch to football stadium lights. The person riding shotgun let down his window, and propped an Uzi on the car door ledge. She turned to observe the vehicle for a moment, and was shocked at what she saw. Seeing the man with an automatic weapon pointed at her, she pushed the door open and dove in, swinging it shut as fast as she could. With her in mid-air, the man let go a burst of gunfire spraying the front of the house. Several bullets lodged in the door ripping out splinters of wood as it slammed shut. Other bullets shattered the windowpanes into thousands of chards, while the remaining bullets chipped and ricocheted off the pale yellow stucco exterior sending chips flying into the flowerbeds.

Jim was startled from his sleep, and sat straight up in bed at the horrendous sounds of the Uzi blasting its quick rounds. He flicked on the lights as he bounded to his feet, running full-bore downstairs to investigate what the commotion was. Rachel and Christine also awakened and turned on their lights, but instead of running to see what the loud noises were, Christine ran into Rachel's room, and jumped into bed with her under the covers finding comfort with her big sister.

Paula did not know what had happened except that someone in a car just rode by in what appeared to be a Hummer, or something of that size, evidently trying to kill her. She composed herself enough to catch her breath. Her heart pounded with her breast as she looked up to see Jim standing over her. Protectively, he bent down with an eye peering out the window to the front of their property.

"What the hell just happened here, Paula?" Jim, visibly shaken, trembled with anger and fear.

Paula had never seen such a look of terror on his face, and did not like what she witnessed. The man and her family, which she loved more than life itself, were now in danger as the result of her job duties. She had no reason to think it could be anything else.

"I'm not sure, Jim. I got out of the car, and was on my way inside. When I reached the porch steps, I noticed bright lights from a huge vehicle shine on the front yard. The tires were burning rubber. I glanced sideways to the road and saw it out of my peripheral vision, a huge, black SUV."

Paula sat up from her prone position, and heard her daughters' movement above on the second floor. Awakened by the barrage of bullets and the destruction of property, they heard their mother and Jim talking, and decided to run down to the foyer. The girls reached the bottom of the stair and were horrified to see the damage to the door and windows, fragments of wood and glass scattered on the hardwoods and rugs. As the couple sat on the floor, arms around each other, they turned to see Rachel and Christine standing together at the base of the stairs, shivering in fear.

"Go back to bed, girls. We'll be up there in just a minute," said Paula.

"What happened, Mama?" asked Rachel.

"Nothing, sweetheart. Please, you two, go back upstairs," she said.

Having heard the shots and seeing all the glass on the floor, the girls knew their mother was withholding information that she felt they did not need to know at the moment. None-the-less, they went to Rachel's room instead of their separate bedrooms because Christine was still too afraid to go back to her room alone. Paula took a deep breath, and continued explaining where she left off.

"There was a man leaning out of his car door with an automatic weapon. He began firing what looked an Uzi. I dove inside to the floor as quickly as I could and managed to kick the door shut behind me. And you see the rest," said Paula.

She stood up, with Jim's help, brushing herself off and straightening her clothes. Paula, normally calm and collected, held back tears of anger that these perpetrators attacked her at home, her haven, where the people she loved the most were sleeping.

"How dare those bastards shoot-up my home!"

"They're gone, honey," said Jim.

"They could come back," she said.

Jim held her in his arms, not knowing what else to do at that moment. He did not understand things about the criminal mind the way she did. Paula's mind went into overdrive. Quickly she calmed herself down enough to think clearly then fished her cell phone out of her leather jacket pocket and dialed 911.

"I'll talk to them, Paula."

"I got it, honey, thanks. Would you please go check on the girls? I don't know how much they saw, or how this is affecting them."

"Okay, I'll be right back," he said.

"This is the 911 dispatcher speaking. State your emergency."

"Hello, this is Mrs. Paula Roberts. There has been a shooting at my house about five to ten minutes ago. The person doing the shooting was in a vehicle that drove by. He sprayed my house with some type of automatic weapon. I believe the shooter was trying to kill me."

"Mrs. Roberts, is anyone hurt? Do you need an ambulance?"

"No, I'm fine. There is evidence, though, and a statement that I'm sure the police will want. Send someone ASAP."

"Okay, I will do that, Mrs. Roberts. Are you able to describe the vehicle, or the persons within the vehicle?"

"Yes, I am."

"Hold a moment, Mrs. Roberts; I'll switch you to the Charleston Police Dispatch."

"Charleston Police dispatcher, Officer Williams speaking, can I help you?"

"Yes, I need to report a shooting and an attempted murder in my neighborhood."

"Yes, please go ahead with your name, address, location, and description of what happened."

"Officer Williams, I remember seeing a large dark colored SUV. The wheels were large, silver, and very shiny. It was too dark to capture much more. The windows were darkly tinted. Both the driver and person firing the weapon were wearing ball caps pulled down on their heads."

The dispatcher typed the information into her computerized form, and agreed to send a police officer to investigate the crime scene and write a full report. The rest of the Charleston Police force on duty was alerted to the incident with a description of the vehicle. The Charleston County Sheriff's department was notified of the shooting, as well, and a collaborative effort was under way to apprehend the vehicle.

Paula went upstairs to check on Rachel and Christine. She found Jim sitting on the edge of their bed with his arm around them, the girls still huddled together under the covers. Two neighbors called to find out what the ruckus was. Paula fielded the calls and assured the neighbors that everything was fine. The police unit arrived and took a brief statement, promising to return in daylight at an appointed time to take pictures, and gather evidence.

Paula, relieved that the police made an appearance and took a statement, joined Jim in getting the girls back to sleep. Afterwards, Paula and Jim joined each other in the master bedroom.

"Jim, I'm exhausted, I'm gonna try to get some rest now."

"Okay, honey. Try to forget about it for now. You need your rest."

"I will, Jim, you too. Thanks for being you. You were "Mr. Steady" in the middle of a crisis."

"I play the part well, but inside don't think I'm not shaken, as well."

They kissed and Jim rolled over on his side, facing away. Paula leaned over to the side of her bed where she had placed her purse, and pulling out her thirty-eight, then placed it quietly on her bedside table for easy access. Her mind replayed the events that had occurred the past two hours. She was not sure if Lane had been able to identify her vehicle, or if he had the resources to have tailed her so quickly. That was the enigma. Who were these people?

Only a couple of hours before the kids have to be up for school, she thought, as she drifted to sleep.

The black Hummer eluded the drag net, which was loosely thrown together by law enforcement in the wee hours of the morning when the late night shift was winding down. Lane and his men returned to the body shop after they were not able to meet their connection on the island, courtesy of an employee he called. Thwarted by the Crescent Moon detectives, Lane was pissed about missing his shipment. He and the two other men got in their vehicles and headed home. Opening his cell, he answered a call.

"We did what you said to do, boss man. We were able to catch up to that woman tailing you."

"What exactly did you guys do?" asked Lane, wanting to know the extent to which they carried out his orders.

"We followed her like you told us to after you left the car lot. She sped around you at the bridge to Johns Island."

"Oh, so that was her speeding around us. That bitch was on my tail with her bright lights blinding me."

"Yeah, we saw that. We followed her across the bridge then followed her home."

"So, what did y'all do to her?"

"We were just trying to scare her, like you said. We shot up her house good. That woman is very nimble on her feet. I know we shook her up with the amount of lead that sprayed her home."

"I wish you had done all that away from the neighborhood, man. So, you shot up her home?"

"She had a head start on us and we lost her for a while, Mr. Lane. When we caught up to her, she was walking in her front door. Nobody saw us and we were out of there in no time."

"Good, then maybe she will stay the hell out of my business next time."

"Yes sir, I believe she will. Is that it, Mr. Lane?" said the man.

"Yeah, that's it. Do not call me again for a while. Things are too hot since you boys chased her into a quiet neighborhood. I heard a lot of chatter on the police band. I'll call you soon and get you straight for what you did. How much do I owe you?"

"Just fifteen hundred, Mr. Lane," said the driver of the Hummer.

"Alright, I'll be in touch. Give me forty-eight hours then come by the lot for the cash," said Lane. And listen; drive something different when you come."

"Will do, sir," said the man.

Lane closed his cell and turned down the street to his neighborhood.

Thirty-Seven

Shaken by the event the night before, Paula went into work as usual but did not feel good about leaving her girls at home after school alone. She arranged for them to go a girlfriend's home, who had a set of daughters the same ages as Rachel and Christine. Arriving to the office after dropping her daughters off at school, Paula noticed that Russ's vehicle was not in his parking spot. *He must be catching up on sleep,* she thought. Exiting her car and walking in the office at normal hours, she was too wired from the shooting to sleep in as planned. She observed Carla busy answering the phone and filing papers, a typical Friday at Crescent Moon Investigations. Paula's direct line rang shortly after she put her things down and sat at her desk.

"Hello, this is Paula Roberts, how can I help you?"

"Yes, Paula, good to hear your voice again, this is Agent John Dibbs. It's been a while. How's married life treating you?"

"Agent Dibbs, it's good to hear your voice, as well. Married life is wonderful. Thanks for asking. How is your family?"

"We're all good. My wife and kids are adjusted to Atlanta and the schools here."

"And your new territory, and office down in the big city, how's that working for you, Agent Dibbs?"

"You don't forget a thing, except to call me John. Things are going well down here. Things are busier, though, than when I had the Charlotte office. And, they've given me a new territory."

"Oh really now, pray tell."

"Yeah, now instead of one state like North Carolina, they've given me part of South Carolina and Georgia."

"I know you can handle it, Agent Dibbs. Well, I know you didn't call me to announce the news, how can I help you?"

"No, I didn't, Paula. I'll get right to it. I thought that you were done with all the dangerous stuff, but I'm hearing you are back in action around Charleston."

"That makes two of us. Are you referring to anything in particular, or just my new vocation? I assume you may know what it is since you called my office."

"Paula, one of our agents assigned to your area informed me about a drug bust in the wee hours of the morning that was planned to go down on Johns Island. He said the DEA had the lead on it and planned to apprehend the men who were buying a cocaine shipment, but the men never made their connection. Can you tell me anything about that?"

"Now, why would I know anything about that, Agent Dibbs?"

"The agent says your house was shot up last night in the early morning hours. When I heard your name, and found out what you were doing now, I thought maybe you knew something. This is serious business, Paula."

"I know it is, Agent Dibbs," Paula said, ignoring his suggestion to call him, John. "I'm not at liberty to say anything on the matter, I'm sorry."

"Not this again, Paula. We've been down this road before. Neither you, nor your boss want to be charged with obstructing justice do you?"

"You will have to take the matter up with him. He will be in later. I assume you know his name?"

"I do. I'll be talking to you later. I am sorry to have contacted you under these circumstances. You take care and give my best to your husband."

"I'll tell Russ you called. Good-bye, Agent Dibbs. You take care."

Paula placed her finger over the hook switch contemplating whether to call her partner immediately, or to wait until he came in. She chose the latter and put the phone on its cradle. She knew that she and her partner had interfered with a potential bust, and that it could become an FBI investigation. The way Russ explained the situation, and the compassion he felt for the family, she willingly went along to help prevent the drug deal from taking place. It was their job to interfere, at the request of Cindy Lane, to allow her time to give her husband one last warning to turn around from his elicit activities. At least, that is the way she and Russ viewed the situation.

Paula did not expect to be followed by people who shot up her home, attempting to kill her. Now, the call from Agent Dibbs, Regional Director of the FBI, gave her cause for concern. Thoughts raced through her head about the safety of her daughters, and her husband. Jim was right about her not working in a dangerous occupation again, and she hated to admit it. *It was too late for an admission*, she thought, *because since the shooting it was obvious to them both.*

Paula took a deep breath then exhaled slowly. "Oh crap! I might as well get it over with," she muttered.

"Excuse me, Paula?" said the polite student worker.

"Oh, nothing, Carla, I'm just thinking aloud."

"Well if there's anything you want to talk about, you can talk to me. I've been part of this investigative family here for some time now, and I know how to keep things under wraps. Mr. Baxter talked to me about that when he hired me, and has confided in me on quite a few things."

"Thanks for saying that, Carla. You've been very steady and reliable. We are both really proud of your performance and impressed by your maturity level, especially for a college student of your age."

"Thanks, Paula. That is very nice of you to say, but I am a little older than I look. I did not have the money to attend college right out of high school so I worked for a few years first. Last Thursday was my two-year anniversary on the job, and Mr. Baxter said we'll be going out to lunch to celebrate as soon as things slow down. He also refreshed me on the importance of confidentiality on the job here. He said it's best that we always keeping things "in house", when it comes to us three, you know what I mean. Then he thanked me for being the first student who had stayed with him this long. I thought I was going to cry."

"That's sweet, and pretty awesome on your behalf, Carla. I do appreciate your willingness to listen, but what is going on with me is more complicated than I want to share right now with anyone. A home situation needs to stay at home. I'll keep it in mind though."

"Sure Paula, I understand, and thanks for the nice things you said."

"It's the truth, Carla. I really like you. I'll open up some time, but now is not the right time. By the way, how's school going?"

"It's going great, thanks. I even met a guy that I like a lot last week. We're going to a movie this weekend."

"I hope that goes well. It sounds promising."

"Yes, it sort of does, doesn't it? I'm usually a gal that works and studies, not much else. Well, I guess I had better get back to work," Carla said.

The women returned to their respective jobs, and shortly afterwards, the phone rang. Carla, as usual, fielded the call. Paula shuffled through some papers, sorting them by priority. As she stacked them accordingly, she ran across a small envelope from Anna Lee Jennings. Opening it, she pulled out a thank you note on exquisite linen-finished paper, and she read:

Paula Roberts P.I. - Johns Island

Dear Paula,

In case you are wondering, I have not dropped off the face of the earth. I am writing to "thank you" for all you have done for me and my family. Mark and I decided to get back together. Everyone is happier now, and he is still clean and sober. He has been going to NA meetings for some time now, and has been promoted at work in a small bank in Summerville. It's a thirty minute ride to work, but he doesn't seem to mind. I had my doubts about us getting together at first, but when I see him and the kids playing in the backyard, or think about us at the dinner table at night, it makes everything worth it. I tried to push down the love I felt for him, but there was no denying it. He is sincerely remorseful, and he shows it to me in many ways by the little things he does.

Again, thanks to you and Russell Baxter, we are a family again, safe and sound, and growing together. Yes, we remarried. Contact me anytime.

Kind regards,

Anna Leigh Jennings

Paula wiped a few tears from her cheek as she soaked in Anna Leigh's words, touched that their family was together again. She was not sure what to think about

Anna Leigh giving Mark a second chance, but she thought that if they could love each other, and the family was happy again then it was not for her to decide. Why should she not be happy for them?

She did not want her new family to go through anything like the Jennings family had, not that her situation was the same as the Jennings, but she worried about her family, at times. Different problems were straining her family, and just as significant. Someone had just shot up her home. Her kids were afraid, and Jim was more upset than she had ever seen him. They had coffee together that morning, but after Jim quickly downed one cup, he left with a grim look on his face without kissing her good-bye, a rarity, which left her wondering what to do.

Paula Roberts P.I. - Johns Island

Thirty-Eight

⚜

Two Days Later:

It was Sunday after church, and Cindy Lane had taken her kids to Sunday school then returned home to make sandwiches. Her husband had slept in, refusing to get up to go to church with them, much to the dismay of his wife, who was raised to attend church as a family. Tommy Lane sat at the kitchen table with toast and coffee, reading the Post and Courier. The kids ran in to change clothes as their mother had directed, speaking to their dad as they flew by. Cindy walked in to the kitchen area where Tommy sat, and placed her purse and church bulletin on the round antique oak table with claw feet.

"Tommy, you've got to stop what you are doing." said Cindy. "I can't keep living like this. Don't think I don't know about the drugs."

"Cindy, shh, the kids will hear you."

"Don't shush me. I'm leaving with the kids, if you don't quit the drugs, and leave this bad crowd you're running around with. They are supposed to be your body shop employees, not guys you hang out with."

"They are my employees, and it's good to have social activities with them. It boosts their morale. We aren't doing anything wrong…just having a few beers and playing cards. You know how it goes."

"Yeah, I know how it goes alright, and I'm not buying it. This town isn't that big, and I also know who these men's families are. I know about them and their activities from other reputable people, as well. I've found white powder on the bathroom counter in our own home and tasted it. It wasn't baby powder. I'm not that stupid."

"No one said you were stupid, Cindy, please stop this. The children might hear you."

"Kids, go outside and play, so that dad and I can talk," said Cindy, projecting her voice to the next room.

"Yes, ma'am," they said, doing what their mom insisted.

With the children out of ear shot, Cindy continued to zero in on her husband without wavering.

"Oh, so now you are concerned about the children. Why aren't you concerned about them when you are out gallivanting all hours of the night, when you should be home with me putting them in bed? You are still trying to hide what's going on, Tommy, and I'm not going to stand for it any longer."

A silence came over the room as neither one of them spoke. The air was so thick one could cut it with a knife.

Tension, sadness, and decision-making time brought them to a crossroads where their lives would forever change, one way, or the other.

"Here's the bottom line, Tommy, I had some people stop you from making your connection a few nights ago because I knew you were going to get busted. If you can't stop on your own, then get some help now. I have two numbers for treatment centers in the area. And, you will have got to stop your outside associations with the men who have been involved with you doing drug deals."

"I wondered how my vehicle got spiked. You did that to keep me from getting busted? That could have killed me. The vehicle nearly flipped," said Lane.

Cindy could see that he was genuinely irritated, but ignored his facial expression and pressed ahead with her ultimatum.

"I care about you, Tommy, but not enough to be with you, if you are going to lead a life of dealing drugs. The kids and I deserve better than this. I cannot be married to a drug dealer. You have a good car business, and there's no need for this. Why are you doing it anyway?"

"I don't know, Cindy. I guess it's the thrill of it all, the excitement. It's stupid, and I know you're right. I don't want to lose you and the kids to this nonsense, but I feel like I can't stop. It's got too strong of a hold on me."

For the first time Tommy leveled with his wife and it touched her for a moment. Cindy was not sure if it was contrived, or genuine, but she was committed if he truly wanted to get help.

"I'm here for you if you will allow me to help you. This is your last chance, and I hate to say this, but I mean every word. If you do not get help, I cannot continue with this marriage."

"So, you're giving me an ultimatum. What is it that you want me to do?"

"I want you to check into one of these two centers immediately." Cindy passed the leaflet to him listing the best treatment centers in the area. "Make your calls and do whatever you have to at work. Your manager can run the business. If your manager can't handle something, you can make the tough decisions from the rehab clinic, if you have to. I'll go into the dealership, like I did when you first started out, to keep tabs on things to make sure it runs smoothly."

"Can I have some time to think about this, Cindy?"

"No, there is no more time, Tommy. I can't go another day, or hour, like this. I even heard you were involved in shooting up a private investigator's house, a female no less. It's a wonder you aren't in jail now."

Tommy Lane dipped his head in shame for a second, but raised it quickly in defiance at what he was hearing. After all, in his mind, he was the man of the house, and his wife had no business giving him an ultimatum, one voice said in his head. The other voice of reason called to him to turn away from drugs and back to his family. He arose from the kitchen chair and walked out the door to the patio where the kids were playing in the backyard on their swing-set, and sat in a wooden lounge chair. Lighting up a cigarette, Lane exhaled, and then sighed.

Cindy finished loading the dirty breakfast dishes in the dishwasher, and wiped the table. She took off her apron, and hung it on the back of a chair. Walking into the den she looked out the French doors and saw her husband talking on the phone. Realizing that she was watching, he turned away, ignoring her as he continued his conversation. She walked out on the patio to join the family, and out of curiosity about her husband's suspicious actions. He hung up the phone just as his wife joined them.

"Who were you talking to, Tommy?"

"Don't worry about it. I'm not doing anything wrong."

"Why don't I believe you?"

"You can choose to, or not Cindy. I'm sick of all this inquisition and witch-hunt type stuff. I have no more to say about anything right now. I'll know what to do by tomorrow. Just let me feel like I'm coming to this decision on my own, and give me some space until tomorrow morning. I don't like this pressure."

Tommy left the patio in anger, and cranked his vehicle. The garage door shot up with the push of the remote, as he backed out. Cindy went to the kitchen window and watched him back out of the driveway, then drive down the street. She had a sick feeling in the pit of her stomach, a feeling as if he was rejecting her advice to get help, and her tough-love approach to save their marriage.

Lane approached the four-way stop sign at the corner. He was disgusted with himself, but drove away in defiance. Turning on the radio, he cranked up the music on his favorite classic rock station, and tried to put the dilemma out of his mind. A carnal struggle warred within him winning control and demanding that he go get his next fix. He had made his choice.

Paula Roberts P.I. - Johns Island

Thirty-Nine

⚜

Lane drove from his residence at the Isle of Palms to Folly Beach to the place where he, Mark Jennings, and others had gone to smoke dope, and snort cocaine. The resident, none other than Jimmy Snyder, mutual friend and long time distributor for the bulk of the cocaine financed by Jennings, and now by Tommy Lane. He hoped they could listen to music and smoke away his blues. After Lane knocked on his door, Jimmy opened up.

"What's up, man? I'm surprised to see you at my door. What are you doing out on Folly Beach?"

"Jimmy, I'm sorry for just dropping in without calling. I have got too much on my mind, and just kept driving in your direction while I was thinking. Before I could get it together to call, I was here."

"It's okay, Tommy, come on in, sit down, and relax. We'll fire one up, and chill."

"I was hoping you would say that. My marriage is falling apart and I was nearly busted trying to score the last shipment," said Lane. "How much do you have left?"

"I've got what we need in coke, and I have weed stashed away," said Snyder.

"That's what I thought, Jimmy. Let's get high."

Snyder cranked the music back to the level it was before answering the door. Lane sat with his friend and an unnamed man that Snyder did not bother introducing because he sat in a semi-stupor gazing at the wall, rocking to the music. Rolling up a fat joint, Snyder fired it up, took a hit, and passed it to Lane.

"Go ahead, Tommy, hit it all you want. As you can see we were already getting wasted before you got here."

"Thanks, Jimmy; I need to relieve the stress I'm under right now. My wife is giving me an ultimatum, and the Feds are on my trail. I'm not sure what to do, so I drove out here to get high."

"This sounds very familiar, Tommy. I hate to say it, but Mark said the same thing a little over a year ago."

"What ever happened to him? I can't get him to return my calls," said Lane. "He used to hang out with us some."

"I heard he got religion, and straightened up," said Snyder."

"Get out! No wonder he hasn't returned my calls. He doesn't want any part of this. Didn't he get divorced and move to Miami? Then I heard he moved back."

"Yeah, that's what he did alright. Now I hear he remarried his wife, so you know he had to straighten up. Anna Leigh is no fool."

Lane passed the joint back to Snyder, who took another hit. About the time they got half way through the joint, and Lane began to float into his mind numbing high, several black vehicles rounded the corner of the block where Snyder lived. The unmarked vehicles pulled into Snyder's drive blocking the vehicles of the occupants, and parallel parking by the front lawn. Loaded with DEA and FBI agents and ready to bust anyone on the premises, if illegal drugs were found, the men jumped out of their vehicles, and popped open their trunks. Standing at the back of their cars, they tossed each other shotguns, and ammunition clips with the speed and precision of a well-executed NFL football play. They moved forward to the door of the suspect in seconds flat.

Lane and Snyder heard the vehicles outside and became aware of the sudden grouping of people in his yard, but not soon enough to do anything about it. They had no time to escape, or do much in the way of hiding the drug paraphernalia. Snyder reached under his sofa and pulled out a sawed off shotgun not knowing what was going on, only that several men were gathering at the front of his home.

"Don't do it, Jimmy. You'll get us killed," said Lane.

The unnamed man, alarmed by what was transpiring, stood and peered through the blinds.

"That's right, Jimmy, put that shotgun away. There must be ten to twelve men out there, all with weapons."

"Damn it all! I figured this time would come one day," said Snyder.

In resignation, he thought better than to have a weapon in his hands when the door opened to the authorities, either by consent, or by force. Snyder slid the shotgun back under the sofa while the two other men stashed the pot, and emptied the ashtrays. All of the men were holding small amounts of cocaine. The unnamed man gathered the small bags from the other two men and ran down the hall then flushed them down the toilet.

An officer made five loud raps on the door. "Open up, we're agents with the D.E.A. and F.B.I. We have a search warrant for the premises," said Agent Glen Ross.

Two agents with the DEA and FBI stood shoulder to shoulder at the front door directly behind Agent Ross. Three other men from both groups fanned out to the front windows. The final four of the ten men ran to the back of the house to prevent a backdoor escape.

"I'm coming," responded Snyder. Lane and the other man lit cigarettes, and sat down, flipping on the television, as if nothing was happening. Snyder opened the front door acting very surprised to see law enforcement.

"James Snyder?"

"Yes sir, that's me."

"I'm Agent Ross with the Drug Enforcement Agency. We have a warrant signed by a federal judge to search your premises for illegal drugs. Is anyone else in your home at this time?

"Yes sir. There are two other men in the den listening to music and visiting with me."

"Are they armed?"

"No sir."

"Do you have any weapons in the house?"

"I do have a small shotgun under my sofa for protection, sir, and a pistol in my bedroom."

"Alright, let's go inside," said the agent. Agent Ross motioned with his head, his weapon drawn, and at his side.

"May I see your warrant?" asked Snyder.

Agent Ross unfolded the warrant from its tri-fold and allowed Snyder to view it.

"I don't know why you men are doing this, but come on in. We don't have any drugs."

The two agents backing up Agent Ross rushed in the foyer and bolted into the den with guns drawn where the other two men were gathered.

"Down on the floor with your hands behind your back," shouted one of the agents. Three of the agents conducted pat down searches on the men.

"All clear," said the first agent, after all three men were searched.

"Cuff 'em," said Agent Ross to his men. He addressed Jimmy Snyder, Tommy Lane, and the unnamed man. "Men, in accordance with our search warrant for this premises, you are being detained. We have reason to believe that this home is being used as a staging operation for cocaine and marijuana distribution. You have the right to remain silent. Anything you say may be used as evidence against you in a court of law. You have the right to an attorney, and if you cannot afford one, you will be appointed one by the state of South Carolina. Is that clear, gentlemen?"

"Yes, sir," the men spoke in quick succession.

As the paraphrased civil rights warning was recited all three men were handcuffed. Three of the four agents at the back door entered from the rear and fanned out, joining the others in a complete search of the home. One agent stood guard at the back door. Two agents kept the men seated in the den while the search was under way. Agent Ross walked around the home supervising the search.

"Agent Chapman, go up in the attic," said Ross. "You go behind and assist him, Agent Duffy."

The agents did as directed. Agent Chapman grabbed the white, nylon cord that attached at the end of the attic door, which lay flush with the ceiling. Pulling down a folding staircase, the agents climbed into to the attic.

"See the light, there, by the rafter, Chapman," said Agent Duffy.

The second agent stood close behind the first agent on the folding staircase. Agent Chapman flipped the switch on, but the one naked sixty-watt bulb did not provide much light. He pulled his flashlight from his back pocket and shined into the dimly lit spaces. Seeing many cardboard boxes and plastic bags, the agents began to shift them around examining each, as they went.

"This one appears to be full of Christmas decorations, but I do smell something funny, and I don't think it's a cedar wreath," said Agent Chapman.

He pulled another bag from beneath the stack. Lifting the top of the bag, he cut the plastic tie, raised it to his nose.

"Smells like weed to me. That's got a strong scent. Do you smell it?"

"Oh yeah, I smelled it the moment you pulled the bag of decorations off that pile. Let's look at these other three bags. I'd bet we've got something there, as well," said Agent Duffy, as he moved closer to Chapman and lifted a bag from another pile.

The men carefully ripped into the tops of the bags with pocketknives at the tops, where they were tied with yellow nylon strips.

"This one is weed. It's wrapped in bricks," Duffy said.

"So is this one," Chapman responded. "How much would you say we've got here all totaled?"

Picking up the bag so he could get a feel for the weight, Agent Duffy said, "About two pounds in this bag, and that one looks about the same, wouldn't you say, Ross?"

"That would be my guess too," Chapman replied.

Duffy dropped the bag of marijuana aside and lifted the third bag that had a very different feel. It was smaller, and more compact, but seemed to be rather heavy. He cut into the top of the bag and a white powder drifted up in the air. Carefully, he set the bag back down, the white haze drifting upward.

"It looks like we have cocaine here. Come look at this bag, Chapman.

"Good job there, Duffy." Chapman scooted over next to Duffy, and took the bag for moment holding it for weight by the top of the bag. I think we have about a kilo of cocaine on our hands in this bag. It will be tough to carry without spilling. We need to be careful."

"You're right, Chapman. Let's go ahead and verify it."

Duffy put his knife in the white powder, and lifted out a minute amount on the tip of the blade, touching it to his tongue.

"It's cocaine, I'm sure of it. It's the pure stuff, too. The instructors at the FBI Academy demonstrated with something like this. All of us had to taste it."

Agent Ross shouted from the bottom of the staircase in the hallway to his men searching the attic.

"Okay men, whatcha got up there? I can hear your excitement," said Ross, who had circled back to the foot of the folding staircase to check on his men.

"We have two large leaf bags full of marijuana, and one large freezer-bag full of cocaine, sir."

"Pass the bags down men, and get down here as soon as you complete your search," said Agent Ross. "You other men down the hall get in here and take these bags of drugs. We have hit the mother lode."

Chapman and Duffy passed the bags down to the waiting agents. After checking the remaining items scattered about the attic, the agents turned out the attic light, and made their way down. Agent Ross patted both Agents Chapman and Duffy on the back as soon as their feet hit the floor.

"Good job, men," said Agent Ross. "Take the evidence out to the car that I'm riding in. We've got room in the trunk to secure it. Chapman and Duffy, you stay with my vehicle since it was your find."

Agent Ross returned to the den where the three men in custody were located. The men looked at Ross and the other agents standing around him.

"That's quite a shipment of drugs that you had in your attic, Mr. Snyder. You wanna tell us how you came to having all this contraband in your attic?"

"I don't know anything about it," said Snyder.

"I see, Mr. Snyder. I figured somehow you wouldn't know anything about it."

"It's not mine!" said Snyder.

"What about you other men? Can you tell us anything about these drugs?" said Agent Ross.

"No sir," they both said.

Tommy Lane and the other man did not offer a word, nor looked in Agent Ross's direction as he addressed them. They were shell-shocked from the events and did not want to speak without the representation of an attorney.

"Take 'em down to the station and book 'em all on possession of marijuana and cocaine with intent to distribute. Seize and impound their vehicles. Let's get out of here men," said Agent Ross.

The agents nodded, and as quickly as they had assembled, they went to work wrapping up the bust. Jimmy Snyder, Tommy Lane, and the unnamed man were escorted to the black unmarked cars equipped with steel cages where they were placed in the backseats. The team of agents felt an exhilaration akin to a sports team winning an important game, giving each other high fives, as they piled into their cars. Agent Ross of the DEA, and Agent McElroy of the FBI rode together to collaborate their reports of the incident so that both agencies were on the same page with no contradictions, which could later prevent an attorney from finding fault due to discrepancies in their respective reports.

Forty

❦

Mark and Anna Leigh Jennings sat side by side in separate seats holding hands and gently rocking back and forth on a swing-set at the neighborhood park. They enjoyed their feeling of oneness once again, something that had been taken away, but that they were blessed to partake of a second time. Marrying, divorcing, and marrying again was something that they never foresaw, but that someone bigger than them had no doubt orchestrated. Watching Samantha and Nathan play with their friends, running, jumping, laughing, playing tag around the playground equipment felt right, and they were thankful.

Russ Baxter and Paula Roberts' efforts had not gone in vain for this family. One man and his family were saved from the awful emotional upheaval that divorce can ravage upon a couple. Anna Leigh and Mark had a lot to do with the turnaround by her decision to forgive, and his decision to return to the faith he had once followed, which strengthened him within to be totally happy as a family man. That, along with the faithful love of the woman he loved since she was in grade school with pig tails.

They also found help in pastoral counseling sessions to overcome their marital issues, which gave them a new foundation of understanding to find their footing in starting over. And, although others did not approve at first, the Jennings soon won back the respect of their families and neighbors by being a commendable and tight family unit. It didn't take them long to volunteer at Sam and Nathan's school functions, and to become an integral part of the community again.

Mark attended all of Nathan and Samantha's extracurricular activities, something he did not do before. Anna Leigh did her usual stellar job of nurturing the whole family with love and good home cooked meals. Mark knew that she would be the rock in his family from the time he had met her on campus in college. She was active in a Christian group at the small college where they met and got him going to Bible studies where he had first had prayed to God for guidance in his life. He always admired the innate sense of peace that Anna possessed, and the way she carried herself. He knew it was special, and wanted to possess it like she did. For the first time in his life, he believed he did.

Tommy Lane, on the other hand, now going through the worst nightmare of his life, was incarcerated for the first time. With the other two men split up in separate interrogations, Jimmy Snyder spilled his guts on Lane, telling the authorities everything about him financing the operations. Lane tried to implicate Jennings for past drug dealings thinking it could help his case, but Snyder did not corroborate his story. Snyder did not care to bring his best friend from high school into a current situation. He knew Jennings was clean and wished him the best.

Additionally, the thought of bringing someone else into the investigation without any proof, other than one drug dealer's confession, did not interest the District Attorney. Jennings had been gone from the area for over a year, and had been back for three months with his wife and a new job. He was humbled and thankful when Anna Leigh accepted his proposal, and was resolved never to look back again.

"Anna, what's going on with the lady from Russ Baxter's office?" asked Mark Jennings.

"Oh you mean, Paula Roberts. She's fine. I talked to her a while back. Just recently I wrote her a letter thanking her and Mr. Baxter for helping us like they did. Of course, I had to tell her about us."

"That's fine. I really don't care who knows. You know, I was thinking about how things transpired, and I realize I'm a very fortunate man. God was surely looking out for me through all of this mess. It's been a long hard road back into your good graces, but worth every bit of it. I'm sorry for my past screw ups, Anna."

"I know you are Mark...one request though," she said.

"What's that, Anna?"

"No more apologies, okay? I'm just glad you were able to work things out in your personal life, and that we are together again. That's all I ever wanted, for us to be a family that loved each other and who pulled the wagon together."

"Me too, Anna, but I feel bad for Tommy Lane, said Jennings. "He called me a couple of times, but I put him off because I was afraid to get involved. He wanted someone to run around with, but I know what the likely result would have been. Besides, the times that we hung out were a long time ago, and I have moved on. Now, he's been busted along with Jimmy, and a couple of more men. I knew most of them."

"There's nothing you could have done but get yourself in the middle of it," said Anna Leigh. "When you showed me the paper about the bust, and then I saw it on television, I shuddered because I know you were close to some of these men. I also read where the authorities are still looking for the men who shot up the Roberts' home."

"I hope they don't contact me for information about the past. I wouldn't know how to handle it," said Jennings.

"I don't think they will, if you let sleeping dogs lie. I mean, unless you are called upon to testify, and then of course, you have no choice. I can't see why they would. You've been out of the loop for quite some time."

"Thanks honey. I was wondering how you felt about that. I agree. I would call my attorney in any case, if they did. That old life seems so far behind me now, and that's where I want to leave it."

Anna Leigh squeezed her husband's hand a little tighter then turned and gave him a smile of approval. Mark reciprocated with a wink then leaned over in his swing meeting Anna Leigh in the middle, sealing their private conversation with a gentle kiss.

The kids finished playing with their friends and ran up to their parents, Mr. B running alongside.

"Mom, can we go now, I'm getting hungry?" asked Nathan.

"Yeah Mommy, everyone else is leaving," said Samantha, echoing her big brother's sentiment.

"Sure we can kids. Let's go."

Packing up in Anna Leigh's station wagon, the Jennings family returned home for their normal dinner routine at home.

Forty-one

A few weeks had passed since the incident that rocked the Roberts family to the core. Having shots fired at her, especially while entering her home while the family was sleeping was not Paula's cup of tea, to say the least. Since then, Russ Baxter had refused to assign her anything he considered dangerous. Jim Roberts buried himself in his work, staying a little late at work a few nights per week. She knew the reason why her husband stayed late, but hoped he would come out of it. The neighborhood had been put on an aggressive crime watch by the Charleston Police Department with officers circling through the residential area twenty-four-seven. Though the Roberts felt safer now, the men had not been apprehended.

Saturday night came and Jim and Paula hired a sitter so they could get away for the evening. They did not do it often, but when they did, they liked to go downtown Charleston to a fine restaurant for fresh seafood, or a steak. This evening they chose an atmosphere where the food was excellent with a live band performing slow jazz tunes. The female artist performing resembled Sade and had a similar style.

They entered the old, classy restaurant's foyer. A hostess stand positioned close by was vacant. To the left of the stand was a long, antique, mahogany bar with a huge mirror, and bar stools. To the right was a small stage in one corner where a small band was busy setting up. Jim and Paula waited for the hostess to return.

Twenty-four tables with starched white linen tablecloths were scattered across the warmly carpeted dining area. A single red rose placed in a vase accompanied by a burning candle accented each table and set an elegant mood for the patrons. Comfortable leather chairs added to the ambience. Framed portraits of historic figures, and colorful seascapes decorated the walls. Each painting was lit at the bottom accentuating a short description and title.

"Two for dinner?" said the hostess.

"Yes, two for a table near the windows, please, and put us back a little ways from the band, if you can manage that," said Jim.

An arm tucked under the crook of his elbow, Paula stood with her husband surveying the dining room, and the band. She loved to see Jim wearing a dress shirt and sport coat, which he rarely did. It gave her a chance to dress, as she was, in one of her rarely worn evening gowns, cultured pearl necklace with matching bracelet, and a smart, white leather purse.

"Let me see. I think I can arrange that," said the perky college student. She excused herself to have a table cleaned and prepped, and returned in a couple of minutes with menus in hand and wearing a dazzling smile. "Right this way, please."

Shortly after being seated, the waiter came and they placed their orders. Jim handed the menus to the waiter, and wasted no time in saying what was on his mind, though looking at Paula in the candlelight the way she was dressed gave him second thoughts. He did not want to spoil the moment, but the topic weighed him down like a ton of bricks. He reached over the table and took her hand in his.

"Paula, you know that I love you as much as life itself and will do anything to protect you and our daughters..."

Jim paused, gathering his thoughts, looking down at the burning candle for a brief moment, then back at her. Paula always loved the look of his face with candlelight flickering. She had a weakness for his more serious look, as well. She felt protected, loved, and wanted to interrupt him with a kiss on the lips.

"I know you would, Jim, and I love you in the same way. I think you know that. What's on your mind?"

"Honey, I'm not comfortable with you working as a private investigator at Moonlight anymore."

"I'm aware of that, darling. I knew that from the beginning," said Paula, smiling. We both knew that, but we have goals we want to accomplish and one thing led to the other. You do know that, don't you?"

"Yes, I do. I just don't understand you sometimes," he said.

"What do you mean, dear?"

"Like your desire to hang on to that kind of job, for one thing."

Paula could see that Jim was doing his best to be forceful with her without seeming combative. "Is there anything else that's troubling you?" Paula asked.

"No, I guess that's it really. Isn't that enough? Look, Paula, we encountered the recent problems that were not only dangerous to you, but could be harmful to Rachel and Christine's development too. I mean they could need counseling because of this event if they develop unusual fears. We really can't say how this could scar them. Also, police have not even captured those men that shot up our house."

"Jim, I know you are right. I'm just having a hard time turning loose of this job. I love it for some strange reason. I worked for a living all my life, since I got out of college, and even before that, really. I went back to work each time I had a child because we couldn't make it on my ex-husband's income alone. The girls depend on me to give them the extra things they need. Even now, though I know you are generous, and doing well, I want to continue to put money aside for their college education, as well as help us have a good standard of living," said Paula.

Tears welling in her eyes, she quickly grabbed a cloth napkin from the table and dotted the corners of her eyes to absorb the moisture. She did not want to appear the least bit weak at a time when she felt that she was being put on the defensive.

"I know you do, dear, and that's one of the many wonderful things about you. Let me just say again that the business is doing really well. Sales have quadrupled since moving to Charleston. You know we had a decent amount of traffic and business in Georgetown, but since moving here things have blown up. It's incredible the amount of walk-in traffic we're getting."

"Honey, that's great to hear. I knew you were much busier, but four times the revenue is amazing," she said.

"Thank you, honey." Jim leaned in close. His eyes portrayed the seriousness in his voice. "Here's the bottom line Paula, you don't need to work anymore at an outside job. I'll be glad to put away the same amount of money that you are doing now for Rachel and Christine's education, provide them with music lessons, or other things you do for them. I'll still be able to do the same things I'm doing for my boys."

"I'm having such a hard time with that idea, Jim. It's the independent streak in me, I guess. I would have difficulty accepting that from you. That's money you can use to keep growing your business, and for your sons," Paula said, biting her lip.

The band began to play a tune, which interfered with them talking without raising their voices, so the couple deferred to the soulful jazzy sounds. The female singer came to the microphone in a shimmering dress that showed off her curves after the musical intro. The vocalist began with an Eric Clapton tune, *You Look Wonderful*

Tonight. Kanda, and her band, which played up and down the Southeast coast continued with three more songs before a brief intermission. As the band began to disperse to the bar for refreshments, and their appetizer arrived. Jim continued the conversation they had started.

"As I was saying, Paula…"

"Jim, darling, I want to enjoy this time we have with each other. We don't come often, and everything is so romantic. If you don't mind, let's not spoil it with this topic. I mean, it can wait until after we eat, can't it, dear?"

"Fair enough, Paula. I'm sorry." said Jim. He took his cloth napkin and put it in his lap."

"Thank you, honey."

"Yum, Jim, calamari, and bacon wrapped scallops."

"I know. They are delicious."

He reached to the center of the table plucking a second marshmallow-sized scallop by the green toothpick inserted within. Paula joined him in selecting one of the succulent delicacies. The waiter arrived with their salads, and noticed the half-empty wine glasses.

"More wine for you this evening, folks?"

"Yes, thank you, half-glasses only, please," said Jim, for both of them. Paula nodded her head in agreement, her mouth full of an appetizer.

After completing their salads, the plates were taken away, and the main course arrived. Jim had ordered blackened salmon, while Paula chose a Mahi-Mahi with an Asian sauce. The couple ate their dinner and enjoyed the atmosphere without discussing the controversial topic. They kept things light exchanging stories about their kids, and reminiscing about good times at the beach when Jim had his boys during the summer. Jim shared that he received a call earlier in the day from his boys, Clark and Rob, who were excited about their trip to Charleston in the upcoming summer.

The band resumed playing, and the couple ordered cherries jubilee. At the close of the second set, the band again sought refreshments. Paula and Jim resumed the heavier topic of conversation.

"Paula, what about this idea, as far as work goes? You can come to work at the store if that makes you feel better. We can make room for you either in sales, or in the office. I'm sure you will be an asset."

"On the surface that sounds good, Jim, but we've never tried working together all day, and then come home to each other. Do you really think that would work? I mean, what if we got tired of each other?" she said.

"We could try it, Paula, and if it didn't work out, then you are free to not work, or try something different."

"That's a logical plan, and probably a smart choice, but since the incident, Russ has assigned me administrative stuff, getting contracts signed, and the like. He's being sensitive to what just happened."

"I understand that, Paula. I know there are details to work out as with any professional job. Listen, I know you love your work, even though it is dangerous, I just feel like it's gotten to the place that we can't afford to take any more chances. I don't want to be in constant fear that something could happen to you, or the family, for that matter," he said.

"I know you are right, Jim. I really didn't expect this type of outcome working there. You know that, and as much as I like Russ Baxter, at times I do question whether he was being candid with me in our initial interview about the possible dangers."

"I've wondered the same thing," said Jim.

"I tell you what, Jim; I'll meet with Russ first thing Monday and have a good discussion with him about everything. Russ and I had planned to talk about things very soon, anyway. If I do leave, he will have to buy me out, so that will take a little time to hash out. And, on existing cases I would certainly want to finish up anything I've started."

"Of course you would. I understand that," he said.

"Okay, well, let's not talk about it anymore tonight, dear."

"I agree, Paula. Let's spend the rest of the evening enjoying each other. Like you said, we don't get to do this as much as we used to."

The band played their last set and the couple left midway through then returned home after a walk around the Market. Paula thought about how she would wind down her work at Crescent Moon Investigations. Jim was gratified that she was willing to begin phasing out a job she loved for the sake of her family.

THE END

Daniel Easterling

Made in the USA
Charleston, SC
28 June 2015